The Forgotten War

Based on Historical Events

David Lee Corley

Copyright © 2024 David Lee Corley

All rights reserved.

DEDICATION

Dedicated to all the men and women that fought and sacrificed for their country.

Table of Contents

Quote *3*

Prologue *4*

Ba Chuc *6*

Invasion *31*

Pagoda *86*

Opium *102*

Risky *128*

The Fortress *152*

Boat People *192*

The Deal *222*

The Fall *246*

Road to Battambang *305*

Letter to Reader *326*

Author's Biography *328*

DAVID LEE CORLEY

Quote

"In the time of deceit, telling the truth is a revolutionary act."

– George Orwell

Prologue

A Tale of Two Revolutions

In the spring of 1975, Southeast Asia witnessed the birth of two communist nations, emerging from the ashes of prolonged civil wars. On April 17, 1975, the Khmer Rouge captured Phnom Penh, establishing Democratic Kampuchea. Merely thirteen days later, on April 30, 1975, Saigon fell to North Vietnamese forces, leading to the creation of the Socialist Republic of Vietnam.

Despite their shared communist ideology, Vietnam and Democratic Kampuchea (Cambodia) embarked on drastically different paths. Vietnam adopted a more pragmatic approach to communism, maintaining some economic ties with non-communist nations and focusing on gradual societal transformation. The Vietnamese leadership sought to modernize while preserving aspects of traditional culture.

In stark contrast, Democratic Kampuchea under the Khmer Rouge implemented an extreme form of agrarian socialism. They pursued complete isolation from the outside world and initiated rapid, forced societal changes. The regime, led by Pol Pot, aimed to create a classless society by eliminating intellectual and cultural heritage.

The Khmer Rouge began implementing radical policies immediately upon taking power. They forced the evacuation of cities, abolished money, private property, and religion. Families were separated, daily life was collectivized, and intellectuals, professionals, and perceived opponents were executed en masse.

Meanwhile, Vietnam grappled with post-war reconstruction and reunification challenges. Despite their wartime alliance, tensions between Vietnam and Democratic Kampuchea escalated due to several factors. Territorial disputes, particularly in the Mekong Delta region, caused friction. Ideological differences and mutual mistrust grew, and Cambodia increasingly feared Vietnamese domination in Indochina.

By early 1978, reports of mass killings and extreme hardship in Cambodia began to reach Vietnam. Refugees fleeing across the border brought harrowing tales of the Khmer Rouge's brutality. The Vietnamese leadership, while concerned, remained hesitant to intervene, wary of international repercussions.

As border skirmishes increased in frequency and intensity, both nations stood on the brink of conflict. The stage was set for a confrontation that would alter the course of Southeast Asian history—a war that would challenge conventional notions of sovereignty, humanitarian intervention, and the limits of revolutionary ideology.

Ba Chuc

March 4, 1978 – Beijing, China

The late afternoon sun cast long shadows across the manicured gardens of Zhongnanhai, the secluded compound at the heart of Beijing that served as the nerve center of China's Communist Party. Within one of the compound's traditional pavilions, its sweeping eaves and intricate wooden latticework a stark contrast to the weighty matters discussed inside, General Secretary Hua Guofeng paced back and forth, his brow furrowed in frustration.

Marshal Ye Jianying, Hua's trusted deputy and the venerable vice chairman of the Central Military Commission, sat calmly at a ornate rosewood table, his weathered hands folded before him. The scent of jasmine tea wafted through the air, mingling with the faint aroma of ink from the calligraphy scrolls adorning the walls.

"This situation with Vietnam and Cambodia is spiraling out of control," Hua said, his voice tight with tension. He paused by a window, gazing out at the serene surface of the nearby lake, its tranquility a mockery of the tumultuous political landscape. "Le Duan is overstepping. His interference in Cambodia threatens to destabilize the entire region."

Ye nodded slowly, his expression grave. "Indeed, Comrade Hua. Le Duan's ambitions seem to have outgrown Vietnam's borders. But we must tread carefully. Our support for Pol Pot's regime in Cambodia is not without its... complications."

Hua turned sharply, his eyes flashing. "Complications? The Khmer Rouge are carrying out the revolution as it should be done. Yes, their methods are harsh, but they're cleansing their society of capitalist and imperialist influences. Vietnam has no right to interfere with this process."

"Perhaps," Ye conceded, reaching for his teacup. "But reports of the Khmer Rouge's excesses are troubling. We must consider the long-term implications of our support."

Hua waved a hand dismissively. "Long-term implications pale in comparison to the immediate threat. If Vietnam succeeds in toppling Pol Pot, they will have effectively expanded Soviet influence right to our southern border. We cannot allow this."

Ye sipped his tea thoughtfully before responding. "What do you propose, Comrade Hua?"

"We must send a clear message to Hanoi," Hua said, his voice hardening. "Increase military aid to Cambodia. Step up our diplomatic pressure on Vietnam. And..." he paused, weighing his next words carefully, "we should begin preparations for a possible... demonstration of force along our shared border with Vietnam."

Ye's eyebrows rose slightly. "A bold move, Comrade. One that could lead us down a dangerous path."

"Sometimes, old friend, we must be willing to walk dangerous paths to secure the revolution," Hua replied, his gaze drifting back to the placid waters outside. "History will judge us not by our caution, but by our resolve."

As the last rays of sunlight painted the sky in hues of orange and purple, the two men continued their discussion, the fate of Southeast Asia hanging in the balance of their words. Outside, in the meticulously maintained gardens of Zhongnanhai, life continued its peaceful rhythm, oblivious to the storms brewing within the halls of power.

April 12, 1978 – Phnom Penh, Cambodia

The cigarette smoke hung heavy in the dimly lit room, deep within the maze-like compound known as K-1 in Phnom Penh. Pol Pot, the enigmatic leader of Democratic Kampuchea (Cambodia), sat behind a simple wooden desk, his eyes darting nervously from the letter in his hands to the shuttered windows. The spartan room, devoid of any personal touches or luxuries, reflected the austere ideology of the Khmer Rouge regime.

Outside, the sounds of the capital city were muffled and distant. The once-bustling metropolis now lay eerily quiet, its population forcibly evacuated to rural labor camps. Armed guards patrolled the perimeter of the compound, their presence a constant reminder of the paranoia that gripped the leadership.

Pol Pot's deputy, Nuon Chea, stood silently nearby,

his impassive face betraying no emotion as he waited for his leader to speak.

Finally, Pol Pot looked up, his voice barely above a whisper. "Our Vietnamese brothers mock us, Nuon. This reply from Le Duan... it's nothing but empty words and veiled threats."

Nuon Chea nodded slowly. "They underestimate our resolve, Brother Number One. What do you propose?"

Pol Pot rose abruptly, crumpling the letter in his fist. He began to pace, his movements jerky and agitated. "We've tried diplomacy. We've shown patience. But the Vietnamese... they only understand strength."

He paused, glancing suspiciously at the walls as if they might be listening. Leaning in close to Nuon Chea, he continued in a hushed tone, "We must teach them a lesson they won't forget. A message written not in ink, but in action."

Nuon Chea's eyes gleamed with understanding. "The Revolutionary Army stands ready, Brother. What are your orders?"

"Two divisions. Send them across the border - two kilometers into Vietnamese territory. Let's see how Le Duan responds to a diplomatic overture."

"It will be done," Nuon Chea replied, his voice steady. "But the international community—"

Pol Pot cut him off with a sharp gesture. "The international community? They're all against us, Nuon. Spies and traitors, everywhere. We can trust no one but ourselves. We know what is best for our people."

He moved to the window, carefully peering through a crack in the shutters. The paranoia that had become his constant companion seemed to deepen the lines on his face. "Our revolution is pure. We will not let the

Vietnamese or anyone else corrupt it. This 'incursion' will remind them of our strength and that we do not fear them."

Nuon Chea bowed slightly. "I'll give the order immediately, Brother Number One."

As his deputy turned to leave, Pol Pot called out, "And Nuon... trust no one with this information. The walls have ears, and our enemies are everywhere. Even here, in the heart of our revolution."

The door closed behind Nuon Chea, leaving Pol Pot alone in the shadowy room. He returned to his desk, his eyes fixed on a large map of Southeast Asia spread across its surface. With a trembling hand, he traced the border between Kampuchea and Vietnam, his finger lingering on the spot where, soon, his troops would cross.

In the stifling silence of K-1, as the capital lay quiet around him, Pol Pot set in motion events that would escalate the brewing conflict with Vietnam, pushing the region further towards the brink of war.

Ba Chuc, Vietnam

The afternoon sun bore down on Rene Granier and Spitting Woman as they observed Ba Chuc from their concealed position at the edge of a tree line. The village, normally visible from their vantage point, lay shrouded in a thick, smoky haze. No movement disturbed the eerie stillness, yet both scouts felt the weight of unseen eyes upon them.

Granier adjusted the focus on his binoculars, scanning the perimeter. Spitting Woman, her weathered face a mask of concentration, kept watch on their surroundings. Her hand rested lightly on her weapon, ready for any threat. After several minutes of tense observation, she tapped Granier's shoulder and pointed towards the eastern approach to the village.

They moved silently through the dense vegetation, their progress slow and deliberate. Every rustle in the underbrush, every snapping twig underfoot, sent a jolt of adrenaline through their bodies. As they neared Ba Chuc, the acrid smell of smoke grew stronger, mingling with another, more unsettling odor. Granier held up a closed fist, signaling a halt. They listened intently, straining to discern any human sounds amidst the faint rustle of leaves.

With practiced coordination, they entered the village, moving in tandem, watching each other's blind spots. The devastation was immediate and overwhelming. Bodies lay where they had fallen - in the streets, doorways, and courtyards. Many showed signs of extreme violence. Broken implements of daily life were scattered among the victims, telling of sudden, terrifying chaos.

Granier surveyed the scene, his expression tightening. He glanced at Spitting Woman, who met his gaze with a slight nod. Without a word, they began their grim task, always keeping each other in sight, always alert for movement in the shadows.

They moved methodically through Ba Chuc, Granier noting details in his field notebook and snapping photographs while Spitting Woman kept count of the victims and watched their backs. At regular intervals, they would pause, listening for any sign that the perpetrators of this massacre might still be nearby.

In one home, they found a family huddled together, parents still shielding their children. A half-prepared meal lay abandoned on a table, chairs overturned nearby. Granier paused, taking in the scene, before adding to his notes. Spitting Woman positioned herself in the doorway, her eyes scanning the street outside.

As they progressed, the scale of the massacre became clear. Houses, community buildings, and the local temple all bore witness to the brutality. No one had been spared - the elderly, adults, and children alike had fallen victim to the Khmer Rouge's savagery.

Hours passed. The sun dipped towards the horizon, casting long shadows across Ba Chuc. These lengthening shadows seemed to move of their own accord, keeping both scouts on edge. Granier closed his notebook and looked to Spitting Woman.

"The count?" he asked quietly.

"Over three thousand," she replied, her voice low and level.

Granier nodded, processing the information. "We should go."

Spitting Woman gave a curt nod. They took one last look at the village before starting their return journey, moving with the same caution that had brought them in. As they walked, the weight of what they'd witnessed settled over them, accompanied by the constant vigilance against unseen threats that might still lurk in the gathering dusk.

As they approached a small dwelling near the edge of the village, a faint sound caught their attention. Granier and Spitting Woman exchanged glances, hands tightening on their weapons. They moved cautiously towards the source of the noise.

Inside the house, they found a scene of horror similar to many others they had encountered. But amidst the stillness, there was movement. A small boy, no more than three years old, clung to the body of a woman, presumably his mother. The child's eyes, wide with terror and incomprehension, locked onto the two scouts.

Granier slowly knelt down, keeping his movements deliberate and non-threatening. Spitting Woman positioned herself in the doorway, dividing her attention between the street outside and the unfolding scene within.

"It's okay," Granier said softly in Vietnamese, reaching out a hand. "We're here to help."

The boy didn't move, his small fingers gripping his mother's clothes tightly. Tears streaked his dirt-smudged face.

Granier looked up at Spitting Woman. Their eyes met in a moment of shared anguish and determination. The mission had changed. They now had a life to save, a witness to protect.

"We need to get him out of here," Granier said quietly.

Spitting Woman nodded. "I'll keep watch. You get the boy."

With gentle persistence, Granier coaxed the child away from his mother's body. The boy was weak, likely having gone days without food or water. Granier cradled him carefully, feeling the child's rapid heartbeat against his chest.

As they prepared to leave Ba Chuc, the full weight of what they'd witnessed settled over them. The village stood as a grim testament to the Khmer Rouge's brutality. But in their arms, they held a flicker of life - a survivor who might one day bear witness to the tragedy.

They began their cautious journey back, the child a

precious cargo that heightened both their sense of urgency and their vulnerability. As the sun dipped towards the horizon, casting long shadows across the landscape, Granier and Spitting Woman moved silently away from Ba Chuc, guardians now of both the tragic truth they'd uncovered and the young life they'd saved.

Hanoi, Vietnam

The Politburo office was austere, its walls adorned with a single portrait of Ho Chi Minh. Le Duan sat behind a heavy wooden desk, his face impassive as Granier and Spitting Woman stood before him. The room was silent save for the quiet whir of a ceiling fan and the distant sounds of Hanoi filtering through the windows.

Spitting Woman placed a thick folder on Le Duan's desk. "The report from Ba Chuc," she said, her voice level despite the weight of its contents.

Le Duan opened the folder. His eyes widened almost imperceptibly as he leafed through the photographs and documents. The images told a story of brutality that words alone couldn't convey - bodies strewn across dirt roads, homes turned to charnel houses, the small boy they'd rescued, his eyes vacant with shock.

"How many?" Le Duan asked, his tone clipped.

"Over three thousand civilians," Spitting Woman replied. "Men, women, children. No one was spared."

Le Duan's jaw tightened. He stood abruptly, turning to face the window. A well-kept garden stretched before him, soothing and peaceful, a sharp contrast to the photos on his desk.

"How sure are you that this was done by the Khmer Rouge?" Le Duan said, still facing away.

"There is no way to know for sure, but we have seen first-hand the Khmer Rouge tactics. They are beyond brutal. Ba Chuc was... it was a slaughterhouse. The Khmer Rouge moved through with precision. They didn't just kill; they annihilated the entire village."

"Houses were burned with people inside," Spitting Woman added. "Those who tried to flee were gunned down in the streets. We found entire families..."

She paused, composing herself. "Entire families huddled together, as if they tried to protect each other in their final moments."

Le Duan turned back, his face a mask of controlled fury. "And the boy? The survivor you mentioned in your initial report?"

"Safe," Granier answered. "He's being cared for in a secure location. He hasn't spoken since we found him."

"That is inconvenient. He might shed light on the identity of the attackers."

"He is a child. I doubt he could shed light on anything beyond his mother's death."

Le Duan nodded, then moved around the desk, picking up one of the photographs. "We've tolerated their excesses, their 'purification' of their society. But this..." He shook his head, letting the photo fall back to the desk. "This crosses a line we cannot ignore."

"Comrade," Spitting Woman began, "what are your orders?"

Le Duan looked at her, then at Granier. His decision was visible in his eyes before he spoke. "Pol Pot brags that one of Khmer Rouge is worth thirty Vietnamese soldiers. He's overconfident. He shall soon be humbled. We're going in. Thirteen divisions. One hundred and fifty thousand of our best troops."

Granier and Spitting Woman exchanged glances. The scale of the proposed action was unprecedented.

"The incursion will be bloody. The international community—" Granier started.

"Will understand once they see this," Le Duan cut him off, gesturing at the report. "We cannot allow this to continue on our border. The stability of the entire region is at stake."

"And China?" Spitting Woman asked, her voice low. "They've been supporting Pol Pot."

Le Duan's expression hardened. "China will have to accept the reality of the situation. We're not seeking to conquer Cambodia, only to remove this madman from power."

He walked back around his desk, sat down heavily. "You two," he said, looking up at Granier and Spitting Woman, "I need you to scout ahead of our troops. Your knowledge of the terrain, of Khmer Rouge movements, will be crucial."

"When do we leave?" Granier asked.

"Immediately," Le Duan replied. "Our forces are already mobilizing. You'll rendezvous with the lead elements at the border."

Granier shifted his weight, a rare sign of discomfort. "Comrade, if I may... The terrain along the border is treacherous. The Khmer Rouge know it well. They've had years to prepare defenses."

Le Duan leaned forward, his eyes intense. "Which is precisely why we need you two. Your experience will be invaluable. What can we expect?"

"It's hard to say," said Spitting Woman. The Chinese have sent over 10,000 advisors to train the Khmer Rouge forces. I suspect they are no longer just a loose group of guerilla fighters. No longer undisciplined. They'll hit our supply lines and draw our forces into ambushes."

Granier spoke up. "Minefields will be an issue. They've seeded the border areas heavily."

"You will find a suitable path for our troops," ordered Le Duan. "We'll need to strike quickly. The longer this campaign drags on, the more international pressure we'll face."

"We agree. Speed will be vital, but the Khmer Rouge will do their best to slow us down," said Spitting Woman.

Le Duan nodded, absorbing the information. "And Pol Pot himself? What do you know of his likely movements?"

"He's paranoid, constantly on the move," Granier replied. "But he has a network of hideouts. If we can identify and target those..."

"Do it," Le Duan said firmly. "Find him. This ends only when Pol Pot is removed from power and a new government replaces the old. Do whatever it takes."

Le Duan fixed on them with a steely gaze. "I need you two to be the eyes and ears of this operation. Your reports will guide our strategy. The lives of our soldiers and the future of this region depend on your accuracy and judgment."

"We will do our best," said Spitting Woman.

Le Duan nodded. "Good. Now go. Every moment we delay gives Pol Pot more time to prepare. Dismissed."

As they left the office, the weight of what was to come settled over them. They were the vanguard of Vietnam's response. The tip of the spear. "Are you okay with this… fighting for Vietnam?" said Spitting Woman.

"I'm not fighting for Vietnam. I am fighting for the people of Cambodia… like the kid we found," said Granier. "A child shouldn't see that kind of cruelty. Never. I fight for him."

Spitting Woman nodded as they left the politburo compound.

Cambodian-Vietnamese Border

The American-made jeep bounced along the rutted road, its chassis groaning in protest. A faded red star, hastily painted over the remnants of a U.S. Army insignia, adorned the hood. Granier gripped the wheel tightly, navigating the uneven terrain. Beside him, Spitting Woman sat in silence, her eyes scanning the passing landscape. Two American-made sniper rifles accompanied their gear.

"Merde," Granier muttered as the jeep hit a particularly deep pothole. "This road gets worse every time."

Spitting Woman grunted in agreement. "At least we're not walking."

As they crested a hill, the full scale of the Vietnamese military operation sprawled before them. The valley below bustled with activity, a mismatched array of Soviet, Chinese and American-made vehicles and artillery pieces creating a cacophony of diesel engines and clanking metal.

Granier slowed the jeep, taking in the scene. "Would you look at that," he said, gesturing towards a column of tanks. "Talk about a hodge-podge."

Spitting Woman leaned forward, her eyes narrowing. "M41 Bulldogs... and are those M48 Pattons? Alongside T-54s?" She shook her head. "This army is a war museum on tracks."

They drove past a line of M113 APCs, their boxy shapes a stark contrast to the sleeker Soviet-designed vehicles nearby. A group of soldiers huddled around an M67 "Zippo", its flamethrower attachment drawing wary glances from those nearby.

"Over there," Granier pointed, "M56 Scorpions. I thought those were all scrapped."

Spitting Woman snorted. "Nothing gets scrapped here. If it can still fire, it's used."

They turned off the main road, following a track that led to a makeshift airfield. A pair of Cessna A-37 Dragonflies screamed overhead, the roar of their engines drowning out all other noise for a moment.

As they approached the field commander's headquarters, a sprawling complex of tents and hastily erected structures, the true diversity of the artillery became apparent. 130mm M-46 field guns stood alongside 155mm M114 howitzers. Chinese-made 105mm Type 91 howitzers were being positioned, their crews working with grim efficiency.

Granier parked the jeep and they both climbed out, stretching stiff muscles.

"I count at least five different types of artillery," Spitting Woman said, her tone a mix of admiration and disbelief.

"Soviet, Chinese, American..." Granier shook his head. "They'll be lucky if they can keep them all supplied with the right ammunition."

A young officer approached them, saluting sharply. "The general is waiting for you."

Following the officer, the cacophony of preparations surrounded them - the clank of artillery being positioned, the rumble of tank engines, and the shouts of soldiers readying for battle.

General Le Duc Anh emerged from the tent, his face a mask of barely concealed suspicion as he approached the two scouts. "So, Hanoi's special operatives finally grace us with their presence," he said, his tone clipped.

Granier nodded respectfully. "General, we have information that could be crucial to the success of the invasion."

The general's eyes narrowed. "And why should I prioritize your intel over my own recon teams? Teams that have been here, on the ground, for weeks?"

Spitting Woman stepped forward, her posture rigid. "Because we've been operating behind enemy lines for months, General. We know the terrain, the Khmer Rouge positions, and their likely strategies."

Inside the tent, Granier spread a detailed map across the central table. Officers crowded around, their curiosity overcoming their initial skepticism.

"Here," Granier said, pointing to a section of the border. "This area is less fortified. The terrain is challenging, which is why the Khmer Rouge haven't concentrated their defenses here. But it's passable for your armor, especially the M41 Bulldogs and M48 Pattons."

The general leaned in, studying the map. "And Pol Pot? Any intel on his whereabouts?"

Granier shook his head. "Pol Pot will remain in Phnom Penh. He's not a field commander. His lieutenants will be directing the defense."

Spitting Woman traced a route on the map. "We propose to scout ahead, here and here. We'll identify ambush positions and minefields before the main force moves in."

The general straightened, his face thoughtful. "It's risky. We could lay down smoke cover as you cross-"

"No," Granier interrupted firmly. "No smoke, no change in bombing or artillery, nothing that could draw attention to our position or mission. The risk of a Khmer Rouge patrol finding us would be far more dangerous than dodging a stray bomb or artillery shell."

A tense silence fell over the tent. The general's eyes moved from Granier to Spitting Woman, then back to the map. Finally, he nodded. "Very well. You have until sundown tomorrow. After that, we move, with or without your intel."

As Granier and Spitting Woman prepared to leave, the general called out, "For the revolution." The traditional Buddhist blessings were noticeably absent, a reminder of the ideological shift that had occurred.

"For the Cambodian people," Granier replied, meeting the general's gaze.

Outside, as they walked back to their jeep, Spitting Woman muttered, "He doesn't trust us."

Granier nodded, checking his gear one last time. "Can you blame him? We're wild cards in his carefully planned operation."

They climbed into the jeep, the weight of their mission settling over them. Ahead lay the border, and beyond it, the unknown territories of a country torn apart by the Khmer Rouge. As they drove towards the frontier, the sounds of the Vietnamese war machine faded behind them.

The invasion of Cambodia was about to begin, and Granier and Spitting Woman would be the first to cross the line.

The afternoon sun dipped low, casting long shadows across no-man's-land. Granier and Spitting Woman lay prone in a patch of elephant grass, the coarse blades scratching at their faces. Before them stretched a no-man's land, a hundred-meter strip of cleared earth separating Vietnam from Cambodia. Soon, darkness would offer them cover, but it would also hide whatever dangers awaited on the other side.

Granier peered through his binoculars, methodically scanning the terrain. "Two watchtowers. North and south. Each manned by two guards."

Spitting Woman's eyes narrowed. "And the fence?"

"Three meters high. Barbed wire top. Looks new."

They observed in tense silence as a patrol emerged from the tree line on the Cambodian side. Four soldiers moved with practiced efficiency, eyes sweeping the border for any sign of movement.

Spitting Woman whispered. "Do you see the red scarves?"

Granier nodded, watching as the patrol passed dangerously close to their position. The soldiers' faces were young, but their eyes held the hardness of men who had seen too much death.

A sudden crackle of radio static made them both stiffen. The patrol leader barked something into his handset, his words indistinct but his tone urgent.

"Something's got them riled up," Granier murmured.

As if in answer, the distant sound of engines growled to life. Moments later, two military trucks rumbled into view, kicking up dust as they sped along the border road.

"Troop movement," Spitting Woman said, her voice tight. "But why?"

The trucks ground to a halt near the watchtowers. Soldiers poured out, shouting and gesturing. Among them, a figure in a crisp uniform stood out - an officer, clearly agitated.

Granier zoomed in on the scene. "They're reinforcing the border. Setting up more defensive positions."

Spitting Woman cursed under her breath. "They know something's coming."

"We'll need to find a weak spot, fast."

Spitting Woman nodded, her eyes never leaving the frenzied activity before them. "And hope they haven't found our people first."

As twilight deepened, the border bristled with new defenses. Granier and Spitting Woman remained motionless, watching and waiting. Their mission, already dangerous, but with thousands of lives hanging in the balance, they had no choice but to play the hand they'd been dealt.

The relative quiet shattered as artillery shells screamed overhead. Granier and Spitting Woman instinctively pressed themselves flatter against the earth as explosions erupted along the Cambodian side of the border. Granier growled as dirt rained down on them.

The ground shook with each impact. Through the haze of smoke and debris, they watched the Khmer Rouge soldiers scrambling for cover. The officer bellowed orders, his voice barely audible over the din of battle.

A new sound cut through the chaos - the distinctive whine of jet engines. Two Vietnamese Dragonfly jets streaked across the sky, so low the treetops swayed in their wake.

The Dragonflies banked hard, lining up their run. Rockets blazed from their wings, slamming into the hastily constructed defensive positions. Concrete and steel disintegrated under the barrage.

Granier's eyes scanned the sky. "We've got Phantoms up there. At least two. Maybe more."

As if summoned by his words, the American-made F-4s came into view, their silhouettes unmistakable against the dimming sky. They moved in a tight formation, watching for any sign of Khmer Rouge MiGs as the Dragonflies carried out their assault.

Another artillery volley found its mark. A watchtower erupted in flames, toppling slowly like a felled tree. Men ran from the wreckage, some on fire.

"This wasn't part of the plan," Spitting Woman said, her voice steady despite the mayhem surrounding them.

Granier nodded grimly. "Someone jumped the gun. Or the Khmer Rouge provoked this."

A stray shell impacted nearby, showering them with dirt and fragments. As the dust settled, they saw the border fence had been breached in several places.

"We need to move," Granier said, already tensing to spring up. "Use the chaos as cover."

Spitting Woman grabbed his arm. "Wait. Look."

Through the settling dust and smoke, they could see figures moving in the no-man's land. Civilians, dozens of them, fleeing the carnage.

"Villagers," Spitting Woman said.

"Poor bastards," said Granier.

Their mission parameters hadn't accounted for this. But as another explosion lit up the darkening sky, they knew their plans would have to change. The border had become a war zone, and their task had just grown exponentially more complex.

Darkness cloaked the ravaged border as Granier and Spitting Woman crept forward. The acrid stench of cordite hung heavy in the air, mingling with the metallic tang of blood. Sporadic gunfire punctuated the night, muzzle flashes and tracer rounds briefly illuminating the devastation.

They moved in short bursts, using the twisted wreckage of vehicles and fortifications as cover. A dying soldier's moan made them freeze. Granier's hand tightened on his rifle, but the sound faded into the night. They advanced.

"Tripwire," Spitting Woman hissed, her hand shooting out to stop Granier.

In the dim starlight, a gossamer-thin wire glinted, stretched taut across their path. Granier nodded, carefully stepping over it. They skirted a crater, still smoking from a direct hit.

A flare suddenly arced overhead, bathing the landscape in harsh green light. They dropped prone, pulses racing. Boots crunched on debris nearby. A patrol, speaking in clipped Khmer.

Spitting Woman's fingers dug into the earth as the patrol passed mere meters from their position. One soldier paused, sweeping his rifle barrel in their direction. Seconds stretched into eternity.

A distant explosion drew the patrol's attention. They moved on, melting into the shadows.

Granier and Spitting Woman exchanged a glance, then resumed their advance. They reached the remnants of the border fence, its razor wire coiled like angry snakes.

"There," Granier whispered, indicating a gap.

As they slipped through, a scream rent the air. A figure burst from the underbrush - a civilian, clothes torn, eyes wild with terror. Before they could react, the crack of a rifle split the night. The civilian crumpled, falling almost at their feet.

Spitting Woman's breath caught. Granier grabbed her arm, pulling her into the cover of a bombed-out bunker. Flashlight beams crisscrossed the area where they'd just been standing.

"We can't help them all," Granier said, his voice low and tight.

Spitting Woman's eyes blazed in the darkness, but she nodded. Their mission came first.

They pressed on, every sense straining. The border lay behind them now, but the real dangers still lay ahead. As they melted into the war-torn Cambodian jungle, the night seemed to close in around them, filled with unseen threats.

Dawn's first light seeped through the jungle canopy as Granier and Spitting Woman moved with silent efficiency. Granier's map, already marked with a spiderweb of notations, came out at each pause.

"Another 130mm artillery position," he murmured, making a precise mark. "That's the third battery. They're well-dispersed."

Spitting Woman nodded, her eyes constantly scanning their surroundings. "ZSU-23-4 over there. Camouflaged, but I saw the radar dish rotate."

Granier added it to the map. These positions would be priority targets for the pre-invasion barrage.

They froze as voices drifted through the underbrush. Granier raised his binoculars, focusing on a clearing ahead.

"Ambush position," he whispered. "Heavily reinforced. I count at least two DShK heavy machine guns and what looks like a recoilless rifle."

Spitting Woman's hand instinctively moved to her weapon. "We could take them."

Granier shook his head. "Too risky. One burst of fire and every Khmer Rouge for miles would be on us."

Reluctantly, she nodded. They marked the position and moved on.

The day wore on. They discovered more booby traps – tripwires connected to grenades, punji pits lined with rusted spikes, and even a crude but effective deadfall trap that would crush anyone triggering it.

"These aren't just defensive," Spitting Woman observed. "They're buying time. Wearing down the advance."

Granier grunted in agreement, meticulously recording each find.

As afternoon faded towards evening, they crested a small rise and stopped short. Before them stretched a vast, seemingly empty field.

"Minefield," Granier said, his voice barely above a whisper.

Spitting Woman nodded grimly. "Mixed. See how the grass is disturbed in different patterns? Anti-tank and anti-personnel."

"They're well prepared. Ya gotta give them that."

They spent the next hour carefully mapping its perimeter, noting how it funneled any advance into pre-sighted kill zones.

Finally, satisfied they had charted a viable path through the Khmer Rouge defenses, they began their cautious return journey.

As the sun set, they approached the battered border

zone. Granier paused, studying his map one last time.

"This will work," he said quietly.

Spitting Woman's eyes met his. "It has to."

They slipped across the border, the precious map secure against Granier's chest. Behind them, the Cambodian jungle waited, filled with hidden threats soon to be unleashed.

General Le Duc Anh leaned over the map spread across the command tent's central table, his weathered face illuminated by harsh electric lamps. Granier and Spitting Woman stood beside him, their uniforms still caked with Cambodian mud.

"Walk us through it," the general ordered, his voice gravelly from years of barking commands and cigarettes.

Granier stepped forward, pointing to various markings on the map. "Three artillery batteries here, here, and here. 130mm guns, well-dispersed. We counted approximately eighteen pieces total."

A staff officer scribbled furiously in a notebook. "Crews?"

"Four per gun," Spitting Woman replied. "Plus two to three ammunition handlers."

Granier continued, "Multiple anti-aircraft positions. ZSU-23-4s primarily, but we also spotted several SA-7 teams."

"Troop concentrations?" another officer asked.

"Hard to get an exact count," Granier said. "But we estimate at least a regiment's worth, possibly more. They're dug in deep."

The general's eyes narrowed as Granier detailed the extensive network of booby traps and ambush positions. When he reached the minefield, the tent grew noticeably tenser.

"Dimensions?" the general asked.

"Approximately two kilometers wide, depth varying between 500 meters to a kilometer," Spitting Woman answered. "Mixed anti-tank and anti-personnel. No clear patterns we could discern."

The staff officers exchanged glances. One muttered something about needing more combat engineers.

General Anh straightened, studying the proposed path through the defenses that Granier and Spitting Woman had mapped out. His finger traced the route, pausing at key points.

After a long moment, he nodded. "It's viable. Costly, but viable." He looked up at Granier and Spitting Woman. "Well done. This intel will save a lot of lives and ensure our success."

"Thank you, sir," they responded in unison.

The general turned to his staff. "I want pre-invasion fire plans updated immediately. Prioritize those artillery positions and anti-aircraft sites. Have our aircraft armed with cluster munitions to take out the troop concentrations and ambush positions." He paused, then added, "And get those combat engineers prepped for minefield clearance."

As the staff burst into activity, the general addressed Granier and Spitting Woman once more. "You two have earned some rest. Get some chow and rack time. We'll handle the crossing."

Granier opened his mouth as if to protest, but the general cut him off. "That's an order. We'll need you sharp for what comes next."

They exited the tent. Outside, the night buzzed with pre-invasion energy. Vehicles rumbled past, loaded with troops and equipment. The air thrummed with anticipation and tightly coiled nerves.

Granier and Spitting Woman exchanged a glance. They both knew that their work was far from over, but for now, a moment's respite beckoned. As they headed towards the mess tent, the distant rumbles of artillery fire echoed across the border. The invasion of Cambodia had begun.

Invasion

Cambodian-Vietnamese Border

The Mekong's murky waters churned under the predawn sky, the far bank a dark smudge against the horizon. The Vietnamese unit commander, Lieutenant Dao surveyed the scene from atop his command vehicle.

"All units, prepare for crossing," he barked into his radio.

A chorus of acknowledgments crackled back. The riverbank erupted into motion.

The first wave of Soviet-made PT-76 amphibious tanks rumbled forward, their tracks churning the muddy shore. They hit the water with a series of tremendous splashes, bow waves rising as they forged ahead.

Private Nguyen Thanh, barely nineteen watched from the deck of an armored troop carrier, knuckles white on the railing. He gripped his AK-47 tightly as the amphibious vehicle lurched forward. The acrid stench of diesel fumes filled his nostrils, mixing with the nervous sweat of the men packed around him.

The vehicle lurched, then began to plow through the river.

"Eyes sharp," Corporal Tran muttered beside him. "They're sure to have a welcome party."

As if on cue, the opposite bank lit up with muzzle flashes. Tracer rounds arced across the water, some pinging off the armored hulls, others hissing into the river.

"Incoming!" someone shouted.

A rocket streaked from the far shore, narrowly missing a PT-76. The explosion sent a geyser of water skyward.

Lieutenant Dao's voice cut through the chaos. "Return fire! Suppress those positions!"

The lead vehicles opened up, their mounted machine guns hammering the shoreline. Thanh added his own rifle fire to the barrage, the AK-47 bucking against his shoulder.

Halfway across, disaster struck. A mine, dislodged by the current, detonated beneath one of the troop carriers. The blast lifted the vehicle partly out of the water, flames erupting from its hull.

"Men overboard!" Tran shouted, pointing to soldiers flailing in the current.

Their own carrier slowed, soldiers reaching out to haul the survivors aboard. Thanh helped pull a gasping sergeant from the water, the man's uniform smoking.

As they neared the far bank, the intensity of the Khmer Rouge fire increased. Bullets whined off the armored sides like angry hornets.

"Prepare to disembark!" Lieutenant Dao ordered.

"First wave's always the bloodiest," muttered Corporal Tran beside him. The older soldier's face was stern and unyielding. "Keep your head down and your ass lower, kid."

The vehicles ground to a halt, ramps dropping into the shallow water. Thanh leapt down from the deck of the tank, the river tugging at his legs as he slogged towards shore.

All around him, Vietnamese forces were storming the bank. PT-76s provided covering fire as infantry charged up the slope.

Thanh found himself running, stumbling onto Cambodian soil. Ahead lay a wall of green—thick jungle momentarily quiet in the predawn light.

A series of explosions rocked the earth. Geysers of mud erupted along the shoreline – mines detonating under the weight of advancing troops and vehicles.

"Watch your step!" Tran bellowed, yanking Thanh sideways. A second later, the spot where he'd been about to plant his foot erupted in a shower of dirt and shrapnel.

They reached firmer ground, diving for cover behind the smoking wreck of a Khmer Rouge truck. Thanh's ears rang from the constant gunfire and explosions.

Lieutenant Dao's voice cut through the din. "Push forward! We need to secure that tree line!"

Thanh exchanged a glance with Tran. The older soldier nodded.

Together, they rose and charged towards the thick jungle ahead.

Then all hell broke loose.

The jungle erupted in muzzle flashes and tracer rounds leaping from the foliage. Bullets whipped past, thudding into the mud around Thanh's feet. A man to his left went down screaming.

"Move! Move!" Tran bellowed, shoving Thanh forward in front of him like a human shield.

They sprinted for the treeline, diving behind the meager cover of fallen logs and twisted metal—remnants of the previous night's artillery barrage.

Thanh's ears rang from the gunfire. He peered over the log, squeezing off a few rounds in the general direction of the enemy. His hands shook so badly he doubted he hit anything.

A deafening explosion rocked the ground. One of the APCs behind them erupted in flames, sending a plume of oily black smoke into the sky.

"RPG!" someone shouted.

"We need to take it out," said Tran grabbing Thanh's shoulder. "We push forward on my mark. Ready?"

Thanh nodded, not trusting his voice.

"Now!"

They charged toward the next bit of cover, bullets kicking up dirt at their heels. They slid into a shallow crater, panting heavily.

Tran glanced over the edge spotting the two-man RPG team beside a tree, only a dozen yards away. Ducking back down, he grabbed Thanh's face, locking eyes and said, "RPG Team. Ten yards to the right. On my mark we fire. Ready?"

Thanh checked the chamber of his weapon, then nodded.

"Go!" said Tran as he swung his own rifle over the edge of the crater.

Thanh followed his movements. They fired in unison. The first bullets were wide, hitting the tree. The rounds that followed found their mark as the RPG team took aim at the crater. The gunner, hit in the head, collapsed dropping the launcher. As the loader reached for the weapon, one of Thanh's bullets hit him in the armpit and buried itself deep in his heart. After a dazed moment, he fell dead.

"Good aim, young eyes," said Tran as they ducked back into the crater.

A young lieutenant crawled over, his face streaked with mud and blood. "Second platoon's pinned down on the left flank. We need to—"

His words were cut short as a burst of machine-gun fire stitched across his back. The officer slumped forward, eyes already vacant.

"Shit," Tran hissed. He keyed his radio. "This is Corporal Tran, Second Platoon. Lieutenant's down. We need support on the left flank!"

Static crackled for a moment before a voice responded. "Roger that, Corporal. Armor's on the way. Hold position."

The distinctive rumble of tank treads grew louder. A T-54 crashed through the underbrush, its main gun swiveling towards the Khmer Rouge positions.

The tank fired. The thunderous boom was followed by screams from the enemy lines.

Tran sprang up and shouted. "Let's go!"

Thanh followed, heart pounding, eyes wide. They pushed forward, the tank providing mobile cover. Other soldiers fell in around them, a ragged line advancing into the maelstrom.

As they neared the tree line, Thanh spotted movement. A Khmer Rouge soldier, barely older than himself, raised his hands in surrender.

"Don't shoot!" the enemy called out in broken

Vietnamese.

Tran hesitated, lowering his rifle slightly.

In that split second, the Khmer Rouge soldier's hand darted to his belt. A grenade arced through the air.

"Get down!" Thanh screamed, tackling Tran to the ground.

The explosion showered them with dirt and shrapnel. Ears ringing, vision blurred, Thanh struggled to his feet. The fake surrenderer lay dead on the ground, shrapnel from his own grenade piercing his body.

Tran stared at Thanh, eyes wide with shock and gratitude. "Nice save, kid."

Thanh helped Tran up. The sounds of battle were already fading as Vietnamese forces pushed deeper into Cambodia. They had breached the first line of defense.

He checked his magazine, reloaded, and fell in beside Tran. Private Nguyen Thanh was no longer the same naive boy who had boarded that APC. He had survived his baptism of fire, but was far from safe.

The muddy waters of the Mekong tributary frothed around the tracks of the lead T-54 tank as it edged into the ford. Captain Minh Bao stood in the turret, his binoculars scanning the far bank. The air was thick with diesel fumes.

"Steady as she goes, Hien," he called down to his driver. The tank lurched forward, water sloshing against the hull.

Behind them, a column of armor waited their turn. Minh could feel the eyes of the infantry squads on the banks, their fate tied to this crossing.

Halfway across, a muffled thump sent tremors

through the tank. Minh's stomach dropped as he realized what it meant.

"Mine! Reverse, rever—"

His words were cut short as a massive explosion lifted the tank's front. Water rushed in through ruptured seams. Minh was thrown against the turret ring, pain lancing through his shoulder.

"Bail out!" he shouted, struggling with the hatch.

As he tumbled into the river, the cold shocking his system, chaos erupted on both banks. Machine gun fire raked the water around him. Somewhere to his left, Hien surfaced, gasping.

On the far bank, muzzle flashes lit up the treeline. A sharp crack cut through the din, followed by a streaking contrail.

"Recoilless rifle!" someone screamed.

The round slammed into the second tank in line. Its turret flew off in a ball of flame, landing with a tremendous splash in the river.

Minh struggled towards the shore, lungs burning. A hand grabbed his webbing, hauling him onto land. He found himself staring into the dirt-streaked face of Private Thanh.

"You okay, sir?" Thanh shouted over the bedlam.

Minh nodded, coughing up the river. He looked back to see the ford churning with activity. Infantry were wading across, firing from the hip. The remaining tanks had spread out, their main guns hammering the far bank.

A familiar whop-whop-whop cut through the air. Minh looked up to see a pair of UH-1 Huey gunships, captured American helicopters, now serving the Vietnamese forces, sweeping in low over the river. Door gunners opened up, M60 machine guns hammering the Khmer positions.

The Hueys banked hard and made another pass, rockets streaking from their pylons and exploding among the trees. Branches and debris rained down, along with the screams of Khmer Rouge fighters caught in the barrage.

As they advanced, Minh couldn't help but appreciate the irony. The very machines once used against them were now clearing their path into Cambodia. History had a twisted sense of humor.

"Push forward!" Minh bellowed, finding his feet. He snatched up a fallen AK-47. "We need to secure the bank!"

Thanh fell in beside him. Together, they splashed across the ford, bullets kicking up spray around them. At the top of the bank, Tran provided covering fire.

As Thanh and Minh neared the far bank, a Khmer Rouge soldier burst from concealment, eyes wild. He swung his rifle towards Minh.

Thanh reacted first, his burst catching the enemy's center mass. The Khmer fighter fell backwards, disappearing beneath the muddy water.

Minh nodded grimly at the private. "Good work, soldier. What's your name?"

"Private Thanh, sir."

"Stay close, Private. We're not out of this yet."

They scrambled up the bank, joining a ragged line of Vietnamese troops pushing into the treeline. Overhead, the Hueys made another pass, their machine guns spitting streams of tracer fire.

Minh paused behind a blasted tree stump, surveying the chaos. His tank lay half-submerged in the ford, smoke still rising from its hull. But the crossing continued. More armor was fording the river, infantry swarming across in their wake.

He felt a tap on his shoulder. Thanh pointed to movement in the brush ahead. Minh nodded, readying his rifle.

Minh and Thanh pressed forward, using the Hueys' barrage as cover. The acrid smell of burning foliage mixed with the coppery tang of blood.

"Watch for tunnels," Minh warned, eyes scanning the ground. "The Khmer love their underground networks."

As if summoned by his words, the earth erupted ten meters ahead. A Khmer Rouge fighter emerged from a hidden spider hole, AK-47 blazing.

Thanh reacted instantly, dropping to one knee and returning fire. His burst caught the enemy soldier in the face, sending him tumbling back into his hole.

"Good shot," Minh grunted, then froze. "Wait. Listen."

Through the roar of battle, a new sound reached them. A low, steady rumble, growing louder by the second.

"That's not aircraft," Thanh said.

Minh's eyes widened in realization. "Fall back! Now!"

They scrambled backwards just as a wall of water burst through the treeline. The Khmer Rouge had breached a dam upstream, unleashing a flash flood.

The torrent swept away soldiers on both sides, uprooting trees and carrying debris. Minh and Thanh clung to a sturdy trunk, the flood waters swirling around their chests.

"Crafty bastards," Minh spat, struggling to keep his rifle above water.

As the initial surge passed, leaving behind a muddy

quagmire, the Vietnamese advance stalled. Tanks that had made it across now found themselves bogged down. Infantry slogged through knee-deep mud, easy targets for snipers.

Khmer Rouge fighters seemed to materialize from the sodden earth, emerging from hidden entrances to ambush the struggling Vietnamese forces.

Minh keyed his radio. "This is Captain Minh. We need those Hueys back for close air support. Danger close!"

"Negative, Captain," came the reply. "Hueys are RTB for rearm. Hold your position."

Minh cursed, surveying the chaos around him. The carefully planned river crossing had devolved into a muddy, bloody slugfest.

"Sir," Thanh said, pointing to a ridge overlooking their position. "I think I see a command post up there."

Minh followed his gaze, noting the concentration of radio antennas and the bustle of activity.

"Good eye, Private," he said, a plan forming. "If we can take out their command, we might just turn this mess around."

Thanh nodded, checking his ammunition.

"It's going to be a hell of a climb," Minh warned.

"Better than drowning down here, sir," Thanh replied with a wry smile.

Together, they began to pick their way through the battlefield, mud sucking at their boots with every step. The ridge loomed ahead, promising either salvation or doom for the bogged-down Vietnamese advance.

As Minh and Thanh slogged towards the ridge, the battlefield around them devolved into pockets of intense fighting. The flood had fragmented the Vietnamese advance, turning the coordinated assault into a series of desperate skirmishes.

A burst of gunfire erupted to their left. Thanh instinctively dove behind the twisted wreckage of a jeep, pulling Minh down with him. Bullets pinged off the metal mere centimeters from their heads.

"Sniper," Minh hissed, peering cautiously around the edge of their cover. "In that group of trees, about two hundred meters."

Thanh nodded, taking a deep breath to steady himself. He slowly raised his rifle, using the jeep's frame to stabilize his aim. For a long moment, he remained motionless, scanning for any sign of movement.

A muzzle flash. A bullet landed just inches away from Thanh's face. But the private held steady, unflinching. Thanh squeezed his trigger, the rifle bucking against his shoulder. A cry of pain echoed from the trees.

"Good shot," Minh said, clapping him on the back. "Now move!"

They sprinted from cover to cover, using the chaos of battle as concealment. Twice more they encountered Khmer Rouge fighters emerging from hidden tunnels, dispatching them in brief, violent exchanges.

As they neared the base of the ridge, a deafening explosion rocked the earth. Minh looked back to see one of the bogged-down T-54 tanks erupting in flames, its turret spinning through the air like a macabre top.

"Damn," he muttered. "We're running out of time."

The slope was treacherous, mud and loose rocks threatening to send them tumbling back down with each step. Halfway up, Thanh's foot slipped. He started to fall, but Minh's hand shot out, grabbing his webbing and hauling him back.

"I've got you," Minh grunted.

Finally, they crested the ridge, chests heaving from the exertion. The Khmer Rouge command post sprawled before them – a collection of hastily erected tents and radio equipment. Officers hurried between positions, shouting orders.

Minh and Thanh exchanged a glance, both knowing they were vastly outnumbered.

"We'll only get one shot at this," Minh said, voice low. "See those fuel drums? If we can ignite them..."

Thanh nodded, understanding immediately. "It'll take out the whole post."

"And hopefully break their command structure," Minh finished. "You up for this, Private?"

"Yes, sir."

They split up, circling to opposite sides of the camp. Minh watched Thanh move into position, marveling at the young soldier's newfound confidence.

Minh took a deep breath, sighting down his rifle at the cluster of fuel drums. Across the camp, he saw Thanh do the same. He squeezed his rifle's trigger.

The fuel drums erupted in a massive fireball, sending a shockwave across the ridge. The Khmer Rouge command post dissolved into chaos, tents and equipment consumed by the inferno. Burning soldier running in terror.

Minh ducked behind a boulder, shielding himself from the heat and debris. Through the roar of the flames, he heard panicked shouts and the sporadic pop of ammunition cooking off.

"Thanh!" he called out, scanning for the young private.

A moment later, Thanh appeared through the smoke, soot-streaked but grinning. "We got 'em, sir."

Minh nodded, allowing himself a slight smile. "We got them. Now let's hope it's enough."

He keyed his radio. "All units, this is Captain Minh. Khmer Rouge command post neutralized. Advance! Advance!"

Below, the bogged-down Vietnamese forces surged forward with renewed vigor. The loss of coordinated resistance from the Khmer Rouge was immediately apparent. Their counterattacks became disjointed, lacking the previous precision.

As Minh and Thanh made their way back down the ridge, a familiar whop-whop-whop filled the air. The Huey gunships had returned, their door gunners laying down suppressing fire on the disorganized enemy positions.

"Sir, look!" Thanh pointed towards the river. "Reinforcements."

A fresh wave of Vietnamese armor was fording the water, T-54 tanks and BTR-60 APCs pushing through the muddy terrain. The momentum had shifted.

They rejoined the main force, linking up with a battered but determined infantry squad. The Vietnamese advance rolled forward, steam-rolling over the remaining pockets of resistance throughout the borderland.

By nightfall, they had secured a significant bridgehead. Minh stood on the captured ridge, surveying the battlefield. Fires still burned in places, and the air was thick with smoke and the echoes of sporadic gunfire. But the crossing had been achieved.

Thanh approached, offering a canteen. "Water, sir?"

Minh took it gratefully, realizing how parched he was. "Thank you, Private. You did good work today."

Thanh nodded, his youthful face now bearing the

weathered look of a combat veteran. "Funny. How things change so fast."

"What do you mean?"

"This morning, I was scared to death."

"And now?"

"I'm still scared, but I don't seem to mind it as much."

"I know what you mean. Fear is a good thing as long as it doesn't overwhelm you."

"Yeah. That's it."

As if to underscore his words, a distant rumble of artillery fire rolled across the landscape. The night sky briefly lit up with flashes of light, a harbinger of battles yet to come.

Minh took another swig from the canteen, then handed it back to Thanh. "Get some rest, Private. Tomorrow, we push deeper into Cambodia."

As Thanh saluted and moved off, Minh remained on the ridge, watching as the last light faded from the sky. The river crossing had been won, but at a heavy cost. And he knew it would be a long march to Phnom Penh.

The moon hung low, a sliver of light barely illuminating the war-torn landscape. Granier and Spitting Woman moved quietly through the temporary Vietnamese encampment, their American-made M21 sniper rifles slung across their backs. Granier's rifle was equipped with an AN/PVS-2 Starlight scope, its bulk a testament to its night-vision capabilities. Spitting Woman's M21 bore a standard scope, relying more on her keen eyesight in the darkness.

As they approached the perimeter, they paused to observe the sleeping soldiers. Faces etched with exhaustion, even in slumber, told the story of the brutal crossing. Granier adjusted his Starlight scope, the green-tinted view transforming the night into an eerie day.

"Movement, two o'clock," he whispered, indicating a spot beyond the defensive line.

Spitting Woman squinted, her eyes straining in the low light. "I don't see anything."

"Khmer Rouge scout. He's good, using the shadows."

They slipped past the outer sentries, Granier leading the way. The jungle closed in around them, a suffocating darkness filled with the chirps of insects and the occasional distant explosion.

An hour into enemy territory, they encountered their first target. A Khmer Rouge patrol moved through a small clearing. Granier, his Starlight scope piercing the gloom, spotted them first.

"Five men, twenty meters ahead," he whispered. "Patrol leader second from the left."

Spitting Woman nodded, raising her M21 and squinting through the regular scope. She took a deep breath, compensating for the low light.

The crack of her rifle dropped the patrol leader. Before the others could react, Granier's M21 barked twice more, the Starlight scope allowing him to acquire targets with unnerving speed and accuracy. In the space of seconds, only two enemy soldiers remained, panicked and directionless, searching for cover.

As the survivors fled into the jungle, Granier and Spitting Woman didn't pursue. Their mission wasn't to engage in firefights, but to decapitate the Khmer Rouge leadership.

They pushed deeper into the jungle. The terrain

became increasingly treacherous - hidden punji stick traps waited beneath innocent-looking piles of leaves, while tripwires promised swift death to the unwary. Granier's Starlight scope revealed these dangers, allowing them to navigate safely.

Near midnight, they heard voices ahead. Creeping forward, they saw a Khmer Rouge command post. A dozen soldiers surrounded a crude table where maps were spread out. An officer, distinguished by his cleaner uniform and air of authority, pointed at various locations, clearly outlining plans for a counterattack.

Granier set up his M21, the Starlight scope giving him a clear view of the officer's face. He controlled his breathing, waiting for the perfect moment.

A twig snapped nearby. Both Granier and Spitting Woman tensed. A Khmer Rouge sentry, previously hidden, emerged from the bushes barely ten meters away.

Spitting Woman reacted instantly. Her knife flashed in the moonlight as she sprang forward, clamping one hand over the sentry's mouth while the blade found his throat. They went down in a near-silent struggle.

At the command post, the officer looked up, alerted by some sixth sense. Granier knew their window was closing. He squeezed the trigger.

The officer's head snapped back, and he crumpled over the map table. Chaos erupted in the camp.

Spitting Woman, having dispatched the sentry, opened fire with her M21 from her prone position. Two more Khmer Rouge soldiers fell before the others could scramble for cover.

Granier and Spitting Woman retreated swiftly, using the superior range of their rifles to pick off pursuers as they melted into the darkness. The sounds of disorganized shouting faded behind them, evidence of the command structure they'd shattered.

As they navigated back towards friendly lines, they encountered a new challenge. A concealed bunker, its firing slit barely visible in the undergrowth, opened up with a heavy machine gun. Tracer rounds cut through the night, forcing them to dive for cover.

Pinned down behind a fallen tree, Granier peered through his Starlight scope. "I see three in the bunker. Gunner and two loaders."

Spitting Woman nodded, formulating a plan. "I'll draw their fire. You flank left and take out the gunner."

Granier hesitated. "It's too risky. You can't see them clearly."

"Trust me," she replied, a fierce grin visible even in the darkness.

Before he could protest further, Spitting Woman darted from cover, firing her M21 from the hip. The muzzle flashes drew the machine gunner's attention, bullets chewing up the ground around her.

Granier moved quickly, using his Starlight scope to navigate the treacherous terrain. He circled around, finding an angle on the bunker's firing slit.

Inside, he could see the gunner clearly, the man's face illuminated by the weapon's cycling action. Granier steadied his breath, then fired.

The machine gun fell silent.

Spitting Woman was already moving, charging the bunker before the remaining Khmer Rouge soldiers could regroup. She tossed a grenade through the firing slit, then pressed herself against the bunker's wall.

The explosion was deafening in the confined space. When the dust settled, silence reigned.

Phnom Penh, Cambodia

The dim light of oil lamps flickered across Pol Pot's face, deepening the shadows under his eyes as he listened to the report. The messenger, a young Khmer Rouge officer, trembled slightly as he delivered the news of the border battle's outcome. It wasn't good news.

Pol Pot's fist slammed onto the rough-hewn table, sending maps fluttering to the dirt floor of the command bunker. "Retreating? After all our preparations?"

The officer flinched but continued, his voice barely above a whisper. "The Vietnamese... their weapons, Comrade. American guns, tanks, even aircraft. Our forces couldn't—"

"Enough!" Pol Pot cut him off, rising abruptly. He paced the confined space, mind racing. The other generals present watched warily, tension thick in the stale air.

After a long moment, Pol Pot spoke again, his tone icily calm. "Our soldiers fought bravely. They are not to blame for this setback."

He turned to face his commanders. "The Vietnamese think their stolen American toys make them invincible. They've forgotten the old ways, the ways that defeated those same Americans."

A spark of understanding lit in the eyes of the oldest general present. "You mean to draw them in, Comrade? Use the land against them?"

Pol Pot nodded, "Precisely. We are children of Cambodia. Every tree, every stream, every shadow is our ally. The deeper the Vietnamese venture into our country the more advantage we gain."

He swept his hand across the map, scattering markers representing traditional defensive positions. "No more fixed fortifications. No more pitched battles. We melt away before their advance, then strike from all sides."

The generals murmured their agreement, already envisioning the new strategy.

"Booby traps, ambushes, night raids," Pol Pot continued, his voice gaining intensity. "Let them march deeper into our country. Every step will cost them blood."

He fixed each commander with a piercing stare. "Spread the word. Every village, every jungle path becomes a battleground. We'll bleed them dry in a war they don't understand."

The young officer who had delivered the report straightened, a flicker of hope replacing his earlier fear. "And the people, Comrade? Those in the path of the Vietnamese advance?"

Pol Pot's expression hardened. "They will serve the revolution, one way or another. Use them, move them, do what must be done."

As his commanders filed out to implement the new orders, Pol Pot turned back to the map. His finger traced the route of the Vietnamese advance, already envisioning the quagmire they would soon face.

"Come, then," he muttered to himself. "Come and learn why Cambodia has never truly been conquered."

Borderlands, Cambodia

As dawn began to break, Granier and Spitting Woman approached the Vietnamese perimeter. Exhausted soldiers stirred in their foxholes, preparing for another day of brutal combat. The two snipers' uniforms were caked with mud, their faces full of fatigue.

It was worth it. They had sown chaos among the enemy that night, eliminating key leaders and disrupting operations, giving the Vietnamese soldiers an important advantage. As they reported to the field commander, both knew that tonight they would venture out again. The war ground on, and they would continue their deadly hunt.

The general listened to their report intently, his weathered face betraying little emotion. When they finished, he nodded, " You've significantly disrupted their command structure. Good work."

He turned to a large map of the region, pointing to the southern flank of the Vietnamese advance. "But we have a new issue. The enemy is on the move. Our forces are pushing forward, but I'm concerned about our supply lines."

Granier and Spitting Woman exchanged a glance.

"The Khmer Rouge are crafty," the general continued. "They may be setting traps along our flanks, waiting to cut off our supply convoys. I need your eyes out there."

He traced a route along the map with his finger. "Scout this southern corridor. Look for signs of enemy activity - hidden positions, artillery emplacements, anything that could threaten our supply routes. We can't afford to have our advance stalled."

Spitting Woman studied the map intently. "That's a lot of ground to cover, sir."

The general nodded. "It is and there is not a lot of time. With the Khmer Rouge retreating, our forces will be moving fast."

Granier considered the challenge. "The terrain there is rough."

"Do whatever you need to do," the general replied. "But get me that intel. The success of our entire offensive could hinge on keeping those supply lines open."

Both scout-snipers nodded. Dismissed by the general, they left the command tent.

As they prepared for a few hours of restless sleep before heading out, the sounds of the advancing Vietnamese forces echoed in the distance. Tanks rumbled, soldiers shouted orders, and the occasional crack of gunfire punctuated the air. It wouldn't bother them. They were used to sleeping during a battle.

The Cambodian campaign was entering a new phase, and once again, Granier and Spitting Woman would be at the forefront keeping the troops safe.

Borderlands, Cambodia

The Cambodian sun beat down mercilessly as Granier and Spitting Woman moved through dense undergrowth. Sweat soaked their camouflage, but they pushed on relentlessly.

Granier's fist shot up. Spitting Woman froze.

He pointed, barely whispering, "Wire."

She nodded, eyes tracing the nearly invisible strand to a crude fragmentation mine. They skirted it, Granier marking the map.

As they pressed on, signs of Khmer Rouge activity increased. Punji pits. Tripwires. Mines. Granier's Starlight scope, repurposed for daylight, spotted most from afar.

Spitting Woman wiped sweat from her brow. "Slowing us down."

"Yep."

They crested a rise, dropping prone. Below, a Khmer Rouge position sprawled - trenches and bunkers.

Spitting Woman counted through her scope. "Two dozen. Maybe three. MG nest."

Granier grunted, noting it down.

They circled the position, encountering more of the same. Minefields. Mortar sites. Booby traps.

"Textbook," Spitting Woman muttered, navigating a particularly dense minefield.

Granier's brow furrowed. "Too textbook."

They pushed on. The day wore on, heat intensifying. Three more positions, each like the last.

Sunset found them on another ridge. Granier scanned the seemingly empty jungle below, unease growing.

"Off," he said simply.

Spitting Woman nodded. "Too quiet."

They studied the landscape intently, searching for anything unusual. Nothing.

"Time," Spitting Woman said finally.

Granier nodded reluctantly. As they started back, the feeling they'd missed something crucial gnawed at both of them.

Moving through the jungle, Spitting Woman raised her fist, motioning to stop. Granier moved up beside her. She pointed to her ear… listen – angry voices. They moved in the direction of the commotion.

Granier and Spitting Woman crouched at the edge of the jungle, surveying the scene before them. A village, once likely a peaceful collection of wooden houses and small farms, now resembled a chaotic prison camp.

Thatched roofs sagged under neglect, and several structures showed signs of recent fire damage. The central dirt path, normally a place of community gathering, was now eerily empty save for a few patrolling Khmer Rouge soldiers.

The villagers, gaunt and hollow-eyed, were being herded into groups in the village square. Men, women, and children alike wore simple black pajama-like garments, many tattered and stained. Their movements were sluggish, heads bowed in defeated compliance.

Khmer Rouge soldiers, most barely more than teenagers themselves, barked orders and shoved stragglers with the butts of their rifles. They wore a mismatched assortment of military gear - some in standard uniforms, others in civilian clothes with red scarves as their only identifier. Their faces were a study in contrasts - some bearing the vacant stare of indoctrinated youth, others twisted with a cruelty beyond their years.

In the center of the square, a man in a slightly cleaner uniform - likely a local commander - gestured angrily at a map spread on a makeshift table. He jabbed his finger at various points, shouting at his subordinates.

Granier nudged Spitting Woman, pointing to a group of villagers being led towards the jungle edge opposite their position. The people moved with the stiff gait of exhaustion, carrying crude tools - machetes, hoes, and axes as weapons. Some were given antiquated muskets with powder and ball.

"They're arming them," said Granier.

Spitting Woman's eyes narrowed. "Not arming.

Condemning."

Granier nodded, "And I doubt many of them will survive if they meet the Vietnamese head on."

They watched in tense silence, the reality of Khmer Rouge occupation laid bare before them. This wasn't just a military conflict anymore - it was a fight for the very soul of Cambodia.

They watched as a Khmer officer gestured wildly, indicating positions around the village. His meaning was clear: hide, wait, attack.

"Cannon fodder," Granier muttered.

A young boy, no more than twelve, struggled with a rusty machete nearly as long as his arm. An old woman clutched a pitchfork, her knuckles white with fear.

Spitting Woman's hand tightened on her rifle. "We could take out the officers. Buy them time to run."

Granier shook his head, his voice heavy. "And bring the whole Khmer Rouge down on the village? We'd just be changing the executioners."

They sat in tense silence, watching the preparations continue. The sun dipped lower, shadows lengthening across the doomed village.

Finally, Granier spoke. "We need to report this."

Spitting Woman didn't move, her eyes fixed on a mother clutching her infant, a sharpened bamboo spike in her free hand.

"Hey," Granier said softly, touching her arm. "There's nothing we can do here. But maybe... maybe if command knows, they can find a way to skirt the village."

She nodded, but her expression remained hard as they slipped back into the jungle.

Their return journey was swift and silent, each lost

in their own dark thoughts. As the Vietnamese lines came into view, Spitting Woman finally spoke, "You know what'll happen."

Granier didn't answer immediately. When he did, his voice was barely audible. "Yeah. I know."

They shared a long look, the weight of what they'd witnessed – and what was to come – hanging between them. The war ground on, indifferent to the human cost on all sides.

Command Tent

Granier and Spitting Woman stood before General Anh and his staff in the command tent. Maps covered the table, marked with the day's advances and newly discovered enemy positions.

Granier delivered most of the report in clipped, professional tones. The general nodded, his weathered face impassive as he absorbed the information about minefields, booby traps, and Khmer Rouge defensive positions.

When they reached the part about the village, Spitting Woman stepped forward, her voice tight. "Sir, the Khmer Rouge are arming civilians. Forcing them to fight."

The general's eyes narrowed. "Where?"

Granier pointed to a spot on the map. "Here. Directly in your path of advance."

A heavy silence fell over the tent. The general studied the map, his finger tracing the route.

Finally, he spoke. "There's nothing we can do. We must press on."

Spitting Woman tensed. "Sir, with respect, these are innocent civilians. They have no training in warfare.

They'll be slaughtered."

"And how many more will die if we delay?" the general countered, his voice hard. "Every day this war drags on, more innocents suffer."

"We could find another route," Spitting Woman pressed. "Bypass the village entirely."

The general shook his head. "Time is critical. We can't afford detours."

Granier put a hand on Spitting Woman's arm, a warning, but she shrugged it off.

"These people don't want to fight," she insisted. "They're being forced—"

"Enough!" the general's voice cracked like a whip. "I don't like it any more than you do. But this is war. Ugly choices must be made. We march on Phnom Penh."

He turned to his staff. "Ensure the advance units are aware of the situation. Rules of engagement remain the same. Any armed resistance is to be neutralized."

Spitting Woman opened her mouth to protest again, but Granier's grip on her arm tightened.

The general's gaze softened slightly as he looked at them. "Your concern for civilians does you credit. But the fastest way to save lives is to end this war quickly. We push on."

He nodded, a clear dismissal. Granier turned to leave, practically dragging Spitting Woman with him.

Outside the tent, Spitting Woman wrenched her arm free. "We can't just—"

"We can. And we will," Granier cut her off, his voice low and intense. "Because those are our orders. And because he's right."

Spitting Woman glared at him, then stormed off into the night. Granier watched her go, his own face a mask of conflicted emotions. In the distance, artillery rumbled, heralding the next day's advance. The war ground on, heedless of individual tragedies.

Cambodian Village

The Vietnamese column advanced cautiously through the stifling jungle heat, tanks and APCs rumbling down the narrow road. Captain Minh stood in the turret of his T-54, sweat beading on his brow as he scanned the dense foliage. The eerie quiet set his teeth on edge.

"Too easy," he muttered into his radio. "Where's the resistance?"

Private Thanh, crouched in the back of an APC, shared his commander's unease. His fingers tightened on his AK-47, eyes straining for any sign of movement in the oppressive green wall around them. Corporal Tran rode beside him, also watching.

As the village came into view, a palpable tension rippled through the Vietnamese ranks. Sergeant Linh, commanding an APC near the rear, felt the hairs on the back of his neck stand up.

Suddenly, shots rang out from the village. Minh's blood ran cold as he realized the nature of the "enemy" they faced.

"All units, halt!" he barked. "We've got civilians—"

His words were cut short as the jungle erupted in a maelstrom of gunfire. Khmer Rouge soldiers seemed to materialize from the undergrowth, swarming the Vietnamese positions with a ferocity that belied their earlier absence.

"Ambush!" Minh shouted, ducking as bullets pinged off his tank's turret. "Return fire!"

The air filled with the staccato of small arms, the

deeper boom of tank cannons, and the screams of the wounded and dying. In the village, terrified civilians ran in all directions, caught in the murderous crossfire. Some threw down their crude weapons refusing to fight.

Exiting the armored vehicle, Thanh found himself suddenly exposed as a rocket struck his APC, the explosion throwing him clear. Dazed, he scrambled for cover behind the burning wreck, the heat searing his back. A Khmer soldier charged him, eyes wild with battle fury. They grappled desperately, Thanh's rifle trapped between them. He headbutted the man, feeling cartilage crunch. As the Khmer soldier staggered back, Thanh brought his rifle up and fired, the muzzle flash illuminating a face twisted in hate and pain.

The battle devolved into nightmarish madness. Vietnamese soldiers, trained for conventional warfare, struggled against the Khmer's guerrilla tactics. Every tree, every hut seemed to hide an enemy ready to strike with savage efficiency.

Minh's tank became a focal point of the Khmer assault. RPG rounds screamed in, most missing, but one struck a glancing blow that left his ears ringing. He oriented the main gun towards a concentration of enemy fire, the cannon's roar momentarily drowning out the battle's din.

"We need to fall back!" Minh's voice crackled over the radio, tinged with desperation. "Create distance for air support!"

But disengaging proved nearly impossible. The Khmer pressed their advantage relentlessly, refusing to let the Vietnamese regroup. They had their enemy by the belt and they wouldn't let go. They seemed to be everywhere at once, striking and melting away only to reappear where least expected.

Sergeant Linh watched in horror as another rocket struck his APC. The vehicle erupted in flames, screams of the wounded cutting through the chaos. He dragged two of his men free, their uniforms smoldering, before a burst of enemy fire forced him to dive for cover.

The fighting devolved into a series of brutal, close-quarters engagements. Thanh found himself in a desperate hand-to-hand struggle with a Khmer fighter, both their weapons lost in the melee. They rolled in the mud, each seeking a killing advantage, the acrid smell of blood filling their nostrils.

Hours seemed to pass, though it was only minutes. The Vietnamese forces, bloodied and battered, finally managed to create some space between themselves and the Khmer attackers.

"Now!" Minh ordered, his voice hoarse from shouting. "Call in the strike!"

Moments later, artillery shells began to rain down, the whistle of their approach a banshee wail promising destruction. The distinctive whine of Huey gunships joined the symphony of death, rockets streaking from their pods to explode among the Khmer positions.

The village and surrounding jungle were transformed into an inferno. Trees splintered, huts disintegrated, and the earth itself seemed to erupt. Screams of the dying – Khmer, Vietnamese, and civilian alike – pierced the thunderous barrage.

As quickly as it had begun, the battle was over. The surviving Khmer melted back into the jungle, leaving behind a scene of utter devastation. The acrid smoke stung Minh's eyes as he surveyed the carnage from his battered tank. The village was gone, reduced to smoldering ruins. Bodies littered the ground, some still twitching in their death throes.

"Casualties?" he asked, his voice barely above a whisper.

"Heavy, sir," came the grim reply. "At least a third of our force. Maybe more."

Thanh, covered in blood both his and others', stumbled through the aftermath in a daze. The ground was slick with gore, spent cartridges crunching underfoot. He passed the mangled body of a young boy, a rusted machete still clutched in his lifeless hand, and felt bile rise in his throat.

Minh nodded, the weight of command pressing down on him like a physical thing. They had survived, pushed back the Khmer, but at what cost? The road to Phnom Penh stretched ahead, and he knew with certainty there would be more fights like this one – bloody and vicious.

As medics tended to the wounded – their agonized cries a counterpoint to the moans of the dying – and engineers cleared the path forward, Minh couldn't shake the feeling that they had walked into exactly the trap the enemy had planned. The jungle seemed to watch them, waiting for the next act in this heartless theater of war.

The column slowly reformed, the survivors shell-shocked and wary. Every shadow now promised death, every rustle of leaves a potential threat. They had won this engagement, but the victory tasted of ash and blood. As they prepared to push on, the heaviness of the lives lost – soldiers and civilians alike – hung over them like a shroud.

Command Tent

General Anh's face was a mask of barely controlled rage as Granier and Spitting Woman stood at attention before him. The command tent, usually a hub of controlled chaos, was eerily silent. The staff officers present seemed to hold their breath, waiting for the storm to break.

"Explain yourselves," the general growled, his voice low and dangerous.

Spitting Woman opened her mouth to speak, but the general cut her off with a sharp gesture.

"No. Let me tell you what happened," he continued, his tone dripping with sarcasm. "While you two were busy wringing your hands over villagers, an entire Khmer Rouge force slipped right past you. Right. Past. You."

He slammed his fist on the map table, causing markers to jump and scatter. "We lost over a third of our lead battalion. Good men and women butchered because you failed in your primary mission."

Spitting Woman tensed, her jaw clenching. "Sir, we reported everything we—"

"Everything except the enemy lying in wait to ambush us!" the general roared, his composure finally shattering. "Your job wasn't to play savior to every village. It was to protect our troops, to be our eyes!"

He turned to Granier, eyes blazing. "And you. I expected better from you. You let her distract you from the mission."

Granier remained stoic, but a muscle in his cheek twitched. "General, we—"

"I don't want to hear it," General Anh cut him off. "Your failure has cost us dearly. Not just in lives, but in momentum. The entire offensive has been delayed."

He paced the length of the tent, then turned back

to face them. "You will get your asses in front of my army and scout the path ahead. Do your duty. No more detours. Is that clear?"

Granier and Spitting Woman nodded.

"Make it so!"

The dismissal was clear in his tone. Granier and Spitting Woman turned to leave.

As they reached the tent flap, the general's voice stopped them. "And remember this – every day this war drags on because of setbacks like this, more civilians die. Your misplaced compassion may have cost more innocent lives than it could ever have saved."

The words hung in the air as Granier and Spitting Woman exited the tent. Outside, the sounds of the camp – the rumble of vehicles, the chatter of soldiers – seemed muted, distant. They walked in silence, the general's accusations and their own perceived failure pressing down on them.

Finally, out of earshot of others, Spitting Woman spoke, her voice barely above a whisper. "He's right. We missed them. How did we miss them?"

Granier shook his head, his expression grim. "They're adapting. Changing tactics. We need to adapt too."

They shared a long look, understanding passing between them. The war had entered a new phase, and they would have to evolve with it – or risk more lives lost to their mistakes.

Cambodian Jungle

As ordered, Granier and Spitting Woman made their way to the frontline and then moved farther into enemy territory. The humidity of the Cambodian jungle clung to Granier and Spitting Woman like a second skin as they moved silently through the dense undergrowth. Sweat trickled down their faces, mixing with the camouflage paint that masked their features. The air was thick with the sweet, rotting scent of vegetation and the distant rumble of the approaching Vietnamese forces.

They paused frequently, crouching low to scan their surroundings. The jungle was alive with sounds - the chatter of monkeys, the buzz of insects, and the occasional snap of a twig underfoot. Each noise set them on edge, potentially signaling an enemy presence.

Granier took point, his experienced eyes searching for signs of recent passage or hidden traps. Spitting Woman covered their rear, her rifle at the ready. They communicated mostly through hand signals, preserving the silence that was their best defense.

As they approached a small clearing, Granier held up a fist - the signal to stop. He pointed to a barely visible tripwire stretched across their path. They carefully navigated around it, marking its location on their map for the following troops.

The vegetation thinned slightly as they neared the edge of the jungle, offering glimpses of the terrain ahead. They could see the faint outline of hills in the distance, potential vantage points for Khmer Rouge observers or snipers.

Spitting Woman tapped Granier's shoulder, gesturing to a patch of disturbed earth. Upon closer inspection, they discovered a hastily covered fighting position, recently abandoned. They documented its location, noting the fresh cigarette butts and food wrappers left behind.

As they pressed on, the distant sound of vehicles and marching troops grew louder. They knew the main Vietnamese force wasn't far behind, relying on their reconnaissance to avoid ambushes and navigate the treacherous terrain.

Every step was measured, every decision weighed against the potential risks. They were the eyes and ears of the advancing army, and the success of the operation - as well as countless lives - depended on their ability to detect and report any threats that lay ahead.

Granier froze suddenly, raising a closed fist. Spitting Woman immediately dropped into a crouch, her eyes scanning their surroundings. Years of working together had honed their silent communication to near perfection.

Through gaps in the foliage, they caught glimpses of Khmer Rouge soldiers moving in a loose patrol formation. Granier and Spitting Woman exchanged a glance, then began to slowly retreat, seeking better cover.

A twig snapped underfoot with a sound that seemed to echo like a gunshot in the tense silence.

The jungle erupted in chaos. Muzzle flashes lit up the underbrush as the Khmer patrol opened fire in the direction of the sound.

Bullets whizzed past, thudding into trees and kicking up dirt around them. Granier and Spitting Woman dove for cover behind a massive fallen log, the bark splintering as rounds impacted mere inches from their heads.

"Shit!" Spitting Woman hissed, pressing herself flat against the ground. She returned fire, her M21 cracking in the confined space.

Also returning fire, Granier peered through the smoke and foliage calling out targets. "Two at your eleven, behind the big banyan!"

Spitting Woman shifted her aim, squeezing off two quick shots. A cry of pain confirmed at least one hit.

"I count eight, maybe ten," she said, ejecting a spent magazine and slapping in a fresh one with practiced ease.

Granier nodded, firing at a Khmer soldier attempting to flank their position. "We're outnumbered. We need to break contact, warn the main force."

But the Khmer patrol pressed their advantage, their fire intensifying. Granier and Spitting Woman found themselves pinned down, unable to maneuver. The air grew thick with gunsmoke.

A grenade arced through the air, landing just behind their cover.

"Grenade!" Granier shouted. They scrambled, diving away as the explosion showered them with dirt and wooden shrapnel.

Ears ringing, slightly dazed, they crawled to new positions. Spitting Woman's arm was bleeding from a wooden shard, but she gritted her teeth and kept firing.

Suddenly, the tenor of the firefight changed. New weapons joined the fray – but they weren't firing at Granier and Spitting Woman. Confused shouts in Khmer rang out, followed by the distinctive sound of bodies falling.

An RPG streaked through the jungle, detonating near the center of the Khmer patrol's position. The explosion was deafening, sending a shockwave that Granier and Spitting Woman felt in their chests.

In a matter of seconds, the Khmer patrol's fire ceased completely. The jungle fell eerily silent, save for the ringing in their ears and the crackle of small fires ignited by the RPG.

Granier and Spitting Woman remained frozen, fingers on triggers, unsure of what had just transpired. Smoke drifted through the underbrush, limiting visibility.

"Americains?" a voice called out cautiously. "Francais?"

Granier and Spitting Woman exchanged a puzzled look, both breathing heavily from the intense firefight.

"Neither," Granier replied in careful English, his voice hoarse. "We're with the Vietnamese forces."

A tense moment of silence followed. Then, a figure emerged from the smoke-filled underbrush – a Cambodian man, dressed in a motley assortment of civilian clothes and military gear. He held an AK-47 at the ready, but not pointed directly at them.

"Cambodian resistance," the man said, his English accented but clear. "We've been tracking that Khmer Rouge patrol for days."

More figures appeared, materializing from the jungle. Their appearance and equipment varied widely, but all carried themselves with the wariness of experienced fighters. Some bore old American weapons, others Chinese-made rifles, and a few even clutched ancient bolt-action guns that looked left over from colonial times.

Spitting Woman slowly stood, wincing at the pain in her arm, her own weapon lowered but ready. "Thank you for the assist. But why help us?"

The leader's expression hardened. "The enemy of my enemy is my friend. For now." He gestured at the bodies of the Khmer patrol, some still smoldering from the RPG blast. "We fight for a free Cambodia. The Khmer Rouge are butchers, but we're not keen on trading one occupier for another."

Granier rose as well, studying the resistance fighters carefully. "We're just here to stop the killing, not occupy."

The leader laughed bitterly. "Noble goal. Good luck with that." He turned to his men, speaking rapidly in Khmer. They scavenged weapons and ammunition from the fallen Khmer Rouge soldiers.

The resistance leader, who had introduced himself as Sophal, crouched beside Granier and Spitting Woman in the dense undergrowth. His weathered face was etched with lines of worry as he spoke in hushed tones.

"There's a re-education camp about three kilometers northeast of here," Sophal said, pointing in the direction. "It's where the Khmer Rouge send those they deem... impure."

"We appreciate the intel, but that's not our mission," said Granier.

Spitting Woman shot him a sharp look. "Wait. What do you mean by 'impure'?"

Sophal's eyes darkened. "Intellectuals. Teachers. Anyone with foreign connections. Even people who wear glasses. They're worked to death or executed."

Spitting Woman turned to Granier, her voice low but intense. "We can't ignore this. You know what'll happen if our forces just steamroll through here."

Granier hesitated, torn between duty and conscience. "Our orders are clear. We're here to scout and report, not engage in rescue operations."

"To hell with orders," Spitting Woman hissed.

"This is why we're here. To stop this madness."

"And how do you propose we do that?" Granier countered, his voice rising slightly. "We're two people. Two. Against an entire army of Khmer Rouge."

Sophal interjected, "My men and I have been planning a raid, but we lacked the numbers and expertise. With your help—"

"No," Granier cut him off. "I'm sorry, but we can't. We have a responsibility to our own forces. If we don't report back, we could be jeopardizing the entire offensive."

Spitting Woman stood up, her fists clenched. "And what about our responsibility to basic human decency? We've seen what the Khmer Rouge do, Granier. We know what's happening in that camp."

Granier rose to meet her gaze. "General Anh is right. The only way to stop the killing is to capture the capital and stop the war."

"So we just leave them to die?" Spitting Woman's voice was filled with disgust.

"We report it," Granier insisted. "We make sure command knows about the camp. They can decide how to handle it."

Spitting Woman laughed bitterly. "You know as well as I do what'll happen. They'll bomb it to hell or storm through it. Either way, those prisoners are dead."

The argument continued, growing more heated. Sophal and his men watched silently, tension evident in their postures.

Finally, Spitting Woman played her trump card. "Remember the village, Granier? Remember how we felt, knowing what was going to happen and doing nothing? Can you live with that again?"

Granier's resolve visibly wavered. He ran a hand through his hair, frustration evident. "Dammit, Woman. You fight dirty."

"I fight to win," she retorted. "And right now, winning means saving lives."

After a long moment, Granier nodded reluctantly. "Alright. We'll scout it out. But that's all. We gather intel, we plan, and we report back. No engagement unless absolutely necessary. Agreed?"

Spitting Woman nodded, relief evident on her face. "Agreed."

Sophal gestured to his men, and they began moving through the jungle with practiced stealth. Granier and Spitting Woman followed.

As they approached the camp, the sounds of labor and occasional shouts became audible. They reached the edge of a cleared area. The reeducation camp sprawled before them – a collection of crude wooden buildings surrounded by a barbed-wire fence. Emaciated prisoners in black pajamas worked in the fields under the watchful eyes of armed guards.

Granier peered through his scope, "I count at least thirty guards. Maybe two to three hundred prisoners."

Spitting Woman watched as a guard brutally struck down an elderly prisoner who had collapsed from exhaustion.

Granier and Spitting Woman sat in the dim light of their makeshift shelter, the sounds of the jungle night providing a constant backdrop to their hushed conversation. The day's events - the reeducation camp, the forced labor, the haunted eyes of the civilians - weighed heavily on both of them.

Spitting Woman broke the silence first, her voice low but intense. "We can't just keep passing these camps by, Granier. You saw what was happening back there."

Granier nodded slowly, his face weary from too many difficult decisions. "I know. But what would you have us do? We're two people, Woman. We can't save everyone."

"We can save some," she insisted. "Every life matters. Those people back there, they're being marched to their deaths. We could have done something."

Granier sighed, running a hand through his hair. "And risk compromising our entire mission? We're here to guide the army, to help end this war. That's how we save lives - by finishing this, quickly and decisively."

Spitting Woman stood up, pacing the small space. "And how many will die before we reach Phnom Penh? How many villages will be emptied, how many people worked or starved to death while we march past?"

"Probably thousands," Granier admitted, his voice heavy. "But if we divert our focus, if we slow down to try and save every village we come across, how many more will die because we've given Pol Pot and his butchers more time to carry out their madness?"

Spitting Woman turned to face him, her eyes flashing in the dim light. "So we just accept those deaths? Write them off as necessary sacrifices?"

"No," Granier said firmly. "We remember them. We use them as motivation to push harder, to end this faster. But we can't lose sight of the bigger picture."

"The bigger picture?" Spitting Woman scoffed. "What about the picture I saw today? Children being herded like cattle, old men collapsing under the weight of forced labor. That's the reality. Not some abstract strategic goal."

Granier stood up, facing her. "You think I don't see that? That it doesn't haunt me? But our job, our duty, is to help win this war. To stop Pol Pot and his entire regime. That's how we save millions of lives."

"And what if we're too late?" Spitting Woman challenged. "What if by the time we reach Phnom Penh, there's no one left to save?"

"You're not being realistic. The Vietnamese military is advancing every day. If we clear the way, they should reach the capital in a week, maybe two. Then the real battle begins. We need to focus on the mission. Push hard, fast. Give them less time to carry out their atrocities."

Spitting Woman shook her head. "It's not enough. We need to do more, now. Every village we pass, every group of civilians we see being marched away - that's an opportunity to save lives, right then and there. It's not wishful thinking. It's real."

"And risk slowing down the entire campaign?" Granier countered. "If we're discovered, if we're killed or captured trying to save a handful of people, how many more will die because the army loses its best scouts?"

"So we're just supposed to watch them die?" Spitting Woman's voice cracked slightly. "Stand by and do nothing?"

Granier stepped closer, his voice gentle but firm. "We're not doing nothing. Every trap we disarm, every ambush we uncover, every piece of intel we provide - that's saving lives. It's not immediate, it's not... satisfying in the moment. But it's vital."

Spitting Woman turned away, her shoulders tense.

"It doesn't feel like enough."

"I know," Granier said softly. "Believe me, I know. But we have to trust that by doing our job, by helping end this war as quickly as possible, we're saving more lives in the long run."

They stood in silence for a long moment. Finally, Spitting Woman spoke, her voice barely above a whisper. "I can't just walk away, Granier. Not when I know I could help."

Granier nodded slowly. "I understand. But we need to be smart about it. We can't compromise the mission, but... maybe we can find ways to help when the opportunity presents itself. Small interventions, things that won't slow us down or expose us."

Spitting Woman turned back to face him, a glimmer of hope in her eyes. "You mean that?"

"I do," Granier said. "But we have to be careful. Our primary focus has to remain on the larger mission. We balance when we can, but we can't lose sight of why we're here."

"And what about the reeducation camp we found today?"

Granier sighed. "We'll join with the resistance fighters and liberate the civilians. But that's it. Then it's back on mission."

"Okay. I agree. Back on mission."

The next morning, they scouted the camp's perimeter, noting guard positions and routines. Sophal's men proved to have valuable intelligence on the camp's layout and operations.

As night fell, they gathered to finalize their assault plan. Granier sketched a rough map in the dirt, still voicing objections and concerns.

"This is insane," he muttered. "We're risking everything on this."

Spitting Woman knelt beside him. "We're risking everything by doing nothing, too. Sometimes you have to take a stand."

Granier nodded reluctantly. "Alright. We'll need to take out the guard towers first," he said, pointing to key positions. "Silenced weapons only. Then we breach the fence here and here."

Spitting Woman added, "Once inside, we prioritize freeing the prisoners and arming those who can fight. Sophal, your men will need to guide them to safety."

Sophal nodded.

"What about the guards who surrender?" said Spitting Woman.

"We kill them," said Sophal.

"Is that really necessary?"

"We have no prison camp. If we free them, they will just rearm and come back to fight us another day."

"I agree," said Granier. "No quarter asked, and none given."

The jungle night was oppressively silent, the air thick with tension. Granier lay motionless on a ridge overlooking the camp's eastern perimeter, the starlight scope on his M21 rifle trained on the central compound. Through his scope, he could make out the slow patrol of guards, their shadows stretching in the dim light of scattered lamps.

Across the camp, concealed in the dense foliage of a massive banyan tree, Spitting Woman mirrored his position. Her keen eyes scanned the western approach, counting guards, noting patrol patterns. Both snipers remained perfectly still, their breathing slow and controlled.

Below, Sophal and his fighters melted into the shadows at the camp's edge. Each carried a longbow, arrows nocked and ready. They had spent weeks preparing for this moment, memorizing guard rotations, studying the camp's layout, and practicing their aim with the bows.

A gentle breeze rustled the leaves, momentarily masking the sound of a twig snapping under a rebel's foot. A Khmer guard paused, peering into the darkness. Granier's finger tensed on the trigger, but the guard moved on, oblivious to the impending attack.

Sophal raised his hand, signaling his archers to ready themselves. He looked up, catching Granier's eye. A subtle nod passed between them. It was time.

Sophal's hand dropped. In that instant, the night came alive with silent death.

Arrows whistled through the air, finding their marks with deadly precision. Guard tower sentries fell without a sound, their bodies slumping over railings. Patrolling guards along the perimeter dropped mid-stride, shafts protruding from their throats and heads.

For a precious few moments, the camp remained oblivious to the assault. Wire cutters went to work on the fence, creating breaches for the incoming resistance fighters. Sophal motioned for his first wave to move in, their movements swift and practiced.

Suddenly, a guard rounding a corner stumbled upon one of the fallen bodies. His shout of alarm was cut short by another arrow, but the damage was done.

Alarms blared to life, shattering the night's silence. Floodlights snapped on, bathing the camp in harsh illumination. Now, Granier and Spitting Woman sprang into action.

Granier's rifle cracked, dropping a Khmer guard rushing to man a machine gun nest. The bullet caught him in the left side of his chest, spinning him around before he collapsed.

Across the compound, Spitting Woman's shot took out another Khmer guard racing for the armory, the round entering just below his ear.

Sophal and his team breached the perimeter, switching from bows to assault rifles. They moved in a practiced formation, covering each other as they advanced. A Khmer soldier emerged from a barracks, raising his weapon. Sophal dropped low, his rifle's burst catching the man in the torso.

A spotlight snapped on, catching a group of rebels in its glare. Before the operator could call out a warning, Spitting Woman's round shattered the light, plunging that section back into darkness. She quickly swiveled, taking out two more guards trying to flank Sophal's position.

The camp dissolved into mayhem. Prisoners, sensing a chance at freedom, began to pour out of their barracks. Some ran for the breached fence, while others grabbed makeshift weapons to join the fight. A group of emaciated men overwhelmed a guard, beating him with bare fists and scavenged rocks.

Granier spotted Khmer troops taking aim at the fleeing civilians. His rifle sang out repeatedly, downing two guards, then three, then four. But there were too many. Bullets cut through the crowd, bodies falling in the mud. He forced himself to remain focused, to keep firing.

Spitting Woman, seeing the slaughter, shifted her fire to the Khmer soldiers targeting civilians. Her shots were precise, each one finding its mark. A guard's head exploded in a spray of red mist. Another spun and fell, a round through his spine. But the scale of the chaos was overwhelming.

At the center of the camp, Sophal led the charge. He ducked behind a supply crate as bullets splintered the wood around him. Popping up, he fired a burst from his AK-47, catching a Khmer officer in the chest. He signaled to his men, directing them to flank the main force of guards.

A rebel to Sophal's left went down, a bullet catching him in the thigh. Sophal dragged him to cover, quickly applying a tourniquet before rejoining the fight. The resistance fighters pushed forward, using the confusion to their advantage, but the cost was mounting.

Granier spotted a Khmer soldier preparing to throw a grenade. His shot caught the man's arm just as he released, the grenade falling at his own feet. The explosion sent bodies flying, a cloud of dirt and debris momentarily obscuring Granier's view.

Prisoners and fighters alike sought cover as Khmer reinforcements poured from their barracks. A hail of bullets forced Sophal and his men back. For a moment, it seemed the tide might turn.

Granier caught Sophal's eye, pointing urgently to the Khmer's exposed flank. Sophal nodded, understanding instantly. He whistled sharply, rallying his forces, and charged the Khmer position.

Caught between the assault and the precise sniper fire from Granier and Spitting Woman's positions, the Khmer troops began to falter. Sophal's men pushed forward, clearing buildings one by one. The rattle of gunfire was punctuated by screams and the dull thud of hand-to-hand combat.

A Khmer soldier, desperate and cornered, charged at Sophal with a bayonet. Sophal sidestepped, grabbing the man's wrist and using his momentum to drive the bayonet into another attacking guard. In one fluid motion, he drew his knife and finished both men.

The battle raged on, minutes stretching into what felt like hours. Gradually, the Khmer resistance weakened. Seeing their defenses crumble, the remaining troops began a desperate retreat towards the motor pool.

Spitting Woman picked off fleeing soldiers as they ran, her shots precise even at the extreme range. Granier shifted his focus to the motor pool, disabling vehicles with well-placed shots to engines and fuel tanks.

As the last pockets of resistance were neutralized and the surviving Khmer troops retreated into the safety of the surrounding jungle, an eerie quiet fell over the camp. The air was thick with smoke and the metallic scent of blood. Sophal and his fighters moved cautiously, securing buildings and freeing shell-shocked prisoners.

Bodies – Khmer, resistance, and civilian alike – littered the ground. The once-orderly camp was now a scene of utter devastation. Bullet-riddled buildings smoldered, and overturned vehicles burned, sending plumes of black smoke into the night sky.

Granier and Spitting Woman maintained their positions, scanning for any remaining threats. They exchanged a long look across the compound, both understanding that while this battle was won, their problems were far from over. The real challenge – dealing with the aftermath…

After securing the camp, Sophal approached

Granier and Spitting Woman. The jubilation of victory had faded, replaced by the harsh reality of their situation. He wiped sweat and grime from his brow, his voice low as he spoke.

"We have a problem," Sophal said, glancing back at the gathered prisoners.

Granier's eyes narrowed. "What is it?"

"I told them they were free to go, but..." Sophal hesitated. "They have nowhere to go. Their village was ransacked and burned by the Khmer Rouge. No food, no shelter left."

Spitting Woman's eyes widened. "All of them?"

Sophal nodded. "And many are too weak for a jungle trek. They'd die trying to make it somewhere safe."

Granier's voice remained steady. "What about the vehicles and supplies here?"

Sophal shook his head. "The vehicles were damaged in the assault. Engines shot, fuel tanks punctured. And the supplies..." He gestured around. "There's barely enough here for a day. The guards relied on daily shipments."

Granier absorbed this information, his mind already working on solutions. "Alright. We created this situation, now we need to deal with it. What are our options?"

Spitting Woman spoke up. "We can't leave them here. The Khmer Rouge will send reinforcements once they realize what's happened."

"Agreed," Granier said. "And we can't move them through the jungle. Not in their condition, not without supplies."

The three stood in tense silence for a moment. Around them, the freed prisoners huddled in groups, their faces a mix of hope and fear.

Spitting Woman broke the silence. "There's one option we haven't considered. It's not ideal, but..."

Granier met her gaze, understanding dawning. "The Vietnamese forces."

Sophal looked between them. "You can't be serious. After everything these people have been through, you want to hand them over to another army?"

"We don't want to," Granier said firmly. "But think about it. The Vietnamese have supplies, medical personnel. They're equipped to handle large groups of civilians."

Spitting Woman nodded. "It's not perfect, but it's their best chance at survival right now."

Sophal ran a hand through his hair, conflicted. "And what happens to them after? Once the Vietnamese are done 'helping' them?"

"That's tomorrow's problem. Right now, our priority is keeping these people alive. We can't do that on our own, not with what we have here."

Spitting Woman added, "We'll stay with them as long as we can. Make sure they're treated well. It's the best compromise we have right now."

Sophal looked out at the gathered prisoners, his expression pained. Finally, he nodded. "You're right. I don't like it, but you're right. It's their best chance."

Granier straightened, his resolve clear. "Alright. Let's gather everyone. We need to explain the situation, prepare them for what's coming."

As dawn broke, the sound of approaching vehicles and the distant thud of artillery signaled the arrival of the Vietnamese forces. Granier and Spitting Woman exchanged tense glances, knowing the next few moments would be crucial.

The lead Vietnamese tank rumbled into view, followed by a column of infantry. Colonel Nguyen, the field commander, emerged from an APC, his face a mask of confusion and anger as he surveyed the scene.

"What in the hell is this?" he bellowed, striding towards Granier and Spitting Woman.

Granier stepped forward, saluting. "We've liberated a Khmer Rouge re-education camp."

"Liberated? How come I haven't heard anything about this? Who ordered you to do that?"

"Nobody. It was our own initiative after we found the camp. These are civilian prisoners who—"

"Prisoners?" Colonel Nguyen cut him off. "We don't have time for prisoners! We're on a tight schedule to reach Phnom Penh."

Spitting Woman interjected, "These people need medical attention and protection. They're victims of the Khmer Rouge, not combatants."

The colonel's face reddened. "And who gave you the authority to make that decision? Your job was to scout, not play hero!"

Sophal and his resistance fighters tensed, hands tightening on their weapons. The atmosphere grew thick with tension as Vietnamese soldiers and resistance members eyed each other warily.

Granier spoke carefully, "Sir, with respect, these civilians are now under our protection. Executing or abandoning them would be a war crime."

Colonel Nguyen's hand twitched towards his sidearm. "Are you threatening me?"

"No, sir," Granier replied evenly. "I'm reminding you of our mission objectives and international law."

A tense silence fell. The fate of hundreds hung in

the balance as the colonel visibly wrestled with his decision.

Finally, he spat on the ground. "Fine. But this is on you. Both of you." He turned to his executive officer. "Call in the medics. And get on the horn to command. Tell them we need transport for..." he glanced at the crowd of emaciated prisoners, "...at least two hundred civilians."

Relief washed over Granier and Spitting Woman, but it was short-lived.

Colonel Nguyen jabbed a finger at them. "You two are done. You've repeatedly compromised this operation with your bleeding hearts. Until the general decides what to do with you, you're riding with the supply convoy. Far away from any more decisions."

Spitting Woman started to protest, but Granier put a hand on her arm, shaking his head slightly.

The colonel wasn't finished. "And you," he turned to Sophal, "take your men and get out of here. We appreciate the assist, but this is a military operation now."

Sophal nodded, knowing better than to argue. He shared a look with Granier and Spitting Woman – a mix of gratitude and concern – before leading his fighters back into the jungle.

As Vietnamese medics began tending to the freed prisoners and soldiers established a perimeter, Granier and Spitting Woman found themselves being escorted to the rear of the column.

"Was it worth it?" Granier asked quietly.

Spitting Woman watched as a medic gently treated an elderly prisoner's wounds. "Ask me again when this war is over," she replied.

They climbed into a supply truck, their role in the

advance effectively over. As the convoy began to move out, they sat in silence, pondering the cost of their actions and the uncertain road ahead. They had saved lives, but at what cost to the larger mission? Only time would tell if their moral stand would prove to be the right decision in the brutal calculus of war.

The supply convoy rumbled along the pockmarked road, each jolt and bump a reminder of their newfound irrelevance. Granier and Spitting Woman sat among crates of ammunition and rations, the harsh smell of diesel fuel hanging in the air.

Spitting Woman broke the long silence. "You think we did the right thing?"

Granier didn't answer immediately, his eyes fixed on the passing jungle. Finally, he sighed. "Does it matter now?"

"Of course it matters," she shot back. "Those people are alive because of us."

"And how many more might die because we've slowed the advance?" Granier countered, his voice tight. "We had a duty. A mission."

Spitting Woman's eyes flashed. "We have a duty to humanity, Granier. Or did you forget that?"

"We're soldiers. We have to see the bigger picture."

"The bigger picture?" Spitting Woman scoffed. "Tell that to the prisoners we saved. Tell that to the villagers we couldn't save."

"I'm not saying we were wrong. I'm saying... it's complicated. This whole damned war is complicated."

They lapsed into silence again, each lost in their own thoughts. The convoy rolled on, the monotonous journey a stark contrast to the intense action of the past few days.

"You know," Spitting Woman said after a while, "Le Duan used to say that duty without conscience is just blind obedience."

Granier nodded slowly. "And conscience without duty is just..."

"Chaos," they finished together, sharing a small smile.

The moment was interrupted by a commotion at the front of the convoy. Vehicles were slowing, coming to a stop.

A young lieutenant appeared at the back of their truck, slightly out of breath. "The general wants to see you. Both of you. Immediately."

Granier and Spitting Woman exchanged a look of surprise and apprehension.

They followed the lieutenant towards the command vehicles.

Command Vehicle

General Anh sat before a map-covered table laid out on the deck of the command APC. As Granier and Spitting Woman entered his makeshift headquarters, he fixed them with a steely gaze.

"I should have you shot," he said gruffly. "You went against my orders… again!"

"We didn't have a choice," said Spitting Woman.

"You always have a choice. You just made the wrong one. Now, we're saddled with two hundred plus civilians to feed until we can find someplace to dump them."

"They're not stray dogs."

"No. They're worse. With dogs we can make a fine meal. The people compromise our operational security and slow our advance."

"That was not our intention," said Granier.

"I don't deal with intentions. I deal with reality."

Neither responded, faces impassive.

The general sighed, rubbing his temples. "I've reconsidered your situation," the general continued. "I'm willing to give you one last chance to prove your worth to this operation before I ship you back across the border."

He pointed to a location on the map. "There's a pagoda here, about five klicks west of our current position. The Khmer Rouge have a sniper, or possibly a team of snipers, operating from it. They've pinned down our forces in the area, preventing any advance."

The general's eyes narrowed. "Normally, I'd just call in an air strike and be done with it. But this pagoda... it's culturally significant. Destroying it would turn the local population against us, maybe even drive them into the Khmer Rouge's arms."

He straightened, his tone becoming formal. "Your mission is to neutralize the sniper threat without damaging the pagoda. Success means you continue with the advance. Failure sends you back to the general secretary and whatever consequences he sees fit for your pitiable performance. You have one hour, after which I will be forced to destroy the pagoda and everything around it. If the locals put up resistance, we will treat them as the enemy."

Spitting Woman stepped forward. "We'll take the mission, sir."

Granier nodded in agreement, though his expression remained guarded.

The general's face softened slightly. "Good. You leave in one hour. This is your last chance. Don't make me regret it."

As they turned to leave, the general added, "And remember – this is about military necessity, not moral crusades. Clear?"

"Crystal clear, sir," Granier responded.

Outside the command post, Spitting Woman turned to Granier. "Well, that could have been worse. At least we have a mission to get us out of the doghouse."

"Let's not fuck it up this time," said Granier.

Pagoda

The ancient pagoda loomed before them, its once-vibrant colors muted by the heavy monsoon rain that had begun to fall. Granier and Spitting Woman crouched in the underbrush, water dripping from their camouflaged faces as they surveyed their target. The ornate structure, centuries old, seemed to crouch against the stormy sky like a wounded beast.

"One hour before they shell this place into oblivion." Granier muttered, checking his watch.

Spitting Woman nodded. "Along with priceless artifacts and a few thousand years of history." Her eyes scanned the building, looking for any sign of movement. "How many do you think we're dealing with?"

Before Granier could answer, a crack of gunfire split the air, followed by a cry of pain from the Vietnamese lines behind them. The sniper – or snipers – were still active, and deadly accurate.

"Let's move," Granier said, leading the way through the muddy ground towards the pagoda. Each step was carefully placed, the soggy earth threatening to betray their presence with a misplaced splash.

They were about fifty meters out when Spitting Woman grabbed Granier's arm. "Wait," she whispered, pointing to a nearly invisible tripwire gleaming faintly in a flash of lightning. "They've rigged the place."

Carefully, they began to navigate the minefield of booby traps. Punji sticks, their sharpened points barely visible above the mud, dotted the approach. Shotgun shells attached to tripwires promised a grisly end to the unwary. More complex explosive devices, their mechanisms obscured by the downpour, turned their advance into a deadly game of hopscotch.

Every step was a risk, every movement calculated. The rain, now coming down in sheets, reduced visibility to mere meters. Thunder boomed overhead, masking the sounds of their advance but also potentially hiding the sound of an approaching enemy.

As they neared the pagoda's entrance, a voice called out in Khmer, barely audible over the storm. "Stay back! We have hostages!"

Granier and Spitting Woman exchanged a look of dismay. The situation had just gotten exponentially more complicated.

"We need to get eyes inside," Spitting Woman whispered, her voice tense.

They split up, circling the pagoda. The rain and gathering fog made visibility poor, adding to the tension. Every window, every shadowy corner could hide a sniper's nest. The constant threat of hidden traps slowed their progress to a crawl.

Granier found a partially collapsed section of wall and carefully peered inside. What he saw made his blood run cold. A group of monks and civilians, perhaps two dozen in all, huddled in the center of the room. They were surrounded by armed Khmer Rouge soldiers, their faces young and frighteningly determined. But it was the snipers that truly shocked him.

He made his way back outside. Spitting Woman crawled over, keeping behind cover. "Well?"

"We've got at least three snipers. And... they're kids. Teenagers at most," said Granier.

Spitting Woman's reply was terse. "Damn. That complicates things."

A thunderous crack shook the pagoda, louder than the thunder outside. Part of the ancient structure was giving way under the strain of the rain and recent shelling. Dust and debris rained down inside, causing panic among the hostages and their captors alike.

"This whole place could come down on top of them," Granier said, his voice urgent. "We're out of time."

"I've got an idea," Spitting Woman replied after a moment's pause. "But you're not going to like it."

As she outlined her plan, Granier felt a mix of admiration and dread. It was audacious, dangerous, and probably their only shot. With less than forty minutes left on the clock, they had to act fast.

Minutes later, Spitting Woman's voice rang out, "Attention Khmer Rouge soldiers. We have you surrounded. Release your hostages and surrender, or we'll be forced to take action."

It was a bluff, but it had the desired effect. Confusion erupted inside the pagoda. Taking advantage of the chaos, Granier slipped inside through the collapsed section.

What followed was a heart-stopping game of cat

and mouse through the pagoda's crumbling interior. Granier worked to free the hostages while Spitting Woman created distractions outside. The young snipers, deadly accurate at a distance but inexperienced in close quarters, were overwhelmed by the rapidly changing situation.

Granier inched forward in the dimly lit corridor of the pagoda, his M21 rifle held at the ready. The ancient structure creaked and groaned around him, dust and small debris raining down with each distant explosion. He could hear the panicked breathing of hostages somewhere ahead, mixed with the sharp orders of their Khmer Rouge captors.

Rounding a corner, Granier found himself face to face with a child soldier. The boy, no older than fifteen, stood trembling, his AK-47 wavering between Granier and the floor. Sweat glistened on the kid's forehead, his eyes wide with a mixture of fear and indoctrination.

Granier slowly lowered his rifle, holding one hand up in a calming gesture. "It's okay," he said softly in Khmer, his voice barely above a whisper. "You don't have to do this. Put the gun down."

The boy's finger tightened on the trigger, his breathing rapid and shallow. Granier tensed, ready to dive for cover, but kept his movements slow and deliberate. He pointed to the boy's rifle, then to the ground, repeating the gesture several times.

"I'm not here to hurt you," Granier continued, taking a cautious step forward. "But I need you to put the gun down. Can you do that for me?"

Outside, Spitting Woman pressed herself against the weathered stone of the pagoda's exterior, rain pelting her face. A muzzle flash from an upper window sent her diving for cover as a bullet chipped stone inches from her head. She counted silently, timing the shots, analyzing the pattern.

Using the storm's cover and the pagoda's intricate architecture, Spitting Woman began to work her way closer to the sniper's position. She moved from shadow to shadow, freezing in place whenever lightning illuminated the scene.

As she reached the base of the tower housing the sniper, Spitting Woman could hear the rapid, youthful breathing of her opponent. Her heart sank, realizing she was dealing with another child soldier. She slung her rifle, opting instead for a non-lethal approach.

Inside, Granier had managed to coax the rifle from the boy's hands. As he secured the weapon, a thunderous crack shook the building. Debris rained down, sending hostages scrambling for cover. Granier shielded the boy with his body as a section of ceiling collapsed nearby.

"We need to move!" Granier shouted over the din. He began herding the hostages towards the exit, all while scanning for other threats. Two more child soldiers emerged from a side room, but Granier's calm demeanor and the sight of their disarmed comrade led them to surrender without a fight.

Spitting Woman, having climbed the tower in the howling wind and rain, now stood face to face with a girl no older than thirteen. The child's rifle was trained on her chest, but Spitting Woman could see the exhaustion and uncertainty in her eyes.

"You've done your duty," Spitting Woman said gently, slowly raising her hands. "But it's time to stop now. Let me help you."

For a tense moment, neither moved. Then, with a choked sob, the girl lowered her weapon. Spitting Woman quickly secured the rifle and gathered the child in her arms.

With minutes to spare before the artillery barrage was set to begin, Granier and Spitting Woman regrouped at the pagoda's entrance. They had secured all the hostages and child soldiers, but the structure was becoming more unstable by the second.

"Go, go, go!" Granier urged, guiding the group through the treacherous, booby-trapped grounds surrounding the pagoda. Spitting Woman took up the rear, ensuring no one fell behind.

As they cleared the kill zone, the first artillery shells began to fall. The pagoda, which had stood for centuries, crumbled behind them in a cloud of dust and debris. Granier and Spitting Woman exchanged a look of satisfaction tinged with sadness. They had saved lives today, but the cost of war – especially its toll on the young – weighed heavily on them both.

The group pressed on into the rain-soaked jungle, the sound of warfare fading behind them. The immediate danger had passed.

They'd neutralized the sniper threat and rescued hostages. But the sight of the frightened, brainwashed child soldiers being led away in restraints left a bitter taste in their mouths.

As the Vietnamese forces moved in to secure the area, Granier turned to Spitting Woman, both of them drenched and exhausted. "Think this is what the general had in mind?"

She shook her head, watching as medics tended to the freed hostages. "Probably not. But it's what needed to be done."

Without warning, Khmer mortar rounds screamed into the Vietnamese position, exploding, creating chaos among the civilians, some diving for cover, others running wildly.

Granier and Spitting Woman were trying to maintain order when suddenly, a young girl, no older than fourteen, broke from the group and sprinted towards the jungle's edge.

"Stop her!" Spitting Woman shouted, already moving to pursue.

A nearby Vietnamese soldier raised his rifle, taking aim at the fleeing child. Without hesitation, Granier lunged, shoving the soldier's arm upward. The shot went wide, disappearing into the canopy.

"She's just a kid!" Granier growled, but there was no time for further explanation.

Spitting Woman was already in pursuit, her legs pumping as she chased the girl into the dense undergrowth. The sounds of the camp faded, replaced by the girl's panicked breathing and the crunch of leaves underfoot.

"Wait!" Spitting Woman called out. "We're trying to help you!"

The girl glanced back, terror evident in her eyes. She pushed harder, branches whipping at her face as she ran blindly through the jungle.

Spitting Woman was gaining ground, her hand outstretched, almost within reach of the girl. Suddenly, there was a metallic click.

Time seemed to slow. Spitting Woman's eyes widened as she recognized the sound – a tripwire. She opened her mouth to shout a warning, but it was too late.

The shotgun shell blast was deafening in the confined space. The girl's body jerked violently, thrown forward by the impact. She crumpled to the ground, motionless.

Spitting Woman skidded to a halt, her breath caught in her throat. The scene before her was grotesque – the girl's small body broken, blood seeping into the earth. The acrid smell of gunpowder hung in the air, mixing with the metallic scent of blood.

She stood there, frozen, her mind struggling to process what had just happened. Her legs gave way, and she sank to her knees, eyes fixed on the lifeless form of the child she'd been trying to save.

Moments later, Granier burst through the foliage, breathing heavily. He took in the scene in an instant – the dead girl, the triggered trap, and Spitting Woman kneeling in shock.

"Oh, God," he breathed, moving quickly to Spitting Woman's side.

She looked up at him, her eyes wide and unfocused. "I... I was just trying to..." Her voice broke, tears welling up.

Granier knelt beside her, pulling her into a tight embrace. She resisted for a moment before collapsing against him, her body wracked with sobs. It was all too much.

"It's not your fault," Granier murmured, his own voice thick with emotion. "You were trying to save her."

Spitting Woman's fingers dug into Granier's shirt. "She was just a child," she choked out. "Just a scared child."

Granier held her tighter, his eyes scanning the jungle around them. The war raged on, indifferent to their personal tragedy. He knew they couldn't stay here long, but for this moment, he allowed Spitting Woman her grief.

"I know," he said softly. "I know. But we have to keep going. There are others who need us."

Spitting Woman's sobs gradually subsided, replaced by deep, shuddering breaths. She pulled back slightly, wiping her eyes with the back of her hand. When she met Granier's gaze, there was a new hardness there, born from anguish.

"You're right," she said, her voice hoarse but steady. "We have to keep going."

As they stood, Granier squeezed her shoulder, a gesture of support and shared resolve. They couldn't save everyone, but they would damned well try. With one last look at the fallen girl, they turned and made their way back to the camp, the weight of war heavy on their shoulders.

Granier and Spitting Woman moved silently through the dense jungle. The night was thick with humidity, the air filled with the chirps of insects and distant explosions. They were making their way back to the Vietnamese forces, their minds still processing the events of the past few hours.

Suddenly, Granier raised his fist - the signal to stop. Spitting Woman froze, her senses immediately on high alert. Granier pointed to his ear, then gestured ahead. Voices. Faint, but unmistakable.

They crouched low, creeping forward with practiced stealth. As they neared a small clearing, the voices became clearer. Granier could make out both Khmer and Vietnamese being spoken.

They found cover behind a large fallen tree, its trunk providing concealment as they peered into the clearing.

In the dim moonlight, they could make out several figures. Four men in Khmer Rouge uniforms stood facing five others in Vietnamese military attire. One of the Vietnamese officers was instantly recognizable - Major Nguyen, a high-ranking member of their own command structure.

The group was speaking in hushed but urgent tones. Several bundles wrapped in wax paper. One of the Vietnamese soldiers tested the contents, a dark gummy substance, in one of the packages. Using his knife, he made a small hole in the wax paper and retrieved a small amount of the substance – raw opium. He licked it, then, waiting a moment for the substance to have an effect, he nodded approval.

Two more Vietnamese soldiers retrieved a wooden case from behind a fallen tree and set the crate in front of the Khmer soldiers. He opened the top revealing the contents, American-made assault rifles. One of the soldiers pulled out one of the rifles and examined it. After a moment, he too nodded his satisfaction.

Granier and Spitting Woman watched the exchange. As they strained to listen, fragments of conversation drifted their way:

"...next shipment will be larger."

"...need to reroute the supply lines..."

As they watched the clandestine meeting conclude, Granier leaned close to Spitting Woman, his breath barely a whisper against her ear. "We need evidence. Something tangible."

She nodded almost imperceptibly, her eyes never leaving the scene before them.

The Khmer troops began to pack up, hefting the heavy crate filled with rifles. They disappeared into the jungle shadows, leaving the Vietnamese officers alone in the clearing.

Major Nguyen and his men started gathering up several small packages - unmistakably blocks of opium. Granier and Spitting Woman exchanged a pointed look. This was their chance.

Granier gestured to himself, then to the far side of the clearing. Spitting Woman understood immediately - he would create a diversion.

With a deep breath, Granier moved swiftly through the underbrush, circling to the opposite side of the meeting spot. Once in position, he deliberately snapped a branch underfoot.

The effect was immediate. "Over there!" one of the officers shouted. Granier caught a glimpse of Major Nguyen barking orders before he took off running, crashing through the foliage to draw attention. One of the Vietnamese soldiers stayed behind to protect the opium.

Spitting Woman seized the moment. She darted into the clearing, then smashed her rifle butt into the face of the Vietnamese soldier as he turned to investigate the noise. The soldier collapsed on the ground, grabbing his broken nose and whimpering in pain. Spitting Woman's hand closed around one of the opium packages, tucking it securely into her vest before melting back into the shadows.

Granier led the Vietnamese soldiers on a wild chase, zigzagging through the dense jungle. His lungs burned, branches whipped at his face, but he pushed on, knowing every second bought was crucial for Spitting Woman's escape.

Finally, confident he'd led them far enough astray, Granier dove behind a massive fallen tree. He held his breath as the soldiers ran past his hiding spot, their curses fading into the distance.

After ensuring the coast was clear, Granier backtracked to their predetermined rendezvous point. Spitting Woman was already there, her face taut with tension but eyes gleaming with triumph.

"Got it," she whispered, patting her vest where the package was concealed.

Granier nodded, "They'll be back. Let's move."

Together, they set off through the jungle, moving quickly and quietly. The shouts of the Vietnamese soldiers could be heard in the distance. Major Nguyen clearly angry, shouting orders.

As Granier and Spitting Woman raced through the dense foliage, the sounds of pursuit growing closer, they found themselves approaching a clearing. Ahead, they could see the remnants of an old temple complex, its crumbling stone structures barely visible in the pre-dawn light.

"In there," Granier whispered, gesturing towards the ruins.

They darted into the ancient complex, weaving between fallen columns and overgrown courtyards. The sounds of their pursuers echoed off the stone walls, making it difficult to pinpoint their location.

Granier pulled Spitting Woman behind a partially collapsed wall, both of them breathing heavily. They could hear Major Nguyen's voice, unnervingly close, barking orders to his men.

"Find them! They can't have gone far!"

Spitting Woman clutched the opium package tightly to her chest, her eyes meeting Granier's in the dim light.

Footsteps approached their hiding spot. A beam

from a flashlight swept over the wall above their heads. Granier and Spitting Woman pressed themselves flat against the cool stone.

The footsteps paused, agonizingly close. Granier's hand moved slowly to his rifle's trigger guard.

Suddenly, a portion of a distant wall collapsed with a thunderous crash, sending a flock of birds scattering into the sky. The footsteps near their position immediately rushed towards the sound.

Granier nodded to Spitting Woman, and they seized the opportunity to slip away, moving as quietly as possible through the labyrinthine ruins. Every snapped twig and rustled leaf sounded thunderous in their ears.

As they neared the perimeter of the complex, they heard Major Nguyen's frustrated shout. "They're getting away! Spread out!"

Without a word, Granier and Spitting Woman plunged back into the jungle. They ran in silence, pushing their exhausted bodies to the limit. The sounds of pursuit gradually faded, but they didn't slow their pace. Both knew the stakes were too high to take any chances.

As the first rays of sunlight began to filter through the canopy, they finally allowed themselves to slow to a jog. They were still a fair distance from friendly lines, but for the moment, it seemed they had successfully evaded their corrupt comrades.

"That was too close," Spitting Woman said between breaths, patting her vest where the opium package was securely hidden.

Granier nodded, his face grim. "And it's not over yet. We still have to make it back and figure out who we can trust with this information."

"What do you mean?"

"We don't know how high this goes."

They pressed on, knowing that every step brought them closer to unraveling the conspiracy that threatened to undermine everything they had fought for.

The remained alert for any sign that their pursuers had picked up their trail again. It didn't take long. The Vietnamese soldiers were once again closing in.

With a final burst of energy, Granier and Spitting Woman burst from the jungle's edge, stumbling into the surprised Vietnamese outpost. Shouts of alarm went up as soldiers rushed to their position, weapons raised.

Behind them, their pursuers pulled up short at the tree line, unwilling to reveal themselves to the regular troops.

Granier and Spitting Woman collapsed to the ground, gasping for air. They had made it, evidence in hand.

Spitting Woman winced as the medic finished bandaging some of her cuts and scraps. The makeshift infirmary tent buzzed with activity. The medic left to tend to a soldier with a chest wound that had just been brought in giving Granier and Spitting Woman a moment of privacy.

Spitting Woman leaned in, her voice barely above a whisper. "What do we do now?"

Granier ran a hand through his hair, his face etched with worry. "I don't know. This... this is big."

"A Vietnamese major," Spitting Woman began, her voice hesitant, "working with the Khmer Rouge. Selling weapons for drugs. How high up does this go?"

Granier shook his head. "We don't know. It could

be an isolated incident, or..."

"Or it could be widespread," Spitting Woman finished, her eyes flashing with anger. "How many of our own people have died because of these backroom deals?"

Granier sighed heavily. "We need to be careful here. If we accuse a senior officer without concrete proof of how far this extends, it could cause chaos in the ranks."

Spitting Woman stood up abruptly, pacing the small space. "So what, we just pretend we didn't see anything? Go back to following orders while some of our officers profit from this bloodshed?"

"I'm not saying that," Granier said, his voice tight with frustration. "But we need to think this through. If we blow the whistle now, in the middle of the campaign, without knowing the full extent, it could create disarray. The Khmer Rouge would take advantage of that."

"And if we wait?" Spitting Woman challenged. "How many more deals will go down? How many more weapons will end up in Khmer Rouge hands?"

They lapsed into silence again, each lost in their own thoughts. The sounds of the camp outside – vehicles moving, soldiers talking, the distant thud of artillery – served as a constant reminder of the war that continued around them, oblivious to their discovery.

Finally, Spitting Woman spoke, her voice low and intense. "We've seen the villages, Granier. We've seen what Pol Pot is doing to his own people. Whatever we do, we can't let this conspiracy hinder our efforts to stop that genocide."

Granier met her gaze, nodding solemnly. "Agreed. Our primary mission hasn't changed. We're here to stop Pol Pot. But now we have a secondary objective."

"Find out how far this corruption goes," Spitting Woman said.

"And put a stop to it," Granier added. "Without compromising the campaign if possible."

The war had just become infinitely more complex, and they were walking a tightrope between exposing corruption and maintaining the integrity of the military campaign. Lives hung in the balance, and the truth, whatever it might be, promised to be as dangerous as any enemy they'd faced on the battlefield.

Opium

Granier and Spitting Woman stood in General Anh's makeshift command tent, their uniforms still caked with mud and sweat from their harrowing escape. The opium package sat on the general's field desk, its presence heavy with implications.

General Anh studied the package, his face an unreadable mask. The tent was silent save for the distant sounds of the camp and the occasional rumble of artillery.

Finally, the general looked up, his eyes meeting theirs. "This is... quite a discovery," he said, his voice carefully neutral. "You're certain about what you witnessed?"

"Yes," Granier replied firmly. "We saw the exchange ourselves. Vietnamese officers trading weapons for drugs with Khmer Rouge forces."

Spitting Woman added, "Sir, we believe this corruption may extend further than we initially thought."

General Anh nodded slowly, his expression thoughtful. "I see. This is indeed a serious matter." He stood, pacing behind his desk. "You've done well to bring this to my attention. I will personally look into this matter immediately."

Granier and Spitting Woman exchanged a quick glance, surprised by the general's apparent acceptance of their report.

The general turned back to them, his demeanor shifting to one of brisk efficiency. "Now, we have pressing operational matters to attend to. We've received intelligence about a suspected Khmer tunnel complex not far from here. I need you two to scout it out."

He spread a map on his desk, pointing to a location. "Our engineers are standing by to collapse the tunnels with explosives, but we need precise coordinates and an assessment of the complex's extent. This is crucial for our advance."

Spitting Woman studied the map, "Sir, given what we've just reported, perhaps we should—"

"This takes priority," General Anh cut her off, his tone brooking no argument. "I assure you, I will handle the matter you've brought to light. But right now, we need to press our advantage against the Khmer Rouge. Is that clear?"

"Yes, sir," Granier and Spitting Woman responded in unison, though both felt a growing unease.

"Good," the general said, rolling up the map and handing it to Granier. "You leave immediately. I expect a full report upon your return."

As they turned to leave, General Anh added, "And excellent work, both of you. The army is fortunate to have soldiers of your caliber."

They nodded their thanks and left.

Tunnel Complex

Granier and Spitting Woman lay prone on a ridge overlooking the supposed location of the Khmer tunnel complex. The jungle clearing below seemed undisturbed, with no signs of recent activity.

"Are you sure we have the right coordinates?" Spitting Woman muttered, scanning the area through her binoculars.

"I'm sure," said Granier scanning the area with his rifle scope. "No patrols, no sentries, not even a footpath."

Spitting Woman nodded, "Let's move in closer. Maybe we're missing something."

They descended the ridge cautiously, every sense alert for danger. As they reached the area marked on their map, the eerie quiet persisted. No bird calls, no rustling in the underbrush – just oppressive silence.

Granier knelt, examining the ground. He dug his fingers into the soil, frowning. "This doesn't make sense. The ground's too hard, too rocky for extensive tunneling. You'd need heavy equipment to dig here."

Spitting Woman kicked at a stone in frustration. "Intelligence screwed up again. There's nothing here."

Suddenly, a distant whistle pierced the air. Granier's eyes widened in recognition. "Get down!"

They dove for cover as the first artillery shells slammed into the earth around them. The bombardment was intense, far heavier than anything they'd experienced from Khmer forces.

As they huddled behind a grouping of large boulders, dirt and shrapnel raining down, Granier shouted over the explosions. "Those are 155mm shells! The Khmer don't have those – we do!"

Spitting Woman's face paled as the realization hit. "They're trying to kill us!"

The shelling continued for what felt like an eternity. Just as it began to taper off, a new sound filled the air – the roar of jet engines.

"No, no, no," Granier muttered, peering out from their shelter. Two Vietnamese Sukhoi Su-17 fighter-bombers swooped low over the treeline, their pylons filled with napalm canisters.

"Napalm! Run!" he yelled, grabbing Spitting Woman's arm.

They sprinted through the chaos of the burning jungle, the heat of the napalm strike searing at their backs. Trees exploded into flames around them, the air thick with smoke and the stench of burning vegetation.

Granier stumbled, his leg caught in a tangle of vines. Spitting Woman hauled him up, half-dragging him as they scrambled down a ravine. They splashed into a shallow stream just as another wave of napalm ignited the jungle behind them.

For several minutes, they lay there, partially submerged, as the inferno raged above. Finally, when the roar of the flames subsided to a dull crackle, they dared to move.

Emerging from the water, they surveyed the devastation. The lush jungle had been transformed into a hellscape of smoldering trees and ash.

Spitting Woman's voice was hoarse from the smoke. "They really want us dead."

Granier nodded, wincing as he tested his injured leg. "They damned near succeeded."

"I believe Anh is behind this. It doesn't make sense.

He's a general for God's sake."

"He's not the first corrupt general in Vietnam."

"Yeah, but drugs for weapons. He's killing his own men."

"His reasons don't matter. What does matter is we're on his hit list and he has an entire army at his disposal."

"So, what do we do?"

"Your guess is as good as mine."

"We can't go back to the base camp. He'll have us killed on the spot."

"I'm not sure that's true."

"What do you mean?"

"He can't kill us directly. It'll expose him too much."

"He can have us hanged for treason."

"Yeah, I suppose he can."

"So?"

"We could find the resistance fighters again."

"How do we know they're not in on it too?"

"We don't. Not for sure. But we're gonna need to trust someone if we're gonna survive."

The jungle still smoldered around them, as they limped away from the scene of their near-death, both knew that they had just become fugitives. The war they thought they were fighting had changed dramatically, and now they were caught in a deadly game where both sides were the enemy.

The humid jungle air hung heavy around Granier and Spitting Woman as they pushed through the dense undergrowth. Their bodies ached from their narrow escape, burns and cuts a constant reminder of their brush with death. They moved as quickly as their battered condition allowed, hoping to find Sophal and his resistance fighters.

Suddenly, Spitting Woman froze, her hand shooting out to grab Granier's arm. "Listen," she whispered, her voice tense.

In the distance, barely audible over the ambient sounds of the jungle, came the faint but unmistakable barking of dogs.

"Khmer or Vietnamese?" said Spitting Woman.

"Does it matter?" said Granier. "Whoever it is are using dogs to track us."

"How far away do you think they are?" Spitting Woman asked, already scanning their surroundings for escape routes.

"Can't be sure. Sound carries strangely in the jungle. But we can't take chances. We need to move. Fast."

"Real fast."

Without another word, they broke into a run. The uneven terrain and thick vegetation made their progress difficult, but adrenaline propelled them forward. Branches whipped at their faces, roots threatened to trip them at every step, but they pushed on relentlessly.

The barking grew louder, more frenzied. The dogs had picked up their scent. Their handlers had released them so they could move quickly through the jungle.

"They're gaining on us," Spitting Woman panted, glancing back over her shoulder.

Granier nodded, his eyes scanning the jungle ahead. "We need to find a way to throw off the scent. Water, if we can find it."

They pushed on, their breaths coming in ragged gasps. The sounds of pursuit grew ever closer – not just dogs now, but the shouts of men and the crash of bodies through the underbrush.

"They're trying to cut us off," said Granier.

Spitting Woman stumbled, her foot catching on a hidden root. Granier caught her arm, hauling her up without breaking stride. "Come on," he urged. "We can't stop now."

The jungle seemed to close in around them, the air thick. Every snapping twig, every rustle of leaves sounded like their pursuers closing in. The distant barking of dogs grew louder, spurring them to move faster despite their exhaustion.

"They're gaining on us," Spitting Woman panted, glancing back over her shoulder.

Granier nodded, his eyes scanning their surroundings. Suddenly, his face lit up with recognition. "I know where we are. There's a pepper plantation nearby. If we can reach it..."

They veered sharply to the right, pushing through the undergrowth with renewed vigor. The scent of pepper began to fill the air, growing stronger with each step.

As they burst out of the jungle's edge, they found themselves facing rows upon rows of pepper vines, their berries ripening in the sun. In the distance, they could see the silhouette of a processing mill.

"The mill," Granier gasped. "If we can get there, we might be able to throw off the dogs."

They raced through the plantation, pepper vines whipping at their faces and arms. The barking grew louder, more frenzied. The dogs were close now, too close.

The pepper plantation sprawled before them, a sea of green vines climbing wooden trellises. Rows stretched to the horizon, heavy with clusters of berries in various stages of ripeness. The pungent aroma of pepper saturated the air.

In the distance, the processing mill stood out against the landscape. It was a large, open-sided structure with a high metal roof. As they approached, they could see the interior bustling with activity.

Mechanical dryers hummed at one end, while grinding machines dominated the center. Workers moved about, faces covered against the pepper dust that hung in the air like a spicy fog. They seemed absorbed in their tasks, paying no attention to the two intruders racing through their workspace.

Enormous burlap sacks of peppercorns were stacked throughout the mill, waiting to be processed or shipped. Conveyor belts snaked between stations, carrying pepper through various stages of production.

The constant grinding of machinery and occasional shouts of workers filled the air, providing cover for Granier and Spitting Woman as they navigated through the complex, desperate for a means of escape.

"Quick," Granier said, gesturing to a pile of finished sacks. "Grab some of the ground pepper."

Understanding dawned on Spitting Woman's face. They each snatched up a sack, tearing them open and scattering the finely ground pepper in their wake as they ran through the mill.

The air quickly became thick with pepper dust. Granier and Spitting Woman pulled their shirts over their noses, eyes watering as they continued to spread the pungent spice.

Just as they reached the far side of the mill, they heard the Khmer patrol burst into the structure. The dogs' frenzied barking suddenly turned into a cacophony of sneezing and whining.

They could hear the confusion in the shouts of the Khmer soldiers, punctuated by their own sneezing fits.

Granier and Spitting Woman used the distraction to slip away, ducking back into the jungle on the far side of the plantation. They flung the remains of the pepper behind them. They didn't slow their pace until the sounds of the disoriented patrol had faded into the distance.

Finally, they allowed themselves to stop, collapsing against a large tree trunk. Both were covered in sweat and pepper dust, their eyes red and streaming.

"Quick thinking," Spitting Woman said between coughs.

Granier managed a grim smile. "Let's hope it bought us enough time. We need to keep moving, find Sophal and his men before the Khmer regroup."

As they caught their breath, they pushed on.

After several hours of trekking through the jungle, Granier and Spitting Woman crouched by a small stream, the sound of running water providing a momentary respite from the constant vigilance of their flight. They drank deeply, savoring the cool water, before filling their canteens.

Granier leaned back against a moss-covered log, wiping his mouth with the back of his hand. "What's our next move after we find Sophal and his men?"

Spitting Woman looked up from securing her canteen, her eyes thoughtful. "We can't just walk away from this, from the Cambodian people. Not after everything we've seen."

Granier nodded slowly. "Agreed. But we can't exactly go back to the Vietnamese forces either. Not with a price on our heads."

"What if..." Spitting Woman hesitated, then pressed on. "What if we found a way to contact Le Duan directly? Tell him what's really happening here."

"Le Duan? That's risky. For all we know, he could be part of this whole mess."

Spitting Woman shook her head emphatically. "No, not Le Duan. He's not like the others. He doesn't care about money or personal gain."

"Everyone has a price," Granier countered, skepticism clear in his voice.

"Not him," Spitting Woman insisted. "Le Duan cares about the revolution, about the Vietnamese people. He wouldn't stand for this corruption, this... betrayal of everything we're fighting for."

Granier considered her words, absently swirling the water in his canteen. "Even if you're right, how would we even reach him? We're cut off, hunted. It's not like we can just walk into party headquarters in Hanoi."

Spitting Woman leaned forward, her voice low but intense. "We find a way. Through the resistance, maybe. Or... there are always back channels, people who can get messages to the top without going through official routes."

"It's a huge risk," Granier said, but his tone was less certain now. "If we're wrong about Le Duan..."

"Then we're no worse off than we are now," Spitting Woman finished. "But if we're right, if we can get the truth to him, we might be able to stop this corruption and actually help the people we came here to protect."

Granier was silent for a long moment, weighing the dangers against the potential benefits. Finally, he nodded slowly. "Alright. We'll try it your way. But we move carefully, verify everything we can before we make any moves."

"Agreed. We do this smart, but we do it."

Granier shouldered his pack, a hint of his old determination in his eyes. "First things first, we need to find Sophal."

With that, they melted back into the jungle.

Village

Granier and Spitting Woman saw the outline of a village through dense foliage at the edge of a treeline. They were cautious, not knowing the villagers' loyalties.

The village was nestled in a small clearing, a modest collection of wooden and thatch structures surrounded by the encroaching jungle. A handful of simple huts formed a rough circle around a central area of packed earth, worn smooth by years of daily activity. Smoke rose lazily from a few cooking fires, carrying the scent of rice and herbs on the humid air.

The surrounding jungle loomed close, its dense foliage a mix of vibrant greens and deep shadows. Tall trees with broad leaves formed a natural barrier, their canopies stretching high overhead. The constant hum of insects and occasional calls of unseen birds provided a persistent backdrop to the village's uneasy quiet.

A narrow dirt path wound its way between the huts, eventually disappearing into the thick undergrowth at the village's edge. Small plots of cultivated land dotted the periphery, where villagers grew vegetables and herbs to supplement their diet of fish from streams and ponds, plus the occasional monkey or parrot.

In the distance, the faint outline of mountains could be seen, their misty peaks barely visible above the treetops. A small stream gurgled nearby, providing the village with fresh water and serving as a gathering spot for women washing clothes and children at play.

The village bore subtle signs of the ongoing conflict - a watchful tension in the eyes of its inhabitants, a scarcity of young men, and the occasional glimpse of hastily concealed weapons. Yet life continued, resilient in the face of uncertainty, with chickens pecking at the dirt and the laughter of children occasionally breaking the wary silence.

Granier and Spitting Woman entered the village warily, their senses on high alert. The few villagers visible quickly retreated into their homes, casting suspicious glances their way.

"We need to be careful," Granier murmured. "We don't know where their loyalties lie."

Spitting Woman nodded, her eyes scanning the area. "Agreed, but we're running out of options. We have to take a chance."

They approached an elderly man sitting on a stool in front of his hut, his face a mask of neutrality.

"Excuse me," Spitting Woman said in Khmer, her tone carefully measured. "We're looking for some people who might have passed through here. People who... help others."

The old man's eyes narrowed slightly, but he remained silent.

Granier stepped forward, choosing his words carefully. "We're friends. We want to help too."

A woman peered out from a nearby hut, quickly ushering a child inside. The atmosphere was thick with unspoken tension.

After several fruitless attempts to engage with different villagers, Granier and Spitting Woman retreated to the village's edge.

"This was a risk and we gained nothing," Granier muttered. "We might have just put ourselves on the Khmer Rouge's radar if any of these people talk."

Spitting Woman nodded grimly. "It's a chance we had to take. Let's move on before we attract more attention."

As they turned to leave, a teenage boy emerged from behind a building, his eyes darting nervously between them and the other villagers. He began to follow them at a distance.

Once clear of the village, the boy caught up. "Wait," he called out in a hushed voice.

Granier and Spitting Woman turned, instantly on guard.

"I know who you're looking for," the boy said, his voice a mix of excitement and fear. "I can help you find them."

Spitting Woman exchanged a cautious glance with Granier. "Why would you help us when the other wouldn't?"

The boy straightened, trying to appear older than his years. "I want to join them. To fight. Take me with you, and I'll show you the way."

Granier knelt down to the boy's eye level, his voice low. "What's your name?"

"Kunthea," the boy replied.

"Kunthea, fighting isn't the only way to resist," Granier said gently. "Your village needs protection too. People who can warn them of danger, help them stay safe."

"But I want to do something important."

Spitting Woman joined them, her voice soft but urgent. "Protecting your home, your family - that is important. And it's safer for you and for us if you stay here."

Granier nodded. "You can be our eyes and ears here. Watch for Khmer Rouge movement, help coordinate with the resistance to keep your village safe. That's a crucial job, Kunthea."

The boy considered for a moment, his young face thoughtful. Finally, he nodded. "Okay. I'll stay. But I'll still show you where to find them."

"Thank you," Spitting Woman said warmly. "You're very brave."

As Kunthea began to describe the location, Granier and Spitting Woman listened intently, aware that this information could be their salvation or their downfall.

Bridge

Following Kunthea's directions, Granier and Spitting Woman approached a rickety wooden bridge spanning the deep ravine. As they took their first steps onto the creaking planks, a sharp crack split the air. Splinters exploded near their feet.

"Snipers!" Granier shouted, grabbing Spitting Woman and dragging her back to the ravine's edge.

They dove behind what little cover the uneven ground and sparse vegetation offered. More shots rang out, bullets thudding into trees and kicking up dirt around them.

Granier scanned their surroundings, "Bad position. They can easily flank us here."

Spitting Woman's eyes darted between Granier and the bridge. Without warning, she suddenly sprang to her feet and sprinted across the bridge.

"What the—" Granier yelled, caught off guard.

Instinctively, he popped up from cover, firing his rifle to suppress the snipers.

Bullets whizzed past Spitting Woman as she sprinted across the bridge. By some miracle, she made it to the other side, disappearing into the dense jungle foliage.

Granier ducked back down, heart pounding. The snipers, momentarily distracted by Spitting Woman's dash, now focused their fire on him.

Minutes ticked by, feeling like hours. Granier remained pinned down, unable to move. Suddenly, a single shot rang out from the jungle on the far side of the ravine. Then another. And another.

Granier realized what was happening. Spitting Woman had found a position and was picking off the snipers one by one as they exposed themselves to fire at him.

After what seemed an eternity, silence fell. Granier waited, tense, for any sign of movement.

"Clear!" Spitting Woman's voice called out from across the ravine.

Cautiously, Granier stood and made his way across the bridge. As he reached the other side, he found Spitting Woman emerging from her hidden position.

Granier's relief quickly gave way to anger. "What the hell were you thinking?" he hissed. "You could have been killed! And you could have gotten me killed trying to save you."

Spitting Woman met his gaze unflinchingly. "I saw no other way out. We were sitting ducks back there."

"You should have warned me," Granier argued, his voice tight.

"There was no time for an argument," she replied firmly. "It was a risk, yes, but a necessary one. We're both alive, aren't we?"

Granier opened his mouth to argue further, then closed it, shaking his head. She was right, even if he didn't like it.

"Don't do that again," he finally said, his tone softening slightly.

"No promises. Come on, we need to move before reinforcements arrive."

As they melted back into the jungle, Granier couldn't help but feel a mixture of frustration and grudging admiration for his partner's bold action. They were still alive, still in the fight, and that's what mattered most.

Vietnamese Main Force Advancing

The Vietnamese armored column advanced along a narrow, winding path cut through dense Cambodian jungle. Towering trees formed a thick canopy overhead, dappling the forest floor with shifting patterns of light and shadow. The air was heavy with humidity, making the armored crews and passengers miserable inside the mobile steel ovens. Still, it was safer than traveling outside on foot.

The jungle was filled with the constant buzz of insects and occasional calls of unseen birds. On either side of the path, lush vegetation pressed close, a mix of broad-leafed plants, tangled vines, and dense undergrowth that severely limited visibility beyond a few meters. The ground was uneven, with exposed roots and occasional muddy patches from recent rains, making progress slow and treacherous for the heavy vehicles.

The jungle hummed with unseen life as Sergeant

Nguyen led his small team of scouts forward. Sweat trickled down his face, stinging his eyes as he scanned the seemingly endless sea of green before them.

"Dinh, take point," Nguyen whispered, gesturing to the youngest member of their team. Private Dinh nodded nervously, his fingers tightening on his rifle as he moved ahead.

Corporal Hoa, the team's most experienced member after Nguyen, brought up the rear. Her eyes darted constantly, watching for any sign of movement in the undergrowth.

As they pushed forward, Nguyen couldn't shake the feeling that they were being watched.

"Hold," he hissed suddenly, dropping into a crouch. The others froze instantly.

Nguyen's eyes narrowed as he studied a patch of jungle ahead. Something seemed... off. He motioned for Dinh to pass him the binoculars.

Peering through them, Nguyen swept his gaze across the area. For a moment, he thought he saw a flicker of movement, but it was gone so quickly he couldn't be sure.

"What is it, Sarge?" Hoa whispered.

Nguyen shook his head. "Not sure. Thought I saw something, but... the jungle plays tricks on our eyes." He handed the binoculars back to Dinh.

"Should I radio the commander to hold up?"

"No. Let's keep moving. Slowly."

They crept forward, unaware that they had just passed within meters of a carefully camouflaged Khmer Rouge soldier, his finger hovering over the trigger of his AK-47. As former guerilla fighters, the Khmer Rouge troops were masters at concealment.

As they continued, they unwittingly skirted the edge

of a minefield, the deadly devices buried just beneath the surface of the seemingly innocent jungle floor. They were heavy duty mines designed to take out armored vehicles, not soldiers.

One of the scouts stumbled slightly, his foot catching on something. He looked down, seeing what appeared to be an oddly shaped root. He looked closer pushing away the foliage surrounding it. He was surprised to see a pyramid-shaped block of concrete similar to a road marker. He didn't know what to make of the "Dragon's Teeth" obstacle, designed to tear the tracks off tanks. It didn't look dangerous. Just a block concrete.

"Keep moving, Private," said Dinh approaching from behind.

The scout decided to ignore the concealed obstacle thinking it was left behind years ago and had been claimed by the jungle. He moved on.

They pressed on, passing a clump of vegetation that, had they looked closer, concealed a well-dug fighting position occupied by two Khmer soldiers armed with a recoilless rifle, their eyes following the Vietnamese scouts' every move, their bodies perfectly still.

As they reached a small clearing, Nguyen held up his fist, signaling a halt. "Let's take five. Hoa, radio back to the column. Tell them the route looks clear so far."

As Hoa made the call, Dinh took a swig from his canteen. Neither noticed the camouflaged netting barely visible in the trees above, hiding a Khmer anti-tank team and their deadly RPG.

"All quiet," Hoa reported, finishing her radio call. "They're asking if we've seen any signs of recent activity."

Nguyen shook his head. "Nothing. It's quiet."

As the scouts prepared to move out again, they remained blissfully unaware of the deadly trap they were walking into – and leading their comrades straight towards.

Private Thanh shifted uncomfortably in the cramped interior of the BTR-60 armored personnel carrier, his rifle clutched tightly. The vehicle rumbled forward, part of the long column of armor pushing deeper into Cambodian territory. Beside him, Corporal Tran sat with his eyes closed, seemingly calm despite the danger.

"How can you be so relaxed?" Thanh asked, his voice barely audible over the engine noise.

Tran opened one eye, a wry smile on his face. "Who says I'm relaxed? I'm just conserving energy. We'll need it soon enough."

The column had been moving for hours. Thanh couldn't shake a growing sense of unease. The jungle pressing in on all sides seemed to watch them, waiting.

Suddenly, the APC lurched to a stop. Thanh nearly lost his grip on his rifle.

"What's happening?" he asked, fear creeping into his voice.

Tran was already on his feet, peering through one of the viewports. "The lead vehicles have stopped. Can't see why."

The radio crackled to life, the commander's voice tense. "All infantry, prepare to disembark. We may need to clear an obstruction."

Thanh checked his weapon. Tran placed a reassuring hand on his shoulder. "Stay close to me, kid. Remember your training."

The rear hatch of the APC began to lower, letting in the humid jungle air. Thanh took a deep breath, refreshing compared to the stale air inside the vehicle.

As they filed out of the vehicle, the scene before them was one of confusion. The lead tank had stopped, its crew examining something on the ground. Other infantry squads were spreading out, forming a protective perimeter around the column.

Tran led their squad towards the front, his experienced eyes scanning the jungle for any sign of threat. Thanh followed close behind, every snapping twig and rustling leaf making him flinch.

They were halfway to the lead tank when all hell broke loose.

A deafening explosion rocked the column as the lead tank erupted in flames. Before anyone could react, the air filled with the whistle of incoming rockets and the chatter of small arms fire.

"Ambush!" Tran roared, diving for cover behind a fallen log. "Get down!"

Thanh threw himself to the ground, the sound of bullets whizzing overhead spurring him to crawl desperately towards Tran's position. All around, chaos erupted as Vietnamese soldiers scrambled for cover and returned fire.

"There!" Tran pointed towards a muzzle flash in the trees. Thanh raised his rifle, squeezing off a burst in that direction. He couldn't tell if he hit anything, but the fire from that spot ceased momentarily.

The column was in disarray. Tanks were trying to maneuver in the narrow jungle path, some becoming entangled in obstacles hidden by the undergrowth. APCs were disgorging more infantry, adding to the confusion.

Thanh watched as a rocket struck a nearby APC, the vehicle exploding in a ball of fire. Screams of wounded men filled the air, mixing with the discord of battle.

"We need to move!" Tran shouted, grabbing Thanh's collar. "This position's too exposed!"

They scrambled from cover to cover, joining a group of soldiers attempting to flank the Khmer positions. Thanh's world narrowed to the few meters around him, his training kicking in as he moved, fired, and reloaded almost automatically.

The battle raged on, the Vietnamese forces struggling to regroup and mount an effective counterattack. Thanh lost track of time, each moment blending into a blur of gunfire, explosions, and desperate maneuvers.

Finally, after what seemed like an eternity, the order to retreat came through. The column began to pull back, leaving burning vehicles and too many bodies behind.

As they clambered back into a battered but still functioning APC, Thanh realized he was shaking uncontrollably. Tran, his face streaked with dirt and blood, gave him a grim nod.

"You did good, kid," he said softly. "We made it."

But as the APC lurched into motion, a rocket slammed into the armor behind Tran. His eyes went wide with shock. "Tran, are you okay?" said Tranh.

Tran couldn't respond. A shard of shrapnel had lodged itself in his back and through his lungs. He would never breath again. He fell forward into Tranh's arms.

"It's okay, Tran. I'll get a medic," said Tranh, panicking. But it was too late. Tran was dead.

As Thanh cradled Tran's lifeless body, the APC lurched violently, nearly throwing him off balance. The acrid smell of smoke and burning fuel filled the air, mixing with the metallic tang of Tran's blood.

"We're hit! Engine's done!" the driver shouted over the din of battle. "We have to get out! We're a sitting target!"

Thanh looked up, his eyes wild with grief and fear.

The rear hatch of the APC creaked open, and the surviving soldiers began to pour out into the chaos of the jungle. Thanh hesitated, reluctant to leave Tran's body behind, but another nearby explosion jolted him into action.

As they stumbled into the open, the full extent of the carnage became clear. The retreat had turned into a rout. Vietnamese soldiers scattered in all directions, trying to escape the Khmer onslaught.

"Fall back to the ridge!" an officer shouted, trying to rally the fleeing troops.

The dense jungle path was enveloped in chaos as the Vietnamese armored column desperately tried to retreat. Captain Minh's voice crackled over the radio, "All units, turn around! We're pulling back!"

The lead T-54 tank lurched into motion, its tracks grinding as it attempted to turn in the narrow confines. Suddenly, a sickening crunch echoed through the air. The tank's left track had snagged on a hidden "Dragon's Teeth" obstacle, concealed beneath a layer of vegetation. The concrete teeth tore into the track, immobilizing the vehicle.

"We're stuck!" the tank commander shouted, panic evident in his voice.

Behind it, a BTR-60 armored personnel carrier swerved to avoid the stricken tank. Its wheels crushed the underbrush, revealing more of the deadly obstacles. The driver desperately tried to navigate through, but the vehicle's undercarriage caught on the jagged metal post, leaving it stranded and vulnerable.

Further back, another T-54 attempted to maneuver around the growing bottleneck. Its commander had spotted a small clearing off to the side and was trying to use it to turn around. As the tank entered the clearing, the ground suddenly gave way beneath its weight. The driver gunned the engine, but it was too late – the tank had driven into a carefully disguised pit trap.

The air filled with the whoosh of incoming rockets as Khmer Rouge fighters seized their opportunity. An RPG streaked out of the jungle, slamming into the side of the immobilized lead tank. The explosion rocked the vehicle, smoke pouring from the hatches as its crew scrambled to escape the burning interior.

Another rocket found its mark on the stranded BTR-60. The armored personnel carrier erupted in flames, the screams of trapped soldiers adding to the noise of battle.

The tank in the pit was a sitting duck. A recoilless rifle round penetrated its thinner top armor, detonating inside. The turret was blown clean off, landing with a thunderous crash in the undergrowth. The entire crew was dead.

Amidst the mayhem, other vehicles frantically tried to reverse or find a way around the devastation. Tracks and wheels churned up the earth, revealing more and more of the hidden obstacles that had turned the jungle path into a killing zone filled with immobilized vehicles.

Khmer fighters, emboldened by their success, pressed their attack. RPG teams moved from position to position, taking calculated shots at the most vulnerable targets. The jungle echoed with explosions, the crack of small arms fire, and the agonized groans of damaged vehicles and wounded men.

What had begun as an orderly retreat had devolved into a desperate fight for survival. The Vietnamese armor, once a symbol of their military might, had become a deadly trap for its own crews. As the battle raged on, the jungle path was transformed into a graveyard of burning metal.

Trying to escape the havoc, Thanh found himself running alongside a group of soldiers he didn't recognize, all of them desperate to reach the relative safety of higher ground. The jungle erupted with muzzle flashes as Khmer fighters pressed their advantage, emerging from hidden positions to chase down the retreating Vietnamese.

A soldier just ahead of Thành fell, struck by a burst of gunfire. Without thinking, Thanh grabbed the man's arm, dragging him behind a fallen tree.

Thanh could see that man's wounds were probably lethal, but he couldn't bring himself to abandon another comrade. He hoisted the man onto his shoulders in a fireman's carry, his legs burning with the effort as he continued towards the ridge.

The Khmer were closing in. Rockets streaked overhead, exploding among the fleeing Vietnamese troops. Shrapnel tore through the undergrowth, adding to the chaos.

As Thanh neared the top of the ridge, he saw a group of Vietnamese soldiers setting up a hasty defensive position. Machine guns chattered, providing covering fire for the retreating forces.

With a final burst of energy, Thanh cleared the crest of the ridge, collapsing behind a makeshift barricade with his wounded comrade.

"Medic!" he shouted, his voice hoarse. "I need a medic here!"

As a combat medic rushed over to tend to the wounded soldier, Thanh turned back to face the jungle below. The Khmer fighters were still coming, their assault relentless.

"We can't hold them here," a nearby lieutenant said in a panic. "We need to keep moving, find a more defensible position."

"No," said Thanh. "We need to buy time for the others retreating. We can hold the position."

The lieutenant thought for a moment, then, "Alright. We hold. I'll call for reinforcements."

Thanh leveled his rifle and aimed at the Khmer troops charging up the slope. "Hold until you can see their faces," said Thanh.

The other soldiers on the ridge held their fire as the Khmer drew closer. At times like this, soldiers cared less about rank and more about who felt like they knew what they were doing.

"Hold… hold… now!"

The Vietnamese troops opened fire, mowing down the Khmer troops. Moments later, the Khmer pulled back, abandoning their chase.

"Cease fire! Conserve your ammunition. We're gonna need it," said Thanh.

The soldiers listened and the fire stopped. They watched for the next assault, but it didn't come. The Khmer had won a great victory and were not anxious to turn it into a defeat.

Thanh finally had time to think about his dead friend, Corporal Tran. Tears well up in his eyes. He would miss him.

TWILIGHT OF WAR

Risky

Granier and Spitting Woman crept through the dense jungle, following the vague directions provided by the village boy. The humidity clung to their skin, clothes damp with sweat and streaked with mud. As they neared the supposed location of the resistance camp, both tensed, acutely aware of the danger they were walking into.

Suddenly, a twig snapped underfoot. Before either could react, voices erupted from the foliage around them.

"Freeze! Don't move!" The command came in rapid-fire Khmer.

They found themselves surrounded by camouflaged figures, weapons trained on them from all directions. Granier slowly raised his hands, Spitting Woman following suit.

"We're friends," Spitting Woman said in Khmer,

her voice calm despite the tension. "We're looking for Sophal."

One of the figures stepped forward, his face hidden beneath a layer of mud and leaves. "Sophal? How do you know that name?" His finger tightened on the trigger of his AK-47.

Granier spoke up, keeping his movements slow and deliberate. "We fought together. Against the Khmer Rouge. We need his help."

The leader's eyes narrowed suspiciously. "You could be spies. Khmer Rouge tricks."

"Do I look like Khmer Rouge?" said Granier.

Before either could respond, another voice rang out from behind them. "Kill them. We can't take chances."

Granier saw the leader's finger begin to squeeze the trigger. In that split second, he made a decision. He dove towards Spitting Woman, intent on shielding her with his body.

"Hold your fire!" A familiar voice boomed through the clearing. Sophal emerged from the undergrowth, his expression a mix of shock and relief. "These are friends!"

The fighters lowered their weapons, confusion evident on their faces. Sophal rushed forward, helping Granier and Spitting Woman to their feet.

"I'm sorry. We've had to be cautious," Sophal said, his voice heavy with regret. " The Khmer Rouge have been probing our defenses."

Granier nodded, his heart still racing. "We understand. We're just glad to see a friendly face."

Spitting Woman brushed herself off, her eyes scanning the surrounding fighters. "Things have... changed, Sophal. We need your help."

Sophal studied their faces, noting the weariness and

urgency in their expressions. "Come. We'll talk in the camp."

As they followed Sophal. The resistance camp materialized out of the dense jungle like a mirage, hidden so expertly that it seemed to blend seamlessly with the surrounding foliage. As Sophal led Granier and Spitting Woman deeper into the encampment, the ingenuity of its design became apparent.

Thatched huts, their roofs covered in living vegetation, were scattered in a seemingly random pattern to avoid detection from the air. Camouflage netting stretched between trees, creating shadowy corridors and concealed gathering spaces. The ground underfoot was carefully maintained with scattered leaves to minimize signs of human traffic.

A small clearing at the center of the camp served as a communal area. Here, a few low fires burned, the smoke dispersed by an ingenious system of bamboo pipes that released it gradually through the dense canopy above. Around these fires, resistance fighters huddled in small groups, their conversations hushed and their eyes wary of the newcomers.

The perimeter of the camp was guarded by concealed lookout posts high in the trees, nearly invisible unless you knew where to look. Crude but effective alarm systems – strings of shells and metal scraps – were strung between strategic points, ready to alert the camp of any intrusion.

The entire camp exuded an air of impermanence, as if it could be dismantled and relocated at a moment's notice. Weapons were everywhere – propped against trees, carried by fighters, or partially hidden under camouflage tarps. The atmosphere was one of constant vigilance.

As they moved through the camp, Granier and Spitting Woman noted the diverse makeup of the resistance force. There were hardened fighters bearing the scars of long conflict, alongside younger recruits with fire in their eyes. Women worked alongside men, their roles seemingly equal in the fight against the Khmer Rouge.

Munching on pieces of mango and rice, Granier finished recounting their discovery, his voice low to avoid being overheard. The dimly lit command hut felt cramped.

Sophal leaned back, his weathered face a mask of controlled anger. "I wish I could say I'm surprised," he said, his voice barely above a whisper. "But we never trusted the Vietnamese. This just confirms our suspicions."

Spitting Woman leaned forward, her eyes intense. "No, Sophal. You can't judge all Vietnamese by the actions of a corrupt few. The soldiers, the ones fighting and dying out there, they're not part of this."

"How can you be sure?" Sophal challenged, his tone skeptical.

"Because we've fought alongside them," Granier interjected. "We've seen their courage, their sacrifice. This conspiracy, it's led by officers, by those at the top who see an opportunity for profit."

Sophal's eyes narrowed. "And yet it's Vietnamese guns in Khmer Rouge hands that kill our people. Khmer-supplied drugs that fund their atrocities."

Spitting Woman shook her head vehemently. "The average soldier knows nothing of this. They believe in the mission, in stopping the Khmer Rouge and freeing Cambodia from Pol Pot's grip. Don't let the actions of a corrupt few taint your view of an entire people."

"She's right," Granier added. "We're here because we believe this corruption needs to be exposed, stopped. But we need your help to do it."

Sophal was silent for a long moment, his gaze shifting between Granier and Spitting Woman. Finally, he spoke, his voice heavy with the weight of decision. "What you're proposing is dangerous. It could upend the entire power structure in the region."

"It needs to be upended," Spitting Woman insisted. "For the sake of both Cambodia and Vietnam."

Sophal nodded slowly. "I understand your position. But understand mine. My priority is protecting my people, my country. How can I be sure helping you won't make things worse for us?"

Granier leaned forward, his voice earnest. "Because if we don't stop this, the war will drag on. More Cambodians will die. More Vietnamese soldiers will die. And the only ones who benefit will be the corrupt Vietnamese officers and the Khmer Rouge leadership."

"What is it that you would have us do?"

"We need to contact the man that originally sent us on our mission. He's powerful and can put a stop to this. We need access to a long-range radio transmitter that can reach Hanoi," said Spitting Woman.

A tense silence fell over the hut. Outside, the sounds of the camp – muffled conversations, the distant clanking of weapons being cleaned – seemed to underscore the gravity of the moment.

Finally, Sophal spoke. "I need time to consider this. To consult with my advisors. What you're asking is not our mission. Helping you is not a decision I can make lightly."

Spitting Woman nodded, "Of course. But please,

Sophal, remember – the longer we wait, the more lives are lost by this corruption."

As they left the command hut, stepping back into the humid jungle air, the fate of their mission, and potentially the course of the war itself, now rested in the hands of Sophal and his resistance fighters. All they could do was wait and hope that their trust in the fundamental decency of those fighting on both sides would prove justified.

Vietnamese Field Headquarters

The command tent buzzed with tension as field commanders gathered around a map-strewn table. The recent ambush had left tempers frayed and nerves on edge.

Colonel Nguyen slammed his fist on the table. "This is unacceptable! Our recon teams failed us completely. How did they miss such an elaborate trap?"

Major Tran, head of reconnaissance, bristled. "My men did their job. The Khmer Rouge have become experts at camouflage. We can't—"

"Excuses!" another commander cut in. "We lost good men and valuable equipment because of this oversight."

General Anh raised his hand for silence, his face a mask of calm authority. "Gentlemen, pointing fingers won't change what's happened. We need to focus on moving forward."

A younger captain spoke up hesitantly. "Sir, what about those two scouts... the Frenchman and the tribal woman? They've provided reliable intel in the past. Where are they?"

Anh's expression didn't flicker as he smoothly

responded, "They're on a deep reconnaissance mission. Critical to our next phase of operations. That's all you need to know."

The lie settled over the group, unquestioned but adding to the undercurrent of unease.

Anh continued, directing their attention to the map. "We have a more pressing concern. Intelligence reports a Khmer Rouge fortress here, directly in our route to Phnom Penh," he pointed to a strategic location. "It threatens our supply lines. We cannot risk bypassing it."

The commanders leaned in, studying the position.

"It's a strong defensive position," Colonel Nguyen observed. "Assaulting it will be costly."

Anh's voice was firm. "We have no choice. This fortress must fall if we're to continue our advance on the capital."

He began outlining the assault plan, detailing troop movements and artillery support. As the commanders focused on the upcoming battle, the earlier recriminations faded into the background.

But beneath the strategic discussion, an undercurrent of doubt remained. The loss of trust in their reconnaissance capabilities, the unexplained absence of their best scouts, and the daunting task ahead all contributed to a sense that this campaign was taking a dangerous turn.

As the meeting concluded and commanders filed out to prepare their troops, General Anh remained behind, his eyes fixed on the map. The fortress loomed large in his mind, not just as a military objective, but as a chance to reassert control over a situation that was rapidly spiraling beyond his grasp.

TWILIGHT OF WAR

Resistance Camp

Sophal led Granier and Spitting Woman to a secluded corner of the camp, then said, "We have decided to help you. But I want to make clear, I will not order my men into any operation that promises high casualties. We cannot afford to lose more men." Granier and Spitting Woman nodded in agreement. Sophal spread a crude map on a makeshift table, pointing to a nearby peak.

"There," he said in a low voice. "The Khmer Rouge have a signal repeater station on that mountaintop. If there's a long-range transmitter anywhere in the area, it'll be there."

Granier studied the map intently. "What kind of defenses are we looking at?"

Sophal's expression darkened. "A squad guards it. At least fifteen men, maybe more. They know the strategic value of the position. We need to avoid a confrontation if possible."

Spitting Woman leaned in, her eyes narrowed. "Any way to approach undetected?"

"There's a narrow ravine on the eastern slope," Sophal replied, tracing the route with his finger. "It's treacherous, but it might get a small team close without raising alarms. The catch is, you'll need climbing gear to navigate it safely."

Granier nodded slowly, "Mountain climbing equipment isn't exactly standard issue out here. Can you get your hands on what we'll need?"

"We've raided enough Khmer Rouge supply convoys to piece together a set. It's not pretty, but it'll do the job. Ropes, carabiners, harnesses – we've got enough for a small team."

"Good," Spitting Woman said, her voice tense with anticipation. "How many can you spare to join us?"

"Four of my best fighters and myself," Sophal answered after a moment's hesitation. "Any more would slow you down and increase the risk of detection."

"It'll have to do," Granier said firmly. "When can we move out?"

"We can hike to the base of the ravine this afternoon," Sophal answered. "Then climb the ravine under cover of darkness. But listen, this isn't just about getting to that transmitter. If we take out that repeater station, it'll cripple Khmer Rouge communications in this entire sector."

Granier and Spitting Woman exchanged a meaningful look.

"We understand," Spitting Woman said solemnly. "We'll make it count."

Sophal nodded, a hint of pride in his eyes. "I'll brief the team and get the climbing gear ready. Get some rest. You'll need every ounce of strength for the climb ahead."

As Sophal moved away to prepare his men and equipment, Granier turned to Spitting Woman. "This just got a lot more complicated," he murmured.

She met his gaze, "Maybe, but it's our best shot. And if we pull this off..."

"We might just change the course of this war," Granier finished.

Mountain Ravine

The dense jungle gave way to steep, rocky terrain as Granier, Spitting Woman, and the five resistance fighters began their ascent. The air grew thinner with each grueling step, muscles burning from the exertion.

Halfway up, the sky opened. Rain poured down in sheets, turning the rocky path into a treacherous slide. They fought for each foothold.

"Keep moving!" Sophal shouted over the downpour. "We can't afford to lose time!"

Hours passed, the group pushing through exhaustion and the relentless elements. As late afternoon approached, they finally reached the base of the ravine. Collapsing under an overhang, they caught their breath, muscles trembling from the climb. The ravine loomed before them, a jagged gash in the mountainside that seemed to stretch endlessly upward.

"We rest here until nightfall," Granier said, his voice hoarse. "Then we make our final push up the ravine."

Moving next to Granier as he leaned against boulder, Spitting Woman rested her head on his chest and quickly fell asleep.

As darkness blanketed the mountain, they began their ascent of the ravine. The climbing gear, a patchwork of scavenged equipment, creaked ominously as they inched their way up the sheer rock face.

The first hundred feet were grueling but manageable. Then the ravine narrowed, forcing them to navigate a series of precarious ledges. Loose rocks skittered away under their feet, plummeting into the unseen depths below.

Halfway up, they encountered a sheer vertical section. Granier paused, studying the wall before them. "We'll need to use pitons here," he called back to the others.

Carefully, he hammered the metal spikes into small

cracks in the rock, creating a makeshift ladder. The sound of metal on stone echoed ominously in the confined space.

As they negotiated this section, a light rain began to fall, making the already slippery surface treacherous. Granier could hear the labored breathing of his teammates, feel the tension in the rope connecting them.

Near the top of the vertical face, disaster struck. One of the rebels, exhausted and struggling with the unfamiliar climbing gear, lost his footing. His startled cry pierced the night as he fell, jerking the safety line taut.

Next in line, Spitting Woman grabbed for a handhold, but it wasn't enough. As the rope snapped taut, she was pulled from the rock face and fell.

The safety line wrapped around his waist, Granier felt the wrenching tug that threatened to pull him off the wall. Muscles straining, he clung to his handhold, acutely aware that he was now supporting not just his own weight, but that of the fallen climber and Spitting Woman as well.

"Hold on!" he grunted, fighting to maintain his grip on the slippery rock.

For several anxious moments, the outcome hung in the balance. Then, with a herculean effort, Granier managed to brace himself.

Spitting Woman scrambled to find a handhold or foothold to relieve some of the weight on Granier.

The fallen rebel whimpered in pain and fear, the sound echoing off the ravine walls.

Above, a Khmer guard's face appeared, peering down into the darkness to investigate the noise.

With fluid grace, Sophal nocked an arrow to his

bow. The whisper of its release was followed by a soft thud as the guard fell, the arrow finding its mark in his left eye.

Spitting Woman began to climb back up the safety line. Inch by agonizing inch, she made her way to the fallen rebel's position. She helped the startled man find his footing and to start once again ascending the rock face.

As they regrouped on a narrow ledge, catching their breath, Granier knew they couldn't afford another close call. Granier collapsed against the rock face, his breath coming in ragged gasps. "Everyone okay?" he managed to ask.

Nods and whispered affirmatives came from the group. Spitting Woman squeezed his shoulder, her eyes conveying both gratitude and concern.

"We need to move," Sophal whispered urgently. "That guard will be missed soon."

With renewed caution, they pressed on. Each foot of progress was hard-won, a battle against gravity, fatigue, and the unforgiving terrain. By the time they neared the top of the ravine, every muscle in Granier's body screamed for relief.

Summoning reserves of strength they didn't know they possessed, the group continued their ascent. As they climbed, the signal repeater station loomed above, their goal now tantalizingly close.

Finally, after what seemed like an eternity, Granier hauled himself over the lip of the ravine onto relatively flat ground. As he helped the others up, a mix of exhaustion and triumph washed over him.

As darkness enveloped the mountaintop, Granier, Spitting Woman, and the rebels crouched in the shadows near the repeater station. The smell of cooking food wafted from the nearby barracks, confirming their intel that the Khmer guards were distracted with their evening meal.

Granier nodded to Spitting Woman. "Now's our chance. Go."

She slipped silently into the station, while Granier and the rebels took up watchful positions outside.

Inside, Spitting Woman quickly located the transmitter. Her fingers flew over the controls, resetting the frequency. Taking a deep breath, she began to tap out a coded message to Le Duan, using the secret cipher they had developed years ago during her time as his bodyguard. Only Le Duan would recognize the code and only Le Duan could decipher it.

Minutes ticked by. Granier peered inside, tension evident on his face. "Any luck?"

Spitting Woman shook her head. "I've sent the message. Now we wait for a response. It could take some time."

"The longer we're here, the greater the risk of discovery."

"I know," she replied, her eyes never leaving the transmitter. "But there's nothing I can do to speed this up."

Reluctantly, Granier returned outside to confer with Sophal. "We have to wait for a response," he explained in a hushed tone.

Sophal's eyes narrowed, scanning the quiet compound. "We can't risk being discovered. If they raise the alarm, we're trapped up here." He paused, then added grimly, "We should take them out now, while we have the element of surprise."

"We'll be outnumbered."

"We always are and yet it never stops us."

Granier hesitated, weighing their options. Finally, he nodded. "You're right. We should attack."

Sophal quickly outlined a plan of attack. Moments later, they were in position around the barracks. On Sophal's signal, they lobbed grenades through the windows. The explosions shattered the night's silence, followed immediately by the rebels storming in, assault rifles blazing, racking the Khmer troops, killing them all.

The initial attack was devastatingly effective, catching most of the Khmer guards completely off guard. But the element of surprise didn't last long. Shouts and gunfire erupted from other parts of the compound as more guards rushed to defend against the unexpected assault.

A fierce firefight ensued. Granier and Sophal fought side by side, their weapons chattering in the confined space of the barracks. Two of the rebels fell to enemy fire, their cries of pain lost in the chaos of battle.

Just as it seemed the tide might turn against them, Spitting Woman emerged from the repeater station, adding her firepower to the fray in a flanking assault. Her sudden appearance from an unexpected quarter threw the Khmer guards into disarray, and within minutes, the last of the enemy resistance crumbled.

As the echoes of gunfire faded, replaced by the groans of the wounded, Granier turned to Spitting Woman. "Did you get a response?"

She nodded. "Yes, but it's not what we hoped for."

She quickly relayed Le Duan's message. General Anh had accused them of being the ones behind the weapons-for-drugs conspiracy. Le Duan, unwilling to risk the entire incursion by accusing his field general without proof, had ordered Spitting Woman and Granier to return to Vietnam for interrogation.

A heavy silence fell over the group. Sophal was the first to speak, his voice tight with anger and disappointment. "So it was all for nothing? We lost good men for this?"

Granier shook his head, his mind racing. "Not nothing. We can still destroy the tower and disrupt Khmer Rouge communications in this sector. That's a significant blow."

"Well, that at least something," said Sophal.

Granier and Sophal took up defensive positions while Spitting Woman went to work.

Inside the repeater station, Spitting Woman moved with practiced efficiency. She retrieved several blocks of plastic explosive from her pack. Carefully, she placed the charges at key structural points and around the critical transmission equipment.

Once the charges were set, Spitting Woman exited the station. "It's done," she announced to Granier and Sophal. "We need to move. Now."

Spitting Woman unspooled the wire connected to the blasting caps as she moved down the mountain. The group quickly gathered their gear and began their descent as well. When they were at a safe distance, Spitting Woman paused, turning back to face the station silhouetted against the lightening sky. She stripped the ends of the wire and attached to the leads on the detonator. Without a word, she plunged the detonator.

The explosion rocked the mountaintop, a brilliant flash followed by a thunderous boom that echoed through the valleys below. The repeater tower swayed for a moment before collapsing in on itself, taking the transmitter and all its equipment with it.

As debris rained down and smoke billowed into the air, Spitting Woman allowed herself a small, grim smile. "That ought to give them something to think about," she murmured.

"Good work. Now let's get out of here before reinforcements arrive," said Granier.

The group melted back into the jungle, leaving behind a smoldering ruin where once stood a key piece of Khmer Rouge infrastructure.

The jungle's intense humidity clung to them as Granier and Spitting Woman made their way back to the makeshift camp. The adrenaline from their successful mission to destroy the radio repeater was wearing off, replaced by a bone-deep weariness.

Sophal and his men had gone ahead to secure the perimeter, leaving the two of them alone for the moment. They collapsed beside a small stream, grateful for the chance to rest and refill their canteens.

Granier splashed water on his face, the coolness a stark contrast to the hot air. He glanced at Spitting Woman, noticing the distant look in her eyes.

"What's on your mind?" he asked, breaking the silence.

She took a long drink before responding. "There're two questions that are bothering me."

Granier settled back against a moss-covered log. "Go on."

"Where are the Khmer Rouge getting the opium? Opium is not grown in Cambodia, at least not in large quantities."

"Good question," Granier mused. "Laos? Thailand?"

"Maybe, but I was thinking Burma."

"Why Burma? It's a bit off the beaten path."

"It's part of the golden triangle."

"So are Thailand and Laos, and both share a border with Cambodia. A much shorter supply route."

Spitting Woman leaned forward, her voice low but intense. "Burma is going through its own revolution led by warlords. Just like the Khmer Rouge, they need weapons."

"American weapons?" Granier asked, catching on.

"Why not? They're the best in the world. What better way of overthrowing a government than superior firepower?"

Granier nodded slowly, considering the implications. "Okay. For argument's sake, let's say Burma is the supplier. How does that help us?"

"If we can cut off the supply, the drugs-for-weapons deals will dry up."

"How do we find Burma's opium supply route?"

"We ask our friends in the resistance."

"Why would they know?"

"Revolutions have strange bedfellows. Besides, from what I've seen, they're very resourceful."

"I may have another source for that kind of information, but I don't want to use unless I absolutely have no choice."

"Okay. Good to know."

A moment of silence passed as they both pondered the complexities of such a situation. Finally, Granier spoke up. "What's your second question?"

"Who is buying the raw opium from the Vietnamese?"

"Maybe they're selling it to their own opium houses," Granier suggested.

Spitting Woman shook her head. "Maybe, but that's a lot of opium. Besides, if the Vietnamese government ever found out who was selling that much opium to their people, I'm pretty sure heads would roll."

"And finding the buyer helps us how?"

"I guess it depends on the identity of the buyer."

Granier's eyes narrowed. "Are you thinking the Corsicans?"

"It's possible. Their supply chain in Laos has been cut off. Finding a new supplier would be a top priority."

"So, why don't the Corsicans just buy opium directly from the Burmese?"

"I'm not sure, but I imagine they've tried, and they still have a supply problem. Revolutionaries can be very picky."

Granier sighed, running a hand through his sweat-damp hair. "Okay, but I still don't see how that helps us."

Spitting Woman leaned in closer, her voice barely above a whisper. "What's the one person a Vietnamese general would fear?"

Realization dawned on Granier's face. "The head of the Corsican mob?"

"I sure wouldn't want to piss him off. And if Anh loses his shipment, well…"

The implications of their conversation hung in the air between them. The sound of approaching footsteps cut short any further discussion. Sophal emerged from the undergrowth, signaling that it was time to move out.

As they gathered their gear, Granier and Spitting Woman exchanged a meaningful look. Their mission had just become far more complex, but they also had new leads to follow.

As the group made their way back through the dense jungle, Granier caught Spitting Woman's eye and nodded subtly towards Sophal. She understood immediately.

"Sophal," Granier called out softly, "a word?"

The resistance leader slowed his pace, allowing the others to move ahead. Once they had a semblance of privacy, Granier spoke in a low voice.

"We need to ask you something, and we need your absolute discretion."

Sophal's eyes narrowed, but he nodded. "Go on."

Spitting Woman leaned in. "We have reason to believe there's a trade route bringing opium from Burma into Cambodia. Do you know anything about this?"

Sophal's face remained impassive, but a flicker of something—recognition? concern?—passed through his eyes. He was silent for a long moment.

"That's... a dangerous question," he finally said, his voice barely above a whisper.

"We know," Granier pressed. "But it could be crucial to stopping the weapons-for-drugs operation."

Sophal glanced around, ensuring they weren't overheard. "I've... heard rumors. Nothing concrete. Such a route, if it exists, would be heavily guarded. Not just by men, but by silence."

"But you could find out more?" Spitting Woman asked.

Sophal seemed to be weighing his words carefully. "I have... contacts. People who might know things. But asking these questions could put my people at risk. You understand?"

Granier nodded solemnly. "We do. But the

information could be vital."

After a long pause, Sophal sighed. "I'll look into it. Quietly. But I make no promises."

"Thank you," Spitting Woman said, genuine gratitude in her voice.

As they moved to rejoin the group, Sophal added, "Be careful. If such a route exists, it's protected by people who wouldn't hesitate to kill to keep it secret. And in this jungle, bodies disappear easily."

As dawn broke, Sophal led Granier and Spitting Woman through dense jungle to the shores of a vast lake. The water stretched out before them, its surface a mirror reflecting the pink-tinged sky. In the distance, a cluster of wooden structures perched on stilts above the water - the fishing village.

"I grew up here," Sophal said softly, a hint of nostalgia in his voice. He turned to Granier, handing over his rifle. "I can't bring this. It would raise suspicions."

Granier nodded, understanding the delicacy of the situation. "We'll keep watch from here."

Spitting Woman was already scaling a tall tree near the shore, finding a position that gave her a clear view of the village and the surrounding area.

As Sophal paddled a small boat towards the village, Granier settled into a concealed position on the shore, rifle at the ready.

Hours passed. The sun climbed higher in the sky as village life unfolded before them. They watched as Sophal was greeted warmly, shared meals, and engaged in long conversations with elders and fishermen alike.

Finally, as the afternoon waned, Sophal's boat reappeared, cutting a path back to shore. His face was unreadable as he pulled the boat onto the sand.

"Well?" Granier asked, tension evident in his voice.

Sophal nodded grimly. "The route exists. But..." he trailed off, glancing back at the village.

"But what?" Spitting Woman pressed, having climbed down from her perch.

"No one will speak of its location," Sophal sighed. "The fear is real. Whatever protects this route, it's powerful enough to silence an entire village."

A heavy silence fell over the group as they absorbed this information.

After a moment, Granier spoke up. "I need to make an international call. Is there anywhere we can do that safely?"

Sophal raised an eyebrow but didn't ask questions. "There's a phone center in a town about ten kilometers from here. But it won't be secure."

"It'll have to do," Granier said firmly.

As they prepared to move out, Spitting Woman caught Granier's eye. "Who are you calling?" she asked quietly.

Granier's face was grim. "Someone who might be able to help us locate that route… or kill me depending on his mood."

The unspoken question hung in the air between them: was it a risk worth taking?

Washington D.C.

Lucien Conein, the head of DEA Special Operations, sat in his dimly lit office, the blinds drawn against the harsh midday sun. He poured himself a second glass of bourbon, the amber liquid sloshing dangerously close to the rim. The intercom on his desk buzzed, interrupting his solitary lunch.

"Yeah?" he growled, annoyed at the interruption.

His secretary's voice crackled through the speaker. "There's a man on the phone who says he knows you. His name is Rene Granier."

Conein froze, the glass halfway to his lips. "Granier? You're sure?"

"Yes, sir. He was quite insistent."

Conein considered for a long moment before responding. "Put him through to line two."

He stared at the blinking light on his phone, memories of past confrontations with Granier flashing through his mind. They had a history, alright - both ex-CIA operatives from the Vietnam War, and both harboring a deep-seated hatred for each other that had only grown over the years.

Finally, he pressed the button. "I thought you were dead," he said by way of greeting.

"Sorry to disappoint you," Granier's voice came through.

"Where are you so I can finish the job myself?" Conein's tone was half-joking, but there was an edge to it.

"Nice to hear your sunny disposition hasn't changed, Conein. I'm in Cambodia."

"Are you part of that shit storm?"

"Right in the middle of it."

"You always did know how to stir things up. So, I doubt this is a social call. What do you want, Granier?"

"Cut the crap, Granier. What do you want?"

There was a pause on the line. "Intel," Granier finally said. "About opium trade routes from Burma to Cambodia. You're the head honcho at DEA Special Ops. If anyone has that kind of intel, it would be you."

Conein barked out a laugh. "And why the hell would I help you with that?"

"Because it's connected to American weapons being funneled to the Khmer Rouge by the Vietnamese military."

"Why should I care about that as long as they both continue to kill each other? Seems like a win, win to me."

"Alright, let me try a different approach. If I am successful at cutting off the supply route, you can take all the credit. Imagine how that would look to your DEA buddies. The guy who shut down one of the biggest opium pipelines in Southeast Asia."

"Well, that's at least a little more interesting."

Conein leaned back in his chair and took another pull of his bourbon, "Look, I can't get involved in this. The intel is classified."

"Come on, Conein. That never stopped you before. When did you become such a pussy?"

Conein seethed, "Watch yourself, Granier."

"Everyone knows you're a big cheese now, Conein. But maybe you're lost your nerve."

"I haven't lost anything."

"Good. So, tell me where it's located and let's get on with it."

There was another long pause as Conein considered, then… "This changes nothing between us."

"Agreed."

"It starts in Keng Tung, Burma. It travels overland until it reaches the Mekong River on the border with Laos. There it is hidden on to a crude oil barge and travels down the Mekong until it reaches Cambodia. They travel mostly at night and hide in caves during the day to avoid being spotted by aircraft or satellite. That's all I can tell you."

"Well, it's more than I had ten minutes ago."

"Do you think you can find it?"

"I don't know. But I am sure as hell gonna try. One last question… the Corsicans?"

"What about them?"

"Do you still have contacts?"

"Since they tried to kill me… no. I'm afraid that bridge has been burned forever."

"Can you at least tell me who is in charge of Southeast Asia?"

"Vincent Liccioni… unless he's been killed. Crime is a rough game."

"I'm sure. He's in Saigon?"

"I imagine. Probably hangs in one of the mob's restaurants."

"Why don't the Vietnamese throw him out of the country?"

"Bribes I would guess. That and he's French. The Vietnamese still need the French engineers to repair their heavy equipment and to supply spare parts."

"Thanks, Conein. I owe you one."

"You owe me a lot more than one to clean our slate."

The line went dead. Conein leaned back in his chair, swirling the remaining bourbon in his glass. After a moment, he reached for his phone again, dialing a number from memory.

"It's Conein," he said when the line connected. "We might have a problem…"

The Fortress

The dense Cambodian jungle gave way to a small clearing, where two Vietnamese scouts lay prone, their bodies almost invisible beneath their camouflage. Captain Minh Dao peered through his high-powered binoculars, his eyes narrowed in concentration as he surveyed the Khmer Rouge fortress looming before them.

The fortress was an imposing sight, perched atop a steep hill that offered a commanding view of the surrounding area. Its walls, a mix of weathered stone and newer concrete reinforcements, stood at least twenty feet high. Rusted barbed wire crowned the top, glinting dully in the afternoon sun.

"What do you see?" whispered Sergeant Linh Bui, Minh's experienced second-in-command.

Minh passed her the binoculars. "Four guard towers, one at each corner. Heavy machine gun emplacements in at least six of them along the top of the perimeter walls."

Linh scanned the fortress, noting the details. The

main gate was a massive iron affair, flanked by two smaller pillboxes. A faded Khmer Rouge flag fluttered above it, its red and black colors a stark contrast against the green jungle backdrop.

"Movement on the walls," Linh murmured. "Regular patrols, looks like teams of two. They're well-disciplined."

Minh nodded, sketching the layout in his waterproof notebook. "Any signs of artillery?"

Linh adjusted the focus, scanning the top of the walls. "Yes... there. Northeastern corner. Looks like a 105mm howitzer. Possibly more, but it's hard to tell from this angle."

As they watched, a truck rumbled through the main gate, kicking up dust. The gate remained open just long enough for Linh to glimpse the inner courtyard. "Vehicle depot inside, near the western wall. I count at least three tanks, maybe more under camouflage netting."

"Any weak points?"

Linh studied the structure carefully. "The southeastern wall... there's some damage. Might be from the last monsoon. It's been patched, but it could be vulnerable to concentrated fire."

Suddenly, Minh held up a hand for silence. A patrol of Khmer Rouge soldiers was making its way along the treeline, dangerously close to their position. The two scouts remained perfectly still, barely breathing, as the patrol passed within meters of their hiding spot.

Once the danger had passed, Minh signaled it was time to withdraw. As they crawled backwards into the dense foliage, Linh took one last look at the fortress. A chill ran down her spine as she realized the true cost of what lay ahead. The Vietnamese army would pay a heavy price to take this stronghold.

Phnom Penh

Pol Pot sat in his austere office in Phnom Penh, his face impassive as he listened to the urgent report from his military aide. The room was spartan, dominated by maps of Cambodia and a single portrait of Mao Zedong.

"Brother Number One," the aide said, "our forward observers report a large Vietnamese force advancing towards the Oknha Khleang Moeung fortress. They appear to be preparing for a major assault."

Pol Pot's eyes narrowed. "Composition?"

"At least a division, possibly more. Tanks, artillery, air support - a full-scale invasion force."

Pol Pot stood, moving to the large map spread across his desk. He studied it intently, his finger tracing the route from the Vietnamese border to the fortress.

"The fortress status?" he asked, not looking up.

The aide consulted his notes. "Fully manned and supplied, Comrade. All defenses operational. They report readiness for a prolonged siege."

Pol Pot nodded slowly, his mind racing through possibilities. "If we reinforce before their assault begins, we can turn this to our advantage." He looked up sharply. "How quickly can we move troops?"

"We have a mechanized battalion ten kilometers away. They could reach the fortress within hours if we move now."

"Do it," Pol Pot ordered. Then, after a moment's thought, "Tell the fortress commander to use hidden assault teams once he has determined where the Vietnamese will concentrate their assault."

"Outside the fortress walls?"

"Precisely. The Vietnamese will focus on breaching the walls. They won't expect an attack on their flanks. We will turn their incursion into an ambush and exact a heavy toll for their audacity."

He turned back to the map, pointing to several locations around the fortress. "We'll have seven teams, each twenty men strong, hidden in these positions and armed with RPGs and recoilless rifles. When the Vietnamese commit to their assault, these teams will strike. They'll target command vehicles, artillery positions, anything to sow chaos in their ranks."

The aide nodded, scribbling notes furiously.

Pol Pot continued, "Tell the fortress commander to draw the Vietnamese in close before revealing our full defensive capabilities. Let them think they're making progress, then spring the trap." Pol Pot moved to the window, gazing out over Phnom Penh. The city was quiet, unaware of the storm about to break on the border.

"And have our anti-aircraft teams hidden in the jungle outside the fortress. When the Vietnamese jets attack, we shall clear the sky like a broom on a dusty path."

"Yes, Comrade. I will see that it is done," said the aide as he hurried to carry out his orders,

"And contact our Chinese allies," he added, almost as an afterthought. "Remind them of our... arrangement. We may need their support sooner than anticipated."

Pol Pot returned to his desk, pulling out a sheaf of coded message forms. It was time to set other plans in motion. The fortress was important, yes, but it was just one piece on a larger board.

As he began writing, dispatching orders across his network of commanders, Pol Pot felt a surge of cold confidence. The Vietnamese might have numbers and firepower, but they lacked imagination. They would expect a straightforward siege, not a multi-layered defense with strikes from unexpected quarters.

He paused in his writing, looking up at Mao's portrait.

"Let them come," he murmured. "This fortress will be their graveyard, a monument to the price of underestimating the Khmer Rouge."

The coming battle would be fierce, but in Pol Pot's mind, the outcome was already decided. His fortress would endure, and the Vietnamese would learn a costly lesson about the perils of invasion.

As night fell over Phnom Penh, Pol Pot continued his work, setting in motion a plan that he believed would not just defend a fortress, but turn the tide of the entire war.

Vietnamese Field Command Headquarters

General Anh stood before a large map of the fortress and surrounding area. The assembled officers listened intently as he laid out the battle plan, their expressions a mix of concern and resolve.

"Gentlemen," Anh began, his voice firm, "based on reconnaissance reports, we're facing a formidable challenge. But this fortress stands between us and Phnom Penh. We must take it, and we must take it quickly before it can be reinforced."

He pointed to various positions on the map as he spoke. "We'll begin with a concentrated artillery barrage here, here, and here. Our 130mm guns will focused on softening up the southeastern wall where our scouts noted structural weakness."

An artillery officer spoke up. "How long will we have for the bombardment, sir?"

Anh's expression tightened. "Not as long as I'd like. We can't afford to get bogged down here. We'll give it three hours, no more."

Murmurs rippled through the group, but Anh continued. "Simultaneously, we'll launch an air assault. Our A-37s and F-5s will target the guard towers and any visible artillery positions. We need to neutralize their ability to rain fire down on our advancing troops."

He turned to the air force liaison. "Can your pilots handle low-altitude strikes in these conditions?"

The officer nodded confidently. "Yes, sir. They've been training for this kind of mission."

"Good," Anh nodded. "Because after the initial bombardment, they'll need to provide close air support for our ground forces during the assault."

He swept his hand across the map. "The main assault will come from here and here. Two pronged attack, with our T-54 tanks leading the charge. Infantry will follow close behind, using the tanks for cover."

A colonel raised his hand. "Sir, what about the minefield our intel suggests surrounds the fortress?"

General Anh nodded at the colonel's question about the minefield. "Good point, Colonel. We'll use armored bulldozers to clear paths through the minefields in front of the southeastern wall and the main gate."

He turned to his logistics officer. "Major Tran, how many armored D7 bulldozers do we have available?"

Major Tran consulted his notes. "We have three operational D7s, sir, all with additional armor plating."

"Excellent," Anh said, turning back to the map. "We'll deploy the bulldozers here and here," he pointed to two locations in front of the planned assault routes. "They'll clear paths wide enough for our tanks and infantry to follow safely."

He looked at the assembled officers. "The bulldozers will move out under the cover of our initial artillery barrage. The noise and smoke should provide some concealment. Once they've cleared the paths, our tanks will immediately follow, with infantry close behind."

A young captain spoke up. "Sir, what if the Khmer Rouge have anti-tank weapons targeting the cleared paths?"

Anh nodded gravely. "A valid concern, Captain. That's why our air support will be crucial. We'll have A-37s making constant passes to suppress any visible anti-tank positions. Additionally, our lead tanks will be equipped with mine rollers as an extra precaution."

He surveyed the room. "Any other questions about the minefield clearing operation?"

The officers shook their heads, seemingly satisfied with the plan.

"Good," Anh concluded. "The bulldozers are key to our initial push. Their operators will be briefed on the critical nature of their mission. If they fail, the entire assault could be jeopardized."

He pointed to the southeastern wall again. "This is our primary target. If our artillery and aircraft do their jobs, we should have a breach point here. That's where we'll concentrate our forces."

Anh paused, looking around at his officers. "Make no mistake, gentlemen. This will be a costly assault. But that fortress is the key to our advance on Phnom Penh.

We must take the fortress or destroy it."

He straightened, his voice ringing with authority. "We move at dawn. Any questions?"

The room was silent, the weight of the coming battle settling over everyone present.

"Very well," Anh concluded. "Prepare your men. Tomorrow, we make history."

As the officers filed out to brief their units, Anh remained, staring at the map. The fortress loomed large in his mind, a formidable obstacle on their path to victory. But beneath his stern exterior, a flicker of doubt nagged at him. The cost would be high, perhaps too high. But he pushed the thought aside. In war, there was no room for such hesitation.

Oknha Khleang Moeung Fortress

The jungle's edge bustled with activity as Vietnamese forces prepared for the assault on the Khmer fortress. Private Thanh crouched behind a T-54 tank, one of twenty forming the spearhead of the attack. The tanks' engines idled, a low rumble that seemed to make the ground vibrate beneath his feet.

Captain Minh stood atop his command vehicle, surveying the scene through binoculars. To the rear, a battery of six 130mm artillery pieces was positioned, their long barrels aimed at the fortress walls. Closer to the front, teams were setting up a dozen 75mm recoilless rifles, their smaller size belying their destructive potential against fortified defensive positions.

"Artillery ready, sir," a radioman reported.

Minh nodded, his face grim. "And the air support?"

"A flight of A-37s on standby, Captain. They'll begin their runs on your command."

Thanh watched as three armored bulldozers were brought forward. These weren't ordinary construction vehicles; they had been hastily modified for this assault. Heavy steel plates reinforced their undersides, offering some protection against mines. The lead bulldozer sported an unusual attachment - a long crane arm extending from its front, ending in a horizontal pipe draped with heavy.

A young lieutenant explained the contraption to his curious troops. "The chains will drag along the ground, setting off anti-personnel mines. The bulldozer's weight should trigger any anti-tank mines. Hopefully the extra armored plating will protect the drivers. It's not perfect, but it's the best we can do on short notice."

Behind the bulldozers, more tanks waited. Infantry units huddled nearby, ready to advance once a path was cleared. Thanh could see the nervousness on many faces, especially among the younger soldiers.

Captain Minh's voice cut through the pre-dawn air. "Listen up! Mortars will lay down smoke. Tanks will advance first, providing cover for the bulldozers. Once they reach the edge of the minefield, they'll hold position. Bulldozers will then move forward to clear the path. Infantry, you follow behind the tanks. Stay in formation and watch for my signals."

He paused, looking over the assembled forces. "This fortress stands between us and Phnom Penh. We take it today, no matter the cost. For Vietnam!"

A chorus of voices echoed his words, the sound swelling through the ranks.

Thanh checked his rifle one last time, then looked to the fortress looming in the distance. The Khmer

Rouge flag fluttered atop its highest tower, a reminder of the enemy that waited within those walls.

The radio crackled to life. "Artillery units report ready, sir."

Minh nodded. The entire assault force seemed to hold its breath, waiting for the signal that would unleash hell upon the Khmer stronghold.

In the tense silence before the storm, Thanh found himself thinking of home, of the village he'd left behind. He pushed the thoughts away, focusing on the task ahead. The battle for the Khmer fortress was about to begin, and he was ready.

General Anh stood atop his command vehicle, a Chinese-made Type 63 armored personnel carrier, binoculars trained on the Khmer fortress silhouetted against the pre-dawn sky. The air was thick with tension as thousands of Vietnamese soldiers waited for his command. He lowered the binoculars and nodded to his radio operator.

"All units, this is General Anh. Commence Operation Thunder Fall. Artillery and air support, you have a three-hour window. Make every shell count."

The radio crackled with acknowledgments. Anh checked his watch. 0500 hours. The assault had begun.

Seconds later, the morning calm shattered as the first artillery shells screamed overhead. Six 130mm guns opened fire in a synchronized barrage, their shells arcing high before plummeting towards the fortress. The initial impacts were precise, concentrated on the southeastern wall where intelligence had indicated structural weaknesses.

As the artillery found its rhythm, the sky filled with the roar of jet engines. Two Mig-17s swooped low, rockets streaking from their wings towards the fortress's guard towers. Explosions blossomed along the ramparts, sending debris raining down on the defenders below.

Twenty minutes into the bombardment, a flight of A-37 Dragonfly attack aircraft joined the fray. The nimble jets came in low and fast, their rocket pods spewing destruction. The first pass targeted the main gate, the rockets' impacts sending shockwaves through the ancient iron-bound wood.

"Direct hit on the gate," the air controller reported. "Significant damage, but it's still standing."

Anh nodded. "Have them make another pass. Focus on the hinges."

The A-37s circled around, this time releasing their payload of 500-pound bombs. The explosions were massive, engulfing the entire gatehouse in fire and smoke. When the dust settled, the once-mighty gate hung askew, barely clinging to its moorings.

"We have a breech," reported the air controller.

The Khmer forces inside the fortress moved quickly to put out the fires and seal the breech at the main gate.

The bombardment intensified as the first hour progressed. Artillery shells rained down in a relentless stream, each impact sending shockwaves through the ground. The air filled with dust and smoke, obscuring the fortress from view. Through his binoculars, Anh could see chunks of masonry blasted away from the walls, leaving gaping wounds in the ancient stonework.

As the second hour began, the recoilless rifles joined the symphony of destruction. Their smaller caliber rounds were aimed with surgical precision at known defensive positions, targeting machine gun nests and sniper perches along the battlements.

"Sir," a junior officer reported, "we're seeing movement inside the fortress. Looks like they're trying to reinforce the southeastern wall."

"Redirect artillery fire. Don't let them shore up those defenses."

The big guns adjusted their aim, their shells now falling in a tight pattern around the damaged section of wall. The defenders scattered, abandoning their repair efforts in the face of the intensified barrage.

Midway through the second hour, the A-37s returned, this time focusing their attention on the fortress's interior. Bombs fell with pinpoint accuracy on suspected ammunition dumps and fuel stores. Secondary explosions rocked the compound, sending pillars of flame and smoke high into the sky.

"Good effect on target," the air controller announced. "We've definitely hit something important in there."

As the third hour drew near, Anh received reports of fires burning out of control within the fortress walls. The smoke was now so thick that it was difficult to assess the full extent of the damage.

With thirty minutes left in the bombardment, Anh ordered a final, all-out push. Every gun, every aircraft, every weapon at their disposal unleashed hell upon the beleaguered fortress. The noise was deafening, the impacts almost continuous as shells and bombs rained down in a storm of steel and fire.

As the three-hour mark approached, Anh raised his hand. The thunder of artillery gradually fell silent, the last echoes fading into an eerie quiet. Smoke drifted across the battlefield, partially obscuring the fortress.

Through the haze, Anh could see that significant

damage had been done. Guard towers were toppled, sections of the outer wall had collapsed, and fires burned within the compound. The main gate was a twisted ruin, and large sections of the battlements had been reduced to rubble.

But despite the ferocity of the bombardment, the core of the fortress remained intact. The main walls, though scarred and crumbling in places, still stood. Anh watched a section of wall crumble, only to reveal another layer of reinforced concrete behind it.

"Impressive construction," he muttered, a grudging respect in his voice.

Anh turned to his staff, "Signal the armored units. It's time for phase two. The walls may still stand, but they've been weakened. Our tanks will finish what the artillery started. Have our mortar teams launch their smoke rounds to cover the advance."

As orders were relayed, the rumble of tank engines filled the air. The ground assault was about to begin, and with it, the true test of Vietnamese resolve against Khmer Rouge resilience.

As he looked over the battlefield, Captain Nguyen of the Vietnamese heavy mortar platoon received his orders.

"Smoke screen ordered to cover the tanks' advance," crackled the radio.

Nguyen surveyed the field before him, calculating distances. "Copy that. Smoke screen incoming."

He turned to his team, seasoned men who knew their roles by heart. "Fire smoke rounds!"

The mortar crews sprang into action, swiftly positioning their 120mm weapons. Nguyen consulted his map, marking the coordinates for maximum effect.

"Fire for effect!" he commanded.

The dull thump of mortar fire broke the morning stillness. Seconds later, white phosphorus rounds burst over the battlefield, billowing clouds of thick, acrid smoke spreading rapidly.

"Adjust fire! Spread pattern alpha!" Nguyen ordered, his eyes fixed on the emerging smoke screen.

More rounds arced through the sky, detonating in a precise pattern designed to create a wide, dense curtain of smoke between the Vietnamese forces and the fortress.

As the smoke intensified, obscuring the target area, Nguyen could hear the distant rumble of tank engines coming to life.

"Maintain barrage!" he shouted over the rhythmic fire of the mortars. "Keep that smoke up until our armor is in position!"

The air filled with the sharp smell of phosphorus as the smoke screen grew denser. Through gaps in the swirling white clouds, Nguyen caught glimpses of tanks moving into their starting positions, invisible to the defenders in the fortress.

The stage was set. Under the cover of smoke, the Vietnamese assault began.

Anh watched as twenty T-54 tanks, their engines growling to life, began to move forward in a formidable line. The ground trembled beneath their tracks, a low rumble that grew to a thunderous roar. Dust kicked up in their wake, shrouding the advancing armor in an ominous cloud of smoke and dust.

Captain Minh, commander of the lead tank, felt sweat beading on his brow despite the relative cool of the morning. His hands tightened on the controls as he keyed his radio. "All units, concentrate fire on the damaged sections of the southeastern wall. Machine gunners, suppress enemy troops on the ramparts."

As one, the tanks' main guns elevated slightly, taking aim at the fortress wall. For a moment, time seemed to stand still. Then, the first salvo erupted. The sound was deafening, a thunderclap of man-made fury as twenty 100mm shells streaked towards their target.

The impact was tremendous. Chunks of ancient stonework exploded outward, dust and debris billowing into the air like a sudden sandstorm. Minh could feel the concussion even through the tank's thick armor.

"Good effect on target!" his gunner shouted, eyes glued to his sight.

The tanks' coaxial and roof-mounted machine guns opened up, their staccato chatter filling the air. Tracer rounds arced towards the top of the walls, forcing the Khmer defenders to duck for cover. Minh caught glimpses of frantic movement along the ramparts as the enemy scrambled to respond.

"Gunner, load HEAT!" Minh ordered, his eyes fixed on a particularly damaged section of wall. "Driver, maintain course!"

The tanks continued their advance, their main guns firing in a rolling barrage. Each impact weakened the wall further, cracks spider-webbing across its surface like a giant, deadly jigsaw puzzle. Plumes of dust and pulverized stone erupted with each hit, obscuring sections of the wall from view.

Suddenly, muzzle flashes sparked along the fortress walls. The Khmer Rouge were returning fire. Small arms fire pinged harmlessly off the tanks' armor, but then came the distinctive whoosh of RPGs.

"Incoming!" Minh yelled.

An RPG streaked past, missing Minh's tank by a mere meter. It exploded behind them, the shockwave rocking the vehicle. Another found its mark on a tank two positions down, but thankfully glanced off its sloped armor.

The intensity of the defensive fire was increasing. Minh could see his fellow tank commanders battening down their hatches, opting for the safety of internal visual systems over direct sight.

They were three-quarters of the way to the wall when disaster struck. A massive explosion rocked the line, so powerful it made Minh's teeth rattle. The tank on the far right had strayed too close to the edge of the minefield, triggering a hidden anti-tank mine. Its left track was blown clean off, and flames erupted from the engine compartment like an angry dragon awakening.

"Tank 17 is hit!" a panicked voice shouted over the radio. "We're burning! Oh God, we're burning!"

Minh watched in horror as the tank's crew scrambled to escape the inferno. One man emerged, his uniform ablaze, and rolled desperately on the ground. Another crawled out of the top hatch, dragging an unconscious comrade. The fourth crew member never emerged.

"All units, hold position!" Minh ordered, his voice hoarse. "Do not advance further. Maintain suppressing fire on the fortress."

The line of tanks ground to a halt, their treads churning up the earth, but their guns continued to hammer the fortress walls. The air was thick with smoke and the acrid smell of burning fuel and cordite. Minh could taste it even inside the tank, a bitter reminder of how close they all were to a similar fate.

"Bulldozer teams, move up!" General Anh's voice cut through the chaos. "Clear a path."

The armored bulldozers, which had been waiting behind the line of tanks, now lumbered forward. Their reinforced blades lowered, ready to scrape away more of the treacherous ground and expand the safe zone. Each was a heavily modified Caterpillar D7 model, transformed from construction equipment into formidable machines of war.

The bulldozers' distinctive yellow paint was now obscured by a coat of matte green, blending them into the jungle surroundings. Thick steel plates, hastily but securely welded, covered their vulnerable areas. The operator's cab was reinforced with additional armor, small vision slits replacing the original windows, giving it the appearance of a tank turret.

The most striking modification was the bulldozer blade itself. Reinforced and extended, it now sported a heavily armored front designed to withstand mine explosions.

Extending from the front of each bulldozer was a long boom, stretching out several meters ahead. At the end of this boom, a horizontal bar held multiple heavy chains that would drag along the ground, designed to trigger anti-personnel mines at a safe distance.

The underside of each bulldozer was fitted with a v-shaped armor plate, designed to deflect the force of explosions away from the vehicle's vital components and operator.

Atop each bulldozer, a pintle-mounted machine gun was fitted, offering some means of self-defense and suppression fire if needed.

They were a curious hybrid of construction equipment and tank, ungainly yet purposeful, a unique solution to the deadly problem of minefields in modern warfare.

Minh silently saluted the bravery of the bulldozer crews, knowing they were even more exposed than the tank units.

As the bulldozers began their work, the tanks kept up their relentless barrage. The fortress wall, though still standing, was now heavily damaged. In several places, daylight could be seen through gaps in the stonework. Each new salvo widened these breaches, bringing them tantalizingly close to collapse.

Minh keyed his radio once more. "All gunners, focus fire on those breaches."

The assault continued, a brutal contest between Vietnamese purpose and the stubbornness of ancient stone. The fortress still stood, but for how much longer remained to be seen. Minh could feel the tension mounting. They were so close to breaking through, yet still frustratingly far.

As he called for another salvo, Minh couldn't shake the feeling that something was off. The Khmer Rouge defense, while fierce, seemed almost... predictable. A nagging suspicion grew in the back of his mind.

The lead bulldozer, piloted by Sergeant Duc, a seasoned combat engineer with haunted eyes that had seen too much war, lurched forward.

As Duc advanced, the chains on the end of the boom dragged along the ground, their weight sufficient to trigger anti-personnel mines but light enough to pass over larger anti-tank mines. The sound of small explosions peppered the air as the chains detonated the smaller mines, sending dirt and shrapnel flying. Each blast made Duc flinch, his nerves frayed by the constant danger.

Behind Duc, the second bulldozer, operated by Corporal Linh, a young woman whose determination belied her years, followed closely. Her job was to widen the path, ensuring enough space for the tanks to pass through safely. Linh's bulldozer was equipped with a mine roller - a heavy cylindrical drum attached to the front, designed to detonate anti-tank mines before they could damage the vehicle's tracks or undercarriage.

The third bulldozer, driven by Private Tuan, a new recruit whose hands shook slightly on the controls, brought up the rear. Its primary role was to smooth out the cleared path, filling in craters left by explosions and ensuring a stable surface for the following armored vehicles.

As they progressed, the tension was palpable. Each meter gained was a potential death trap. Duc's hands were white-knuckled on the controls, his eyes constantly scanning for signs of larger mines or hidden obstacles. Sweat beaded on his forehead.

Suddenly, a tremendous explosion rocked Duc's bulldozer. An anti-tank mine, buried deeper than expected, detonated under the vehicle's left track. The bulldozer lurched violently, tilting at a precarious angle. For a heart-stopping moment, it seemed it might topple over. Duc, his breath caught in his throat, frantically worked the controls. The bulldozer groaned, then slowly righted itself, its reinforced underbelly having held against the blast.

"Close one," Duc muttered, his voice shaky. He keyed his radio. "Lead bulldozer here. Be advised, we've hit a large mine but we're still operational."

Linh and Tuan acknowledged, their voices tense as they adjusted their approach, moving with even more caution.

As they neared the fortress walls, resistance intensified. Sporadic gunfire erupted from the battlements, bullets pinging off the bulldozers' armored shells. The covering tanks returned fire, their main guns booming as they targeted the source of the attacks. The air filled with the acrid smell of cordite and the metallic tang of hot steel.

Despite the increasing danger, the bulldozer teams pressed on relentlessly. Their path zigzagged slightly, following the safest route through the minefield as determined by their pre-operation briefing and real-time observations. Each turn was a calculated risk, balancing the need for speed with the paramount importance of safety.

Halfway to the wall, Tuan's bulldozer suddenly sputtered and died. "I've lost power!" his panicked voice came over the radio. Stuck in the middle of the minefield, Tuan's vehicle was now a sitting duck.

Linh, without hesitation, reversed her bulldozer. "Hang tight, Tuan. I'm coming back for you." Her voice was steady, but the fear was evident in her eyes as she maneuvered back through the partially cleared path.

The acrid smell of smoke and cordite filled the air as Linh popped the hatch of her armored bulldozer. The cacophony of battle assaulted her ears – the sharp crack of rifle fire, the dull thud of distant explosions, and the constant ping of bullets ricocheting off metal.

"I need suppressing fire!" she shouted into her radio, knowing the tanks behind her would intensify their fire at the fortress defensive positions on top of the walls.

Taking a deep breath, Linh swung herself out of the relative safety of her cab. The heavy steel plates welded to the bulldozer's frame offered some protection as she crouched low, making her way to the rear of the vehicle.

A bullet whizzed past, so close she felt the displacement of air. Linh's heart pounded in her chest, but her hands remained steady as she unhooked the heavy tow cable.

Twenty meters ahead, Tuan's bulldozer sat motionless, its engine dead. Linh could see Tuan's frightened face through the armored slit of his cab.

"Hang on, I'm coming!" she yelled, though she knew he couldn't hear her over the din of battle.

Linh took a deep breath and sprinted towards Tuan's stricken vehicle. The ground around her erupted in small geysers of dirt as bullets struck. The thunderous report of the tanks' main guns provided the suppressing fire she needed as the enemy fire diminished for a moment.

Halfway to Tuan's bulldozer, an RPG streaked overhead, exploding beside her in a shower of dirt and sparks. The concussion nearly knocked Linh off her feet, but she pressed on.

Reaching Tuan's bulldozer, Linh dropped to her knees, crawling underneath to reach the tow hook. Her fingers, slick with sweat and grime, fumbled with the heavy cable.

"Come on, come on," she muttered, acutely aware of how exposed she was.

A burst of machine-gun fire stitched a line across the bulldozer's armored flank, mere centimeters above her head. Linh bit back a cry of fear, focusing on the task at hand.

Finally, the cable locked into place with a satisfying click. Linh scrambled out from under the bulldozer, giving Tuan a thumbs up through his vision slit.

The return journey to her own vehicle seemed to take an eternity. Linh's lungs burned, her legs felt like lead, but she pushed on. A sharp pain lanced through her left arm – a bullet graze, her mind registered dimly. She climbed back in her bulldozer and advanced once again.

With Tuan's bulldozer in tow, Linh slowly made her way back to the front of the line. The added weight made her vehicle strain, its engine roaring with effort. Every bump and dip in the terrain was a new challenge, the risk of setting off an undiscovered mine ever-present.

Meanwhile, Duc's bulldozer reached the base of the fortress wall. He raised his blade, scraping it against the ancient stonework, symbolically marking the end of their perilous journey.

"Minefield pathway cleared," Duc reported over the radio. "Path is approximately eight meters wide, stable enough for armor to advance."

As the bulldozers reversed course, making way for the waiting tanks, the soldiers couldn't help but feel a mix of relief and apprehension. They had overcome one deadly obstacle, but the fortress itself still loomed before them, damaged but defiant.

The tanks began to move forward, their tracks grinding over the freshly cleared path.

The jungle surrounding the fortress was unnaturally still, a stark contrast to the thunderous advance of the Vietnamese armor. Hidden within the dense foliage, Khmer Rouge units lay in wait, their camouflage so effective they seemed to be part of the vegetation itself.

Major Sokhom, leader of the hidden forces,

crouched behind a massive banyan tree, his eyes never leaving the binoculars trained on the approaching tanks. Sweat trickled down his face, but he didn't dare move to wipe it away. Every muscle in his body was tense, coiled like a spring ready to release.

He watched as the first T-54 tank cleared the minefield, its tracks leaving deep imprints in the freshly churned earth. The tank's main gun boomed, sending another shell smashing into the fortress wall. Dust and debris rained down, but the ancient stonework held.

Sokhom's radio crackled softly. "Eagle's Nest to Ground Leader, we count fourteen tanks across the minefield. Five more approaching."

"Understood," Sokhom whispered back. "All units maintain position. Wait for my signal."

The minutes stretched on, feeling like hours. Sokhom could feel the impatience radiating from his men. They were young, eager for battle. But he knew timing was everything. Rush this, and they'd lose their one advantage.

As the lead tank came within 100 meters of the fortress, Sokhom's hand tightened on his radio. Not yet. Not yet.

Suddenly, a young soldier to his left shifted, his boot snapping a twig. The sound, though small, seemed to echo in the tense silence.

But the Vietnamese continued their advance, oblivious to the danger surrounding them. Sokhom exhaled slowly. Then, seeing the tanks perfectly positioned, he made his decision.

"All units," he said into the radio, his voice low but clear, "on my mark... three... two... one... Fire!"

The jungle erupted into chaos. Dozens of RPG teams emerged from their hiding spots, the whoosh of rockets filling the air. Recoilless rifles boomed from concealed positions, their rounds streaking towards the vulnerable top armor of the tanks.

The first salvo caught the Vietnamese in a devastating crossfire. An RPG struck the lead tank's track, the explosion ripping through metal and sending the tread flying. The tank lurched to a stop, suddenly immobile.

Before the Vietnamese could react, another rocket found its mark on a tank's turret. The shaped charge punched through the armor like it was paper, igniting the ammunition inside. For a split second, nothing happened. Then, the tank erupted in a massive fireball, its turret blown clean off by the internal explosion.

"Keep firing!" Sokhom shouted, his voice nearly drowned out by the cacophony of battle. "Don't let them regroup!"

More rockets streaked towards the Vietnamese line. A recoilless rifle round penetrated the engine compartment of a third tank, setting it ablaze. Panicked voices crackled over the Vietnamese radio frequencies as commanders tried to make sense of the sudden assault.

The surviving tanks attempted to maneuver, their commanders desperately trying to identify the source of the attack. But in their haste to reach the wall, they had left themselves exposed, caught in a deadly crossfire between the hidden Khmer forces and the fortress defenders.

Sokhom watched as another tank erupted in flames, its crew scrambling to escape. They didn't make it far before being cut down by machine gun fire from the fortress walls.

But even as he allowed himself a moment of

satisfaction, Sokhom knew the tide could turn quickly. The Vietnamese still had superior numbers and firepower. Already, he could see their infantry starting to deploy, taking cover behind the burning hulks of the destroyed tanks.

"All units, prepare to fall back to secondary positions," Sokhom ordered. "We've bloodied them, but they'll be coming for us now. Be ready."

As his forces began to melt back into the jungle, leaving destruction in their wake, Sokhom took one last look at the battlefield. The Vietnamese tank advance had been shattered.

A stray bullet whizzed past his head, embedding itself in the tree next to him with a dull thud. It was time to go. As Sokhom retreated into the shadows of the jungle, the sounds of battle continued to rage behind him. The first round had gone to the Khmer Rouge, but the battle was far from over.

The lumbering BTR-60 APCs rumbled forward, their engines straining as they maneuvered around the burning hulks of destroyed tanks. Private Thanh gripped his AK-47 tightly as he braced against the jolting movement of the vehicle.

"Get ready!" Sergeant Hoa shouted over the din. "We're going in hot!"

The rear hatch of the APC crashed open. Thanh barely had time to register the chaos outside before he was propelled forward by his comrades' urgent push.

As his boots hit the ground, the world exploded into a cacophony of sound and fury. The air was thick with dust and smoke. Bullets whizzed past, uncomfortably close, kicking up dirt at his feet. To his left, a young soldier – Thanh thought his name might be Quoc – stumbled and fell, blood blossoming across his chest.

"Move! Move!" someone yelled.

Thanh sprinted for the meager cover offered by a destroyed T-54, his heart pounding in his ears. He slammed against the charred metal, wincing at the heat that seeped through his uniform. The tank's crew lay nearby, their bodies contorted in grotesque poses.

To his right, another APC erupted in flames, hit by an RPG from the jungle's edge. The screams of the men trapped inside pierced through the general chaos of battle. Thanh fought the urge to vomit.

"We can't stay here!" Lieutenant Bao's voice cut through the noise. "The minefield's at our backs and the Khmer on the fortress wall and in the jungle fire on us. We need to push forward!"

Thanh peered over the tank's hull. The fortress loomed ahead, its walls bristling with Khmer defenders. Every few seconds, muzzle flashes erupted from the ramparts, raining death upon the exposed Vietnamese troops. He could see bodies strewn across the field, some still moving, others terrifyingly still.

"On me!" the Lieutenant shouted. "We're going for the tree line!"

With a deep breath, Thanh readied himself. He muttered a quick prayer, though he wasn't sure if anyone was listening. Then, with a primal yell, he burst from cover, running as he'd never run before.

The open ground was a killing field. Bullets kicked up dirt around his feet, and he could hear the sickening thud of rounds finding human targets. A mortar round exploded nearby, the concussion nearly knocking Thanh off his feet. He stumbled but kept moving, ears ringing from the blast.

Halfway to the jungle, an RPG streaked past, so close Thanh could feel the heat of its passage. It struck an APC behind him, the explosion lifting the vehicle off its tracks. Shrapnel peppered Thanh's back, stinging even through his uniform.

"Keep moving, soldier!" It was Sergeant Hoa, his face streaked with blood and grime. He grabbed Thanh's arm, half-dragging him forward.

Together, they staggered toward the promise of cover. Thanh could see other survivors doing the same, a ragged line of men desperate to escape the murderous crossfire. The air was filled with a deadly mix of Vietnamese and Khmer shouts, the clipped crack of small arms fire, and the deeper booms of exploding vehicles and mortar rounds.

As they neared the jungle's edge, the fire intensified. The Khmer in the fortress, realizing their quarry was about to slip away, redoubled their efforts. Bullets tore through leaves and branches, the vegetation offering little protection. Thanh saw a soldier just ahead of him jerk violently and fall, his body riddled with rounds.

With a final, desperate lunge, Thanh threw himself into the undergrowth. He lay there for a moment, chest heaving, scarcely able to believe he was still alive. The sound of battle seemed oddly muted now, as if the jungle itself was trying to muffle the violence.

"Form up!" Lieutenant Bao's voice called out. "Those Khmer bastards in the jungle are our priority now."

As Thanh pushed himself to his knees, he took stock of their situation. Their numbers had been brutally thinned. Of the fifty men in his platoon, he could see perhaps twenty. Many were wounded, applying hasty field dressings or helping their more seriously injured comrades.

The dense foliage offered some respite from the fortress's fire, but Thanh knew it offered little protection. Somewhere in this green hell, Khmer troops were waiting, ready to spring another deadly ambush.

With shaking hands, Thanh checked his rifle and ammunition. He had three magazines left – not nearly enough if this turned into a prolonged firefight. He'd need to gather more magazines from dead and dying comrades as the battle continued. The jungle seemed to press in around them, full of unseen threats. Every shadow could hide an enemy, every rustle of leaves could signal an impending attack.

As he moved to join the reforming squad, Thanh couldn't shake the feeling that they had escaped one death trap only to walk into another. The assault on the fortress had become a desperate fight for survival, and the outcome was far from certain.

Lieutenant Bao was gathering the survivors, his voice low but urgent. "We need to locate and neutralize those Khmer RPG and recoilless rifle teams. They're tearing our armor apart out there."

Thanh nodded, readying his weapon, anxious to get on with it. As they prepared to push deeper into the jungle, he cast one last look back at the battlefield they'd just crossed. The ground was littered with the broken bodies of his comrades and the burning husks of vehicles. It was a sobering reminder of the cost of war, and the price they might yet have to pay before this day was done.

With a deep breath, Thanh turned back to the task at hand. The jungle awaited, dark and foreboding, hiding both enemy and opportunity.

Thanh and his fellow soldiers crept through the dense undergrowth, every sense on high alert. The sound of ongoing battle – the boom of tank guns, the crack of small arms fire – seemed oddly muffled in the green twilight of the jungle.

Suddenly, Lieutenant Bao held up a closed fist. The squad froze. Thanh strained his ears, trying to hear what had alerted their commander. Then he caught it – voices, speaking rapid-fire Khmer, and the distinctive sound of a recoilless rifle being reloaded.

Bao used hand signals to split the squad. Thanh found himself with five others, tasked with flanking the Khmer position. They moved silently, years of jungle warfare training coming into play.

As they neared the enemy position, Thanh could see the Khmer team – three men manning a recoilless rifle, another two with RPGs slung over their shoulders. They were so focused on their targets in the field beyond, they didn't notice the approaching Vietnamese.

Bao's whistle pierced the air – the signal to attack.

Thanh burst from cover, his AK-47 blazing. Two Khmer went down before they could react, but the others were quick to respond. An RPG whooshed past Thanh's head. It exploded behind him, the concussion throwing him forward.

He hit the ground hard, the breath knocked from his lungs. Through blurred vision, he saw a Khmer soldier charging at him, bayonet fixed. Thanh rolled, the blade missing him by inches. He lashed out with his rifle butt, catching his attacker in the knee. The man went down with a cry of pain.

All around, the jungle had erupted into chaotic close-quarters combat. Thanh saw Sergeant Hoa grappling with a Khmer fighter, both men struggling for control of a knife. Another Vietnamese soldier – Thanh didn't know his name – was locked in a brutal fistfight with a Khmer who had lost his weapon.

Thanh scrambled to his feet, only to be tackled by another enemy. They went down in a tangle of limbs, rolling through the underbrush. Thanh felt his rifle torn from his grasp. Desperately, he reached for his combat knife, but the Khmer soldier was on top of him, hands going for his throat.

Spots danced in Thanh's vision as he fought for air. With a surge of adrenaline-fueled strength, he bucked, throwing the man off balance. Thanh's fist connected with the Khmer's jaw, stunning him momentarily. It was enough. Thanh's knife flashed in the dappled sunlight, finding its mark.

Gasping for air, Thanh staggered to his feet. The battle raged on around him. He saw Lieutenant Bao wrestling with a Khmer over control of an RPG launcher. Without thinking, Thanh charged, slamming into the enemy soldier. The three of them went down in a heap, the RPG discharging harmlessly into the air.

A scream of pain cut through the melee – Sergeant Hoa had been stabbed, but even as he fell, he managed to take his attacker with him, his last bullet finding its mark.

Thanh felt a searing pain across his back – a Khmer soldier had slashed him with a machete. He spun, catching the man's wrist before he could strike again. They grappled, each trying to turn the blade on the other. Thanh's arms trembled with the effort, his wounded back screaming in protest. Just as he felt his strength giving out, a shot rang out. The Khmer soldier slumped against him, dead.

Panting heavily, Thanh looked up to see Private Pham, her rifle still smoking. She gave him a quick nod before turning to engage another enemy.

The fight seemed to last an eternity, but in reality, it was over in minutes. Thanh found himself standing amid the aftermath, his uniform soaked with blood – some his, some not. Of the dozen Vietnamese who had begun the assault, only seven remained standing. But the Khmer position had been neutralized.

Lieutenant Bao, sporting a nasty gash across his forehead, was already organizing the survivors. "Secure those weapons," he ordered, pointing to the abandoned recoilless rifle and RPGs. "We'll turn them on the fortress."

As Thanh moved to help, he caught movement out of the corner of his eye. A wounded Khmer soldier, barely more than a boy, was reaching for a grenade. Thanh saw the boy's fingers close around the grenade, saw the determined look in his eyes.

Without thinking, Thanh threw himself forward. He tackled the boy just as he pulled the pin. They rolled once, twice, and then the world exploded in a flash of light and pain.

When Thanh came to, he was on his back, staring up at the canopy. His ears rang, and every part of his body hurt. But he was alive. Somehow, he was alive.

Hands grabbed him, hauling him to his feet. It was Pham, her face etched with concern. "You okay?" she shouted, her voice sounding distant and muffled.

Thanh nodded, though he wasn't sure if it was true. As his senses slowly returned, he realized the bigger battle was still raging. The Khmer position in the jungle had fallen.

Lieutenant Bao was already directing men to set up

the captured weapons. They had won this skirmish, but Thanh knew the fighting wasn't finished.

Grimacing through the pain, Thanh picked up his rifle. There would be time for rest later. For now, there was still a battle to be won.

The Vietnamese soldiers, battered and bloodied from the intense hand-to-hand combat, quickly regrouped under Lieutenant Bao's orders. Thanh, still dazed from the grenade blast, found himself helping Pham drag the heavy recoilless rifle into position.

"Set it up here," Bao commanded, pointing to a small clearing that offered a clear line of sight to the fortress.

Sweat mingled with blood as the soldiers worked feverishly to prepare the captured weapons. Thanh's hands shook as he loaded the first round into the recoilless rifle, the adrenaline from the recent fight still coursing through his veins.

"Ready!" Pham called out, her voice hoarse from shouting during the melee.

Lieutenant Bao raised his binoculars, scanning the fortress walls. "There," he said, pointing to a section of the ramparts where Khmer defenders were concentrated. "Fire!"

Thanh squeezed the trigger. The recoilless rifle roared to life, its round streaking towards the fortress. Thanh watched through the sight as the projectile found its mark, exploding in a shower of stone and bodies. Cheers erupted from the Vietnamese soldiers.

"Again!" Bao ordered. "Keep firing!"

Thanh and Pham worked in synchronized efficiency, loading and firing in rapid succession. Each shot was answered by screams and confusion from the fortress defenders, clearly shocked by the sudden reversal.

Meanwhile, other soldiers had set up the captured RPGs. "RPG teams, focus on the guard towers!" Bao shouted over the din of battle.

The whoosh of rockets filled the air as the Vietnamese unleashed a barrage on the fortress. Guard towers erupted in flames, their occupants leaping to escape the inferno.

But the Khmer were quick to respond. Mortar rounds fired from inside the fortress began to rain down on the jungle, exploding in earth-shaking blasts that sent shrapnel tearing through the foliage.

"Incoming!" someone yelled. Thanh threw himself to the ground as a mortar exploded nearby, showering him with dirt and debris.

As he scrambled back to the recoilless rifle, he saw Pham clutching her arm, blood seeping between her fingers. "I'm fine," she gritted out, seeing his concerned look. "Keep firing!"

The battle raged on, with the Vietnamese pushing their advantage. The captured weapons had turned the tide, allowing them to suppress the fortress defenses effectively.

Suddenly, a new sound cut through the chaos – the rumble of engines. Thanh looked back to see Vietnamese tanks advancing once more, using the suppressing fire from the jungle to push towards the fortress walls. They fired their main guns at the weak points in the walls tearing new holes in the stone and concrete.

"This is our chance!" Bao shouted. "Pour it on! Don't let up!"

Thanh redoubled his efforts, ignoring the burning in his muscles and the stinging of his wounds. Round after round was sent hurtling towards the fortress, each impact weakening its defenses further.

As the tanks drew closer to the walls, Thanh could see panic setting in among the Khmer defenders. Some were abandoning their posts, fleeing deeper into the fortress.

"We've got them on the run!" Pham yelled, a grin on her face despite her injury.

But Thanh knew better than to celebrate too soon. The fortress still stood, and who knew what surprises the Khmer Rouge might have in store within those walls?

As he loaded another round into the recoilless rifle, Thanh steeled himself for what was to come. The battle was far from over, but for the first time since the assault began, victory seemed within reach.

As the battle raged on, the distinctive roar of jet engines cut through the clamor of gunfire and explosions. Thanh looked up, his eyes widening as he saw four F-5 Tiger IIs streaking across the sky, their sleek silhouettes a stark contrast to the chaos below.

"Air support incoming!" Lieutenant Bao shouted, his voice barely audible over the approaching jets. "Everyone, take cover! They're dropping napalm."

Thanh and Pham scrambled away from the recoilless rifle, diving into a nearby bomb crater. The other Vietnamese soldiers did the same, abandoning their positions and seeking whatever shelter they could find.

The lead F-5 swooped low, its wings laden with deadly cargo. Thanh watched in awe as the jet released its payload. Napalm canisters tumbled through the air, igniting as they made contact.

The fortress walls erupted in a hellish inferno.

Flames engulfed the ramparts, spreading with terrifying speed. The screams of burning Khmer soldiers pierced the air, a horrifying counterpoint to the roar of the flames, many leaping to their deaths rather than burn.

Before the first jet had even completed its run, the second F-5 was already making its approach. More napalm canisters rained down, this time targeting the eastern wall of the fortress. The heat was intense, even from Thanh's position in the jungle. He could feel the warmth on his face, smell the stench of burning flesh.

The third and fourth jets followed in quick succession, their napalm strikes methodically blanketing the entire perimeter of the fortress. The walls that had seemed so impregnable mere moments ago now stood wreathed in flames, black smoke billowing into the sky.

As the F-5s pulled up and banked away, their task complete, an eerie silence fell over the battlefield. The constant gunfire from the fortress walls had ceased, replaced by the crackle of flames and the occasional scream or explosion from within.

Lieutenant Bao was the first to emerge from cover, his face a mask of grim satisfaction. "That's done it. We've broken their backs," he said, surveying the burning fortress. "The walls are clear. Now's our chance!"

Thanh and Pham exchanged a look as they clambered out of their makeshift shelter. The recoilless rifle lay abandoned, no longer needed.

"All units, prepare to advance!" Bao ordered. "We're going to breach those walls while they're still reeling!"

As Thanh readied his AK-47, he couldn't help but

feel a mix of excitement and dread. The napalm strike had undoubtedly turned the tide of the battle.

The Vietnamese soldiers formed up. In the distance, Thanh could hear the rumble of tanks advancing once more, seizing the opportunity created by the air strike.

As they began their charge towards the burning fortress, Thanh's heart raced. The battle was entering its final, decisive phase. Victory was close at hand, but the cost had already been horrifically high.

With a war cry on his lips, Thanh surged forward with his comrades, running headlong into the inferno that awaited them at the fortress walls.

As the smoke from the napalm strike began to clear, Lieutenant Bao's radio crackled to life. "Sapper team en route," a voice announced. "Provide cover fire."

Thanh watched as a group of six Vietnamese sappers emerged from the jungle's edge, each carrying a heavy backpack as they sprinted towards the fortress walls.

"Covering fire!" Bao shouted. "Give them everything you've got!"

Thanh, Pham, and the other soldiers opened up with their AK-47s, peppering the top of the walls with a hail of bullets. The few remaining Khmer defenders, those who had somehow survived the napalm, ducked down, unable to return fire effectively.

The sappers reached the base of the wall, immediately setting to work. They targeted the sections most damaged by the earlier bombardment, quickly attaching their satchel charges to the weakened stonework.

"Thirty seconds!" the lead sapper shouted, his voice barely audible over the gunfire.

As the sappers retreated, sprinting back towards the safety of the Vietnamese lines, Thanh felt his heart racing. This was it – the moment that could decide the entire battle.

"Take cover!" Bao ordered.

Thanh dove behind a fallen tree, Pham right beside him. They waited, seconds ticking by like hours.

Suddenly, the world exploded. The satchel charges detonated in unison with a thunderous roar, sending a shockwave rippling through the air. Chunks of stone and debris rained down, pinging off helmets and armor.

As the dust began to settle, Thanh peered over his cover. Where there had once been an impenetrable wall, now stood a gaping breach. The explosion had torn a hole easily wide enough for several men to pass through side by side.

Bao shouted, his voice filled with fierce determination. "First platoon, with me! We're going in!"

Thanh and Pham scrambled to their feet. They formed up with the other soldiers, everyone anxious and excited.

Bao yelled as they approached the breach. "Watch your corners, stay low, and watch out for each other."

As they reached the jagged opening, Thanh could hear sounds of chaos from within the fortress – shouts, screams, and the occasional burst of gunfire. The Khmer defenders were in disarray, but they were far from defeated.

Bao raised his rifle. "For Vietnam!" he shouted, then plunged through the breach.

As Thanh and Pham entered through the breached wall, they were immediately met with fierce resistance.

Khmer Rouge defenders, desperate and cornered, unleashed a barrage of fire from hastily prepared positions within the fortress.

"Contact front!" Bao shouted, diving behind a pile of rubble.

Thanh and Pham split up, each taking cover behind opposite sides of the breach. The air was thick with dust and a smokey haze. Bullets whizzed past, chipping away at stone and wood.

"Grenade!" someone yelled. Thanh saw the small, deadly object arc through the air, landing just meters from their position. Without thinking, he lunged forward, scooping it up and hurling it back towards the Khmer positions. The explosion sent shrapnel flying, followed by screams of pain.

Taking advantage of the momentary lull, Bao signaled the advance. "Push forward! Don't let them regroup!"

The dim interior was a maze of narrow corridors and small courtyards. Smoke hung thick in the air, limiting visibility. Somewhere ahead, Thanh could hear the sounds of fierce fighting.

Pham eyes darted from shadow to shadow. Thanh tightened his grip on his rifle. They had breached the wall, but only one side would emerge victorious.

The fighting was intense and chaotic. In the narrow confines of the fortress interior, the battle devolved into a series of brutal, close-quarters engagements. Thanh saw a fellow soldier go down, caught by a burst of enemy fire. He pressed on, knowing that hesitation meant death.

Slowly but surely, the Vietnamese forces began to gain ground. Their superior numbers and the shock of the breach were telling. Khmer resistance, while fierce, was becoming increasingly disorganized.

"They're falling back!" Bao shouted over the din of battle. "Press the advantage!"

Thanh and Pham found themselves at the forefront of the advance, pushing deeper into the fortress. They cleared room after room, each engagement a heart-stopping mix of reflexes and luck.

In one courtyard, they encountered a pocket of determined resistance. A Khmer machine gun team had set up behind a barricade, pinning down the Vietnamese advance. Thanh caught Pham's eye and nodded towards a flanking route. She understood immediately.

While the rest of the squad provided suppressing fire, Thanh and Pham maneuvered around the side. The Khmer were so focused on the frontal threat that they never saw the danger approaching from their flank. Thanh and Pham struck simultaneously, their combined fire decimating the machine gun position.

As they pushed on, Thanh began to sense a change in the battle's momentum. The Khmer resistance was crumbling. More and more defenders were throwing down their weapons, surrendering in the face of the relentless Vietnamese advance.

Finally, after what seemed like hours of intense fighting, they reached the central keep. The last pockets of Khmer resistance were quickly overwhelmed. As Thanh watched a group of enemy soldiers lay down their arms, he realized with a start that it was over. They had won.

Bao's voice rang out, filled with triumph and relief. "The fortress is ours! Victory!"

A ragged cheer went up from the Vietnamese soldiers. Thanh felt a wave of exhaustion wash over him as the adrenaline began to fade. He looked at Pham, saw the same mix of relief and disbelief on her face. They smile weakly at each other.

As the dust settled and the last echoes of gunfire faded away, Thanh took in the scene around him. The fortress, once an impregnable bastion of Khmer Rouge power, now lay in ruins, firmly in Vietnamese hands. The cost had been high, but they had achieved their objective.

Bao began organizing teams to secure the fortress and tend to the wounded. But for Thanh, Pham, and many others, the reality of their victory was still sinking in. They had faced seemingly insurmountable odds and emerged victorious.

As the Vietnamese flag was raised over the conquered fortress, Thanh allowed himself a moment to consider what they had accomplished. For now, he had earned his moment of triumph.

Boat People

The Mekong River stretched like a muddy serpent along the eastern edge of Cambodia, its waters a lifeline for countless communities along its banks. As dawn broke, the river came alive with activity of the Boat People who called these waters home.

Sampans and houseboats of various sizes dotted the river, their weathered wooden hulls bobbing gently in the current. The air was thick with humidity, carrying the mingled scents of fish, diesel fuel, and the sweet rot of vegetation. Birds called out from the dense jungle that pressed close to the water's edge, their cries mixing with the distant putt-putt of boat engines.

On one particular houseboat, an elderly woman tended to a small garden of herbs growing in pots lashed to the deck. Her gnarled hands moved with practiced ease, plucking leaves for the day's meals. Nearby, children laughed as they cast small nets into the water, hoping to catch fish for breakfast.

Life on the river was simple but fraught with its own unique challenges. River crocodiles lurked in the murkier sections, their presence a constant threat to the unwary. Stories of massive beasts dragging whole boats under were passed down through generations, keeping even the bravest fishermen vigilant.

But the crocodiles were not the only predators on the Mekong. River pirates, desperate and ruthless, occasionally preyed on the Boat People, striking quickly and disappearing into the maze of tributaries and hidden coves. Their raids left devastation in their wake, robbing families of their meager possessions and sometimes their lives.

Perhaps the most unpredictable threat, however, came from the Khmer soldiers who patrolled the river. Their sleek boats, bristling with weapons, were a common sight on the Mekong. While ostensibly there to maintain order and protect against pirates, many of these patrols were little more than shakedown operations. Greedy soldiers would board boats at will, demanding "taxes" or "inspection fees" from people who could ill afford such extortion.

As the morning progressed, a patrol boat appeared on the horizon, its engine cutting through the usual sounds of river life. The reaction was immediate. Boat People scrambled to hide anything of value, women ushered children below decks, and men adopted poses of subservient humility.

The patrol boat slowed as it approached a cluster of houseboats. A young soldier, his face set in a mask of authority beyond his years, called out orders. His eyes scanned the boats, searching for any sign of resistance or hidden wealth.

This was the delicate dance of life on the Mekong. The Boat People had learned to bend with the current, to weather storms both natural and man-made. They had survived war, political upheaval, and the harsh realities of a subsistence lifestyle. Yet still they endured, their culture and way of life as much a part of the river as the water itself.

As the patrol boat moved on, life on the river gradually returned to its normal rhythm. Fish were cleaned, clothes were washed, boats were repaired. The Mekong flowed on, indifferent to the dramas played out upon its surface, carrying with it the hopes, fears, and dreams of the Boat People.

As the sun climbed higher in the sky, casting shimmering reflections on the Mekong's muddy waters, whispers spread through the floating community. Eyes darted towards a long-tail boat that had recently joined their ranks, its presence a source of both curiosity and suspicion.

The boat itself was a familiar sight on the river - a sleek wooden craft about thirty feet long, with a high, curving prow and a long tail trailing behind, housing the boat's engine and propeller shaft. What set this particular vessel apart was its new owner, a dark-skinned woman with an accent that marked her as an outsider.

She had purchased the boat from Old Man Sokha, a respected fisherman known for his craftsmanship. The transaction had raised eyebrows, not least because of the substantial sum exchanged. The boat's most distinctive feature was a covered area amidships, fashioned from weathered planks and palm fronds, offering shade and privacy - a luxury rarely seen on working boats.

The woman, who called herself Mai, spent her days casting nets into the river with practiced ease. Yet there was something about her movements, a certain precision, that seemed at odds with the casual rhythms of lifelong fisherfolk.

But it was Mai's unseen companion that fueled the most speculation. Glimpses of a large figure moving within the boat's covered area had sparked rumors of a foreigner in their midst. Some claimed to have seen a flash of pale skin, others whispered of a man's voice with an accent unlike any they'd heard before.

On this particular morning, as Mai worked her nets under the watchful eyes of the community, her partner sat in the shadowy confines of their makeshift cabin. Granier's large frame was cramped in the small space, but it afforded him the concealment necessary for their mission.

Through small gaps in the shelter's walls, Granier observed the river traffic with keen attention. His eyes catalogued each passing vessel - noting size, cargo, and any signs of unusual activity.

"Anything?" Mai - or rather, Spitting Woman - asked quietly as she hauled in her net, the action a perfect cover for conversation.

"Not yet," Granier murmured, his voice barely audible over the lapping of water against the hull.

As Spitting Woman hauled in her net, the weight of a good catch evident in her straining muscles, a sudden thrashing caught her off guard. A flash of scales, a glimpse of jagged teeth, and suddenly a five-foot crocodile had latched onto a large fish trapped in the mesh.

"Dammit!" she hissed, her carefully maintained facade slipping for a moment.

The crocodile thrashed, its powerful tail sending water spraying across the boat. Its jaws were firmly clamped around what would have been the centerpiece of their evening meal – a plump silver carp that had been unlucky enough to find itself caught between predator and prey.

Without hesitation, Spitting Woman reached for the knife strapped to her thigh, concealed beneath her loose-fitting fisherman's pants. In one fluid motion, she plunged the blade into the crocodile's skull.

The beast thrashed harder, nearly pulling her overboard. Spitting Woman stabbed again, and then a third time. The crocodile's movements became erratic, then slowed, and finally ceased altogether.

Panting slightly from the exertion, Spitting Woman hauled both the net and the now-lifeless crocodile into the boat. Fish flopped around her feet as she disentangled the reptile from the netting, its jaws still locked around their intended dinner.

Wiping sweat from her brow, she glanced towards the covered area where Granier sat hidden. "Change of plans for dinner," she called softly, "How do you feel about crocodile?"

From the shadows, Granier's low chuckle reached her ears. "Well, that's one way to deal with the local wildlife."

Spitting Woman nodded, immediately becoming more aware of the curious stares from neighboring boats. She made a show of examining the crocodile with exaggerated caution, playing up the role of a lucky fisherwoman rather than a trained operative.

"At least we'll eat well tonight," she murmured, beginning to clean her catch with deliberate, unpracticed movements. As she worked, gutting fish and beginning to skin the crocodile, Spitting Woman maintained a careful watch on their surroundings. The incident had drawn more eyes than she'd like, but with luck, it would be dismissed as an exciting bit of river life rather than anything suspicious.

The sun dipped lower on the horizon, casting long shadows across the Mekong. Another day of waiting and watching was coming to an end, but the night might yet bring the breakthrough they'd been waiting for. For now, though, they had a rather unusual dinner to prepare – and a cover to maintain. The constant traffic on the river – from tiny fishing boats to large commercial barges – provided excellent cover for their surveillance operation.

Granier lifted the anchor. Spitting Woman grabbed a long wooden pole and gave their craft a push closer to shore.

As the sun dipped lower, painting the sky in brilliant oranges and reds, a large barge appeared around the river bend. Its deck was stacked high with rusted barrels, and it was riding noticeably low in the water.

Spitting Woman's eyes narrowed as she studied the approaching vessel. "Do you see that?"

"Yeah, I see it," said Granier watch discretely.

"Look at how it's sitting in the water."

Granier grunted in acknowledgment, as he made his way to the stern of the long-tail boat, where the engine sat mounted on a swivel mechanism.

The engine itself was a sight to behold - a repurposed four-cylinder car motor, stripped down and modified to serve as an outboard. It was a common setup on the Mekong, born of necessity and ingenuity. Recycled parts and makeshift engineering allowed the Boat People to keep their vessels running with whatever resources they could scavenge.

With a flip of the ignition switch, the engine

coughed to life. Granier immediately adjusted the throttle, keeping the motor at a low idle. The put-put-put of the engine blended with the ambient sounds of the river, not loud enough to draw undue attention.

He glanced around, noting the positions of nearby boats and the direction of the current. Satisfied that they weren't attracting curious looks, Granier reached down and engaged the forward gear.

The long tail of the boat - a shaft extending several feet behind the stern - began to move. At its end, the small propeller spun slowly in the air, a metallic blur above the water's surface. Granier lowered it into the river.

As the propeller dipped beneath the waterline, the boat began to move forward with a gentle lurch. Granier kept the throttle low, maintaining a slow, steady pace that wouldn't stand out among the other river traffic.

The boat sliced through the muddy waters of the Mekong, leaving only a small wake behind. To any observer, they would appear to be just another family of river folk, perhaps heading to a favorite fishing spot or to trade goods downriver.

Granier stood at the stern, one hand on the tiller, guiding their course to bring them closer to the barge without arousing suspicion. His eyes continually scanned the river and its banks, ever vigilant for signs of threat or opportunity.

As they drew near, the smell of crude oil became unmistakable, even over the river's usual odors.

"Look there," Spitting Woman whispered, her gaze fixed on a small group of men on the barge's deck. Unlike the usual river crews, these men were alert, their eyes constantly scanning their surroundings. One of them rested his hand casually on the butt of a poorly concealed pistol.

Granier felt a familiar tension coiling in his gut.

As they drifted past the barge, Granier risked a glance at its hull. There, partially obscured by the muddy water, he saw what they'd been looking for – a crude attempt to alter the barge's registration numbers.

"It's them," he muttered.

Spitting Woman nodded, "What now?"

Granier considered their options. They couldn't risk breaking cover, not when they were so close. But they couldn't let the barge slip away either.

"We follow," he decided. "Stay with them until nightfall. We have a nice dinner, then we make our move."

As darkness began to settle over the river, bringing with it a chorus of night insects and the occasional splash of a jumping fish, Granier and Spitting Woman continued their patient pursuit. The crude oil barge loomed ahead of them, a dark silhouette against the starry sky. The barge slowed as the powerful engine ceased.

The Mekong was ever changing, sandbars appearing and disappearing without reason, currents shifting, water-logged tree trunks floating, barely visible, threatening to shatter props. It was far too dangerous for big ships to navigate at night. The crew threw a large anchor overboard in the stern, then another over the bow. The two anchors would keep the barge from shifting during the night.

Granier and Spitting Woman sputtered past the barge and tied up along the shore using dense reeds as cover. From their vantage point they could easily keep tabs on their target. They prepared dinner using the boat's small grill. It was going to be a long night, and they would need the energy the roasted crocodile would provide. The meat was surprisingly sweet and smokey.

The moonless night cloaked the Mekong in an inky blackness, broken only by the occasional flicker of distant lanterns. Spitting Woman maneuvered their long-tail boat into a thick patch of reeds near the riverbank, the gentle rustling of vegetation masking any sound of their presence.

Her eyes strained in the darkness, fixed on the looming silhouette of the crude oil barge anchored mid-river. The vessel's bulk blocked out the stars, a darker shape against the night sky.

Granier's whisper was barely audible over the lap of water against the hull. "Remember, if I'm not back in two hours—"

"I know," Spitting Woman cut him off, her voice tense.

With a nod, Granier slipped over the side of the boat. The water engulfed him silently, its coolness a shock against his skin. He treaded water for a moment, letting his eyes adjust to the gloom, before starting his swim towards the barge.

Every splash, no matter how small, sounded thunderous to Granier's ears. He moved with agonizing slowness, using a modified breaststroke to minimize disturbance on the water's surface. The current tugged at him, threatening to pull him off course.

Halfway to the barge, a spotlight suddenly blazed to life on the vessel's deck. Granier froze, submerging himself up to his eyes. His heart pounded as the beam swept across the water, passing mere meters from his position. After an eternity, the light clicked off. He resumed his approach, muscles tense with the effort of silent movement.

Finally, Granier reached the barge's hull. He clung to the slimy metal, catching his breath and listening intently for any sign that he'd been detected. Satisfied, he began to inch his way along the side, searching for a way up.

He found a rusty ladder leading to the deck and began to climb, each creak of the metal rungs setting his nerves on edge. As he neared the top, voices drifted down from above – the night watch making their rounds.

Granier froze, clinging to the ladder as footsteps approached. Two Khmer-speaking men passed just overhead, their conversation punctuated by yawns. He held his breath until they moved away, then hauled himself onto the deck, quickly rolling into the shadow of a large pipe.

The deck was crowded with oil drums, their dull metal surfaces barely visible in the gloom. Granier's heart sank as he realized the magnitude of his task – there were easily over a hundred barrels, and in the darkness, they all looked identical.

He began to move between the rows of drums, checking for any distinguishing marks. Time ticked by agonizingly slowly, each moment increasing the risk of discovery. Sweat beaded on his brow despite the night's chill.

After what felt like hours, Granier had checked dozens of drums with no success. Frustration and fear warred within him – he couldn't afford to leave empty-handed, but every second he remained on board heightened the danger.

Then, a thought struck him. If he were smuggling valuable cargo, he'd want to keep it close. His eyes darted to the wheelhouse, looming at the barge's stern. Of course – they'd want to keep the opium under close watch.

Granier began to make his way towards the wheelhouse, every shadow seeming to conceal a potential threat. He was keenly aware of his exposure, of how quickly this mission could turn deadly if he was spotted.

As he neared his target, a new sound froze him in place – the unmistakable click of a weapon being cocked...

Granier's blood ran cold at the sound. He dropped instinctively, pressing himself flat against the deck behind the nearest oil drum.

"Come out where I can see you?" a gruff voice called out in Khmer. Footsteps approached, slow and deliberate.

Granier held his breath, mind racing. He was too exposed here, too vulnerable. His eyes darted around, seeking an escape route.

The footsteps drew closer. A beam of light cut through the darkness, sweeping across the deck. Granier could see it reflecting off the oil drums, inching nearer to his position.

He tensed, ready to spring into action if discovered. The light crept closer, illuminating the drum just in front of him. Another step and he'd be revealed.

Suddenly, a loud splash echoed from the opposite side of the barge. The footsteps halted.

"What was that?" another voice called out.

The light swung away, giving Granier a moment's reprieve. He didn't waste it. As silently as he could, he began to crawl away from the approaching guard, using the forest of oil drums as cover.

He made it to the edge of the drum field, the wheelhouse looming just meters away. But between him and his goal was an open stretch of deck, fully exposed.

The guards were still distracted by the noise, their voices drifting from the far side of the barge. It was now or never.

Granier sprinted across the open space. His bare feet slapped against the metal deck, each step sounding like a thunderclap to his ears.

He reached the wheelhouse, pressing himself against its wall, straining to hear if he'd been spotted. The guards' voices were drawing closer again.

Granier edged around the wheelhouse, finding a small alcove filled with more oil drums. These were different – newer, less weathered. His pulse quickened. This had to be it.

He began examining the drums, fingers tracing over their surfaces, searching for any hidden marks or compartments. Time was running out. The guards would be coming around this way soon.

Just as he was about to give up hope, his fingers caught on something – a small, almost imperceptible seam in one drum's surface. He pressed, and felt a slight give.

A hidden compartment. Granier allowed himself a moment of triumph before reality crashed back in. He'd found what he came for, but he was still trapped on a barge full of hostile guards, with no easy way off.

The sound of approaching footsteps snapped him back to the present. He had seconds to decide – try to open the compartment and risk being caught red-handed, or retreat with only the knowledge of its existence.

Granier's fingers traced the seam of the hidden compartment, his heart pounding in his chest. With a soft click, it gave way, revealing bundles wrapped in deep red wax paper – unmistakably opium. The pungent odor hit his nostrils, confirming his suspicions. Working quickly, his hands slightly trembling from adrenaline, he transferred eight bundles into a rubber satchel.

As he sealed the waterproof bag, a floorboard creaked behind him. Granier froze, his breath catching in his throat.

"Hey! What are you doing there?" a gruff voice called out in Khmer.

Granier turned, locking eyes with a guard who had just rounded the corner. The guard's eyes widened, taking in the scene – the open compartment, the satchel, the intruder.

"Intruder! On the deck!" the guard bellowed, reaching for his weapon.

Granier squatted low behind the oil drums and weaved his way through the forest sticking to the shadows. More guards joined the search for the intruder, their flashlight beams skipping over the tops of the drums.

Granier was too far from the edge of barge to make a run for it. He needed a distraction. He reaches for the nearest oil drum, wrenching its cap off with a metallic screech. The guards opened fire, bullets pinging off metal drums as Granier tipped the barrel over. Crude oil gushed across the deck, the acrid smell filling the air.

More shouts erupted from different parts of the

barge. Granier could hear the thundering of boots as reinforcements rushed to the scene. He weaved through the maze-like arrangement of drums, the satchel clutched tightly to his chest.

Bullets whizzed past, uncomfortably close. One grazed his arm, leaving a burning trail across his skin. Granier bit back a cry of pain, focusing on his escape.

In the distance, over the gunfire and shouts, he heard the distinctive roar of a longtail boat engine. Spitting Woman was coming. He just had to make it to the edge.

Granier reached into his pocket, fingers closing around his waterproof lighter. With a flick of his thumb, he ignited it and tossed it onto the pooling oil. The crude burned slowly at first, then began to spread with frightening speed, creating a barrier of flames between him and his pursuers.

The fire cast an eerie, flickering light across the deck. Through the flames, Granier could see the guards' silhouettes, hear their frustrated shouts as the fire hampered their pursuit. The heat was intense, sweat pouring down his face as he navigated the inferno.

But he was running out of time and space. The edge of the barge was just ahead, but so were more guards, converging on his position. Granier could see their weapons raised, ready to cut him down.

Making a split-second decision, he grabbed another oil drum and sent it rolling towards the approaching guards. It crashed into their legs, sending two of them sprawling on the oil-slicked deck. Their shots went wide, giving Granier the opening he needed.

Clutching the satchel tightly, he made a break for it. Bullets peppered the deck around his feet, sending up sparks. He could feel the heat of the spreading fire at his back, hear the creaking of metal as the flames engulfed more of the barge.

Without slowing, Granier reached the edge and leapt. For a heart-stopping moment, he was airborne, the dark water rushing up to meet him. The satchel felt like a lead weight, threatening to drag him down.

He hit the river with a splash, immediately submerging to avoid the hail of bullets. The cold water was a shock after the heat of the fire. When he surfaced, gasping for air, he saw Spitting Woman's boat racing towards him, cutting through the water like a knife.

"Granier!" she shouted, her voice barely audible over the roar of the engine and the crackling of the fire.

She was alongside him in seconds, her hand outstretched. Granier reached up, their fingers interlocking. With impressive strength, Spitting Woman held on, his body and satchel dead weight. She skillfully maneuvered the boat with her other hand.

Bullets snapped around them, sending up small geysers where they hit the water. Granier felt the sting of a near miss across his shoulder but held on as Spitting Woman dragged him for several hundred meters away from the burning barge, away from the light.

The strain was evident on both their faces. Granier's arm felt like it was being wrenched from its socket, but he didn't dare let go. Spitting Woman's knuckles were white on the tiller as she fought to maintain their course.

Finally, with a monumental effort, Granier pulled himself and the waterproof satchel into the boat. He collapsed on the deck, chest heaving, every muscle screaming in protest.

Spitting Woman didn't slow down. She opened up the throttle, the engine roaring as they sped off into the darkness. Behind them, the crude oil barge was now fully ablaze, a beacon of fire on the dark river. The shouts of the guards and the crackling of the inferno faded into the distance.

"Did you get it?" Spitting Woman shouted over the engine's roar, her eyes still focused ahead, watching for any pursuit.

Granier managed a nod, patting the satchel. "Eight bundles. It's definitely opium." His voice was hoarse, his lungs still burning from the smoke and exertion.

Granier struggled to sit up, wincing at his various cuts and bruises. He scanned the river behind them, watching for any signs of pursuit. The burning barge was now just a distant glow on the horizon.

"We need to disappear," he said, having to shout to be heard over the engine. "They'll have patrols out looking for us by morning."

Spitting Woman nodded, adjusting their course. "We should rendezvous with the resistance. They'll know where to hide us."

The longtail boat sped on through the night, carrying its passengers and their dangerous cargo towards an uncertain future. The Mekong, as always, kept their secrets, its dark waters hiding both threat and salvation in equal measure.

Dawn broke over the Mekong, the early morning mist still clinging to the water's surface. The usual tranquility of the river was shattered by the roar of engines as Khmer patrol boats raced up and down, their wakes churning the muddy water into froth.

From their hiding spot behind the decaying houseboat, Granier and Spitting Woman watched the frantic search unfold. The wreck's weathered planks and rusted metal provided a perfect screen, concealing their longtail boat from prying eyes.

"They're certainly not being subtle," Granier muttered, his eyes tracking a patrol boat as it sped past their position, barely fifty meters away.

Spitting Woman nodded grimly. "Look there," she whispered, pointing towards the riverbank.

Granier followed her gaze. Through gaps in the reeds, he could see a dirt road running parallel to the river. A convoy of battered trucks rumbled past, each loaded with Khmer troops, weapons at the ready.

"They've called in reinforcements," Spitting Woman said, her voice tight with tension. "This is more than just a local search."

Granier's hand unconsciously moved to the waterproof satchel tucked securely in the boat. The opium they'd stolen was clearly valuable enough to warrant this level of response.

"They need the weapons the opium would buy."

Phnom Penh, Cambodia

The dimly lit room in Phnom Penh's presidential palace was thick with tension. Pol Pot sat behind a massive wooden desk, his face impassive as he listened to the report from his subordinate.

Nuon Chea, known as Brother Number Two, stood rigidly before the desk, sweat beading on his forehead despite the room's cool temperature. He knew the weight of the news he was about to deliver.

"Brother Number One," Nuon Chea began, his

voice steady despite his nervousness, "I regret to inform you that the opium shipment from Burma has been stolen."

Pol Pot's eyes narrowed slightly, the only indication of his reaction. "Stolen?" he repeated, his voice dangerously calm.

Nuon Chea nodded, swallowing hard. "Yes, Brother. It appears that intruders infiltrated the barge. They set fire to the vessel after taking a significant portion of the shipment."

A heavy silence fell over the room. Nuon Chea braced himself for an outburst, but Pol Pot remained eerily composed.

"We can no longer expect to receive the American weapons from the Vietnamese," Nuon Chea continued, feeling compelled to fill the silence. "Without the opium to trade, they will likely back out of our arrangement."

To Nuon Chea's surprise, a small smile played at the corners of Pol Pot's lips. "It's okay," he said, his voice taking on an almost dreamy quality. "We have something far more powerful than the American weapons."

Nuon Chea blinked in confusion. "Brother?"

Pol Pot stood, walking to the window that overlooked the city. In the distance, a convoy of trucks could be seen entering Phnom Penh, loaded with people from the countryside.

"We have the people," Pol Pot said, his eyes gleaming with a fervor that sent a chill down Nuon Chea's spine. "They are our weapon, our resource, our future. With them, we will build a new Cambodia, one that will make the world tremble."

Nuon Chea nodded slowly, beginning to

understand. "The relocation program..."

"Is just the beginning," Pol Pot finished. "The loss of the opium is inconvenient, but ultimately insignificant. Our real strength lies in the purity of our vision and the labor of our people."

He turned back to Nuon Chea, his face set with determination. "Increase the pace of the relocations. I want every village emptied within the week. And find out who was responsible for the theft. They must be dealt with... permanently."

Nuon Chea bowed deeply. "It will be done, Brother Number One."

As he left the room, Nuon Chea couldn't shake the feeling that he had just witnessed the birth of something terrifying. Pol Pot's calm in the face of such a significant setback was unnerving. Whatever plan was unfolding, it was clear that the stolen opium was just a small piece of a much larger, more ominous puzzle.

Mekong River, Cambodia

As the morning wore on, the intensity of the search only increased. More patrol boats joined the hunt, their crews shouting to each other as they methodically combed the riverbanks. Occasionally, they would stop to question local fishermen, their aggressive tone carrying across the water.

Granier and Spitting Woman remained motionless when boats passed close by. The sun climbed higher, turning their hiding spot into a sweltering oven. Sweat trickled down their faces, but they didn't dare.

A patrol boat slowed near the wrecked houseboat. Granier could see the soldiers on board peering intently at the wreck, clearly considering whether to investigate more closely. Wrecks like this one were dangerous with rotting wood decks and hulls.

Spitting Woman's hand tightened on her weapon, ready for the worst. Granier felt his muscles coil, preparing for a potential fight or flight.

After what seemed like an eternity, the patrol boat's engine revved up, and it moved on. Granier and Spitting Woman exchanged a look of relief.

As midday approached, a new sound joined the drone of boat engines – the distinctive whop-whop-whop of helicopter blades. A military chopper appeared over the treetops, flying low over the river.

"This is bad," Granier murmured. "If they start an aerial search, our cover won't last long."

Spitting Woman nodded, her face set in grim determination. "We need to move. Tonight, when it's dark. We can't stay here."

As they settled in for several more hours of tense waiting, both were acutely aware of the challenges ahead. They had the evidence they needed, but getting it to the right people – and staying alive long enough to do so – would be no easy task.

The Mekong flowed on, indifferent to the drama unfolding on its surface. For Granier and Spitting Woman, the river that had been their cover now felt like a trap, with danger lurking around every bend.

As the sun dipped below the horizon, painting the sky in deep oranges and purples, Granier and Spitting Woman made their move. They abandoned their longtail boat, concealing it as best they could in the dense reeds to keep it from being found by the Khmer search parties. The vessel had served them well, but now it was too conspicuous, too easily linked to the barge incident.

They moved silently through the darkening jungle, every sense on high alert. The sounds of distant patrol boats still echoed across the water, a constant reminder of the danger they faced.

After an hour of progress, the thick vegetation began to thin. Granier held up a hand, signaling a halt. Ahead, through the trees, they could make out the outlines of structures.

"A village," Spitting Woman whispered, her eyes scanning for any signs of movement.

"What is that smell?" said Granier.

"Burnt rice."

They approached carefully, using the lengthening shadows as cover. As they drew closer, details began to emerge, and with them, a sense of unease.

The village was clearly a fishing community, its entire existence centered around the river. Long nets were strung between poles, awaiting repair. The smell of fish permeated the air, emanating from wooden racks where catches were laid out to dry. Several boats had been flipped over on the shore, their hulls exposed for inspection or maintenance. Torches lined the center path through the village, all lit, all illuminating.

But something was off. The village was eerily silent.

"Where is everyone?" Granier murmured, his hand instinctively moving to his weapon.

They moved further into the village, their footsteps seeming unnaturally loud in the stillness. Cooking fires had burned low, pots of rice were smoking as the water had evaporated and the rice inside had burned. Bowls of half-prepared meals abandoned beside them. A child's toy lay discarded in the dirt, as if dropped in a moment of haste.

"It's like they all just... left," Spitting Woman said.

Granier nodded. "And recently too. These fires are still burning."

They exchanged a worried glance, both thinking the same thing. Had the village been evacuated because of the search? Were they walking into a trap?

A sudden clatter made them both spin around, weapons raised. A skinny dog emerged from behind a hut, nosing through a fallen basket of fish. It regarded them warily for a moment before slinking away.

"We shouldn't stay here," Granier said, relaxing slightly but still on edge. "Whoever cleared this place out might come back."

Spitting Woman agreed, "If they're evacuating villages, our options for lying low are getting slim. We need to find out what's going on."

"Maybe the Khmer Rouge didn't want the civilians captured by the Vietnamese."

"Maybe, but where did they take them? Where is safe?"

"I doubt we're going to find the answer here."

They moved off, leaving the abandoned village to the dogs.

Granier and Spitting Woman moved cautiously through the dense jungle as they pushed aside vines and ducked under low-hanging branches. The sounds of distant engines and occasional shouts reminded them of the ongoing search, driving them further from the river and deeper into the wilderness.

As the sun climbed higher, they came upon another village. Like the first, it was a small fishing community, but the scene before them was unsettlingly familiar.

"It's the same," Spitting Woman whispered, her

eyes scanning the abandoned dwellings. "Everything left in place, but no people."

Granier nodded, "This doesn't make sense. One village, maybe. But two? Something bigger is going on here."

They moved through the silent village, noting the signs of hasty departure. A loom sat with a half-finished piece of cloth still attached. Meals lay uneaten on rough wooden tables.

"Could be a government evacuation," Granier mused, "but why? And why haven't we seen any signs directing people where to go?"

Spitting Woman shook her head. "And why leave everything behind? People would take valuables, food... This looks more like they just vanished."

As the day wore on, they encountered a third village, then a fourth. Each told the same story - a community abandoned in haste, as if the inhabitants had simply evaporated.

"This is beyond coincidence," Granier said, frustration evident in his voice. "But what could cause this? Disease? Some kind of threat?"

Spitting Woman's face was etched with worry. "Whatever it is, it's widespread."

They paused at the edge of the fourth village, both lost in thought. The scale of the abandonment was staggering, and the lack of a clear explanation was deeply unsettling.

"We're missing something," Granier said finally. "Something big. And I have a feeling that when we figure it out, we're not going to like the answer."

Spitting Woman nodded in agreement. "For now, we keep moving. But we need to find someone, anyone, who can tell us what's going on. This isn't just about the opium anymore. Something is very wrong here."

As they prepared to move on, the weight of the mystery pressed down on them. They had set out to expose a conspiracy, but now found themselves in the middle of something far larger and more ominous than they had ever anticipated.

Granier and Spitting Woman crouched low in the undergrowth, their eyes fixed on the small clearing ahead. The pre-arranged bird call sounded, and they responded in kind. Moments later, Sophal emerged from the shadows, followed by a handful of his most trusted resistance fighters.

"Glad to see you made it," Sophal said in a low voice.

As they settled into the makeshift camp, hidden deep in the jungle, Sophal's eyes immediately went to the waterproof satchel at Granier's side. "First things first," he said, his voice low and urgent. "Did you get the opium?"

Granier nodded, carefully opening the satchel to reveal the bundles of opium wrapped in red wax paper. "Eight packages. Pure opium, just as we suspected."

Sophal's eyes widened slightly as he examined one of the bundles. "This is high-grade stuff. Worth a fortune on the black market."

"Any idea who the buyers might be?" Spitting Woman asked.

Sophal shook his head. "Could be anyone. Triads in Hong Kong, cartels in South America, even corrupt officials in Saigon. The market for this is global."

"And the profits are funding the Khmer Rouge," Granier added.

"Not just funding them," Sophal corrected. "This kind of operation... it changes things. It gives Pol Pot resources, connections. It makes him more dangerous."

A heavy silence fell over the group as they contemplated the implications. Finally, Spitting Woman spoke up. "There's more. We've encountered something strange on our way here. Villages... abandoned villages."

"You too? We've been seeing the same thing all across the region. And it's not just villages. The reeducation camps have been emptied too."

"But they didn't vanish," one of Sophal's lieutenants interjected. "We've seen them – civilians being loaded onto trucks like cattle."

Granier leaned forward, his interest piqued. "You've witnessed this?"

Sophal nodded grimly. "Several times now. That's why I sent Rith to follow one of the trucks." He gestured to a young scout, who stepped forward.

"I tracked them for nearly two days," Rith reported, his voice tinged with disbelief. "The truck joined a massive convoy, all heading in the same direction – towards Phnom Penh."

"It doesn't make any sense," Spitting Woman said, voicing what they were all thinking. "Pol Pot emptied the cities, forced everyone into the countryside. Why would he be reversing that now?"

Granier tried to connect the dots. "Could it be related to the opium trade?"

Sophal shook his head. "The scale is too large for that. We're talking about entire regions being emptied. This is something else."

"Whatever it is," one of the resistance fighters

added, "it's being done in secret. No announcements, no official orders we've been able to intercept."

"Pol Pot has killed twenty-five percent of the Khmer people. He doesn't care about civilians," said Sophal. "He cares about his revolution, and he'll do whatever it takes to make sure it succeeds."

"Isn't all this pointless? The Vietnamese Army is days away from reaching the capital," said Rith. "So, what if Pol Pot moves people around like they're chess pieces? Once the capital falls, it's game over for Pol Pot and his government. His army of Khmer Rouge will have been destroyed and he will no longer be a threat to the Khmer people."

"It's what happens before the fall of Phnom Penh that worries me," said Sophal. "Pol Pot's up to something and that's never a good thing."

The group fell into a tense discussion, throwing out theories and possibilities. Was it a massive relocation program? Preparation for a major offensive?

As the debate continued, Granier found himself staring at the map spread out before them, his eyes tracing the routes of the truck convoys. Something about the pattern nagged at him, a piece of the puzzle just out of reach. "We need to go to Phnom Penh and see what's happening firsthand," said Granier.

Spitting Woman nodded in agreement.

Road to Phnom Penh

The journey to Phnom Penh was not easy or safe. Granier, Spitting Woman, and Sophal moved mostly at night, using the dense jungle as cover during the day. As they drew closer to the capital, the signs of Pol Pot's massive relocation program became increasingly evident.

Abandoned villages gave way to crowded roads, with long lines of people being herded towards the city by armed Khmer Rouge soldiers. The trio had to be extra cautious, often hiding for hours to avoid patrols and bypass checkpoints.

Granier's presence posed a particular challenge. His Western features made him stand out, a potentially fatal liability in a country where foreign influence was violently purged.

As the Khmer patrols in the surrounding jungle increased, they moved back to the road. They devised a system where Granier would travel hidden in the back of a small cart, covered by sacks and tarps, while Spitting Woman and Sophal posed as ordinary Cambodian peasants.

"Remember," Sophal whispered as they approached yet another checkpoint, "keep your head down and your responses simple. We're just following orders, moving to the city like everyone else."

Spitting Woman nodded, her face a mask of subservient compliance. She could feel Granier's presence in the cart behind her, acutely aware of how vulnerable he was.

The Khmer Rouge guard at the checkpoint looked bored and irritated. He barely glanced at Spitting Woman and Sophal before waving them through. "Move along, the city awaits your contribution to the revolution," he said mechanically.

On the outskirts of Phnom Penh, they found a moment to regroup in an abandoned building. Granier emerged from his hiding place, stretching his cramped muscles.

"The city's changed," he muttered, peering out a

broken window at the streets filled with newly arrived rural Cambodians. "It's like they're rebuilding it from scratch with human labor."

Sophal nodded grimly. "Pol Pot's vision of a new society. But to what end?"

"We need to find out," Spitting Woman said, her voice tight with determination. "But first, we need a safer place to hide. Granier can't keep traveling like this."

They spent the next hour discussing options, weighing the risks of various hideouts. The city was a maze of potential dangers, with Khmer Rouge patrols and informants on every corner.

Finally, Sophal spoke up. "I know a place. An old resistance safehouse. If it hasn't been discovered, it should still be secure."

As night fell, they made their way through the transformed streets of Phnom Penh. Granier, hunched and hidden beneath a large straw hat and peasant clothes, felt exposed with every step. The city he once knew was gone, replaced by a surreal landscape of forced labor and revolutionary zeal.

Granier, Spitting Woman, and Sophal crouched low on a rooftop, their eyes fixed on the bizarre scene unfolding before them. The night was alive with activity, the darkness pushed back by harsh floodlights that illuminated a massive construction project.

"What in the world...?" Granier muttered, his voice barely audible over the distant sound of machinery and shouted orders.

Spitting Woman peered through a pair of binoculars, "It's a trench," she said. "An enormous trench, circling the entire inner city."

Sophal nodded, "Pol Pot's turning the heart of

Phnom Penh into a fortress."

As they watched, the scale of the operation became clear. Thousands of civilians, many looking exhausted and malnourished, worked tirelessly to dig the massive trench. It was easily wide enough to swallow an entire tank, a deadly trap for any advancing armored column.

"Look there," Granier pointed, indicating a series of fortified positions being constructed along the trench's inner edge. "Pillboxes. And those look like mounting points for recoilless rifles."

Spitting Woman swept her binoculars across the scene, taking in more details. "Heavy machine gun nests too. They're creating interlocking fields of fire. Any attack would be funneled into kill zones."

Sophal's face was filled with concern. "This isn't just a defensive measure. It's a challenge. Pol Pot's daring the Vietnamese to come and get him."

As they continued to observe, a new, more disturbing development caught their attention. A section of the trench, freshly dug and still being smoothed out, was suddenly filled with people. But these weren't workers – they were civilians, mostly women, children, and the elderly.

"What are they doing?" Spitting Woman asked, her voice tight with dread.

Granier's jaw clenched as realization dawned. "Human shields," he said, his tone one of disbelief and anger. "The bastard is using his own people as human shields."

"The implications are staggering. Any attacking force would have to choose between abandoning their assault or knowingly killing thousands of innocent civilians. It's a strategy as brilliant as it's horrifying," said Sophal.

"This is madness," Sophal whispered, his eyes never leaving the scene below. "He's turned the entire population into a weapon."

Granier nodded, "Now we know why he's been emptying the countryside. He's not just building a fortress – he's creating an impenetrable human wall."

Spitting Woman lowered her binoculars, her face pale in the dim light. "We have to stop this."

"General Anh is not going to stop. He's hell bent on taking Phnom Penh and capturing Pol Pot to end the war."

As they began to discuss their options, the gravity of their situation pressed down on them. They were witnessing the birth of a nightmare, a twisted strategy that turned an entire population into an instrument of war.

The Deal

As dawn broke over the outskirts of Phnom Penh, the rumble of heavy vehicles shattered the eerie calm. A convoy of Soviet-made trucks lumbered into view, each towing a massive 130mm M-46 field gun. The artillery pieces, their long barrels covered in camouflage netting, were an imposing sight against the backdrop of the jungle-lined roads.

Vietnamese soldiers swarmed around the trucks, their movements practiced and efficient. Officers barked orders, coordinating the placement of each gun with precision. The air filled with the sound of metal scraping against metal as the artillery pieces were unlimbered and set into position.

Crews worked tirelessly, digging gun pits and constructing earthen berms around each position. The dull thud of shovels hitting dirt mixed with the clanking of equipment being unloaded. Ammunition trucks pulled up, and teams of soldiers began the laborious process of stacking shells near each gun.

In the distance, the skyline of Phnom Penh loomed,

a stark reminder of the urban battlefield that lay ahead. Reconnaissance teams with binoculars and range-finding equipment moved to forward positions, calculating firing solutions and marking potential targets on their maps.

The artillery commanders huddled around a makeshift command post, poring over maps and discussing fire plans. Radio operators set up their equipment, establishing communication links with forward observers and the main Vietnamese command.

As the morning wore on, more artillery units arrived – batteries of 122mm D-74 howitzers and mobile BM-21 rocket launchers. Each new arrival added to the growing arsenal, forming a ring of firepower around the Cambodian capital.

By midday, the outskirts of Phnom Penh had been transformed into a formidable artillery park. Dozens of guns stood ready, their barrels elevated and pointing ominously towards the city. The Vietnamese gunners waited tensely, knowing that at any moment, the order could come to unleash their devastating firepower on Pol Pot's last stronghold.

Vietnamese Field Headquarters

General Anh stood in his command tent, surrounded by maps and bustling staff officers, when a lieutenant approached with a sense of urgency.

"Sir, a messenger from the resistance. He says he has a message for your eyes only."

Anh nodded, "Bring him in."

A young Cambodian man, dressed in nondescript civilian clothes, entered the tent. He bowed slightly, then handed Anh a folded piece of paper.

"I've been instructed to wait for your reply, General," the messenger said softly.

Anh unfolded the note, his eyes scanning its contents. His face remained impassive, betraying nothing to the curious officers around him. For a long moment, he stood in silent contemplation, the only sound the rustle of papers and the distant rumble of vehicles.

Finally, he looked up at the messenger. "Tell the sender that I accept. You're free to go."

The young man nodded, bowed again, and quickly left the tent.

As soon as the messenger was out of earshot, Anh turned to his staff. "Major Nguyen, I want a team of our best snipers ready within the hour. Colonel Tran, prepare a platoon of Marines to accompany me this evening."

The officers exchanged confused glances but knew better than to question their commander.

"Sir," Colonel Tran ventured, "may I ask where we're going?"

Anh's eyes hardened. "We have a meeting to attend. In a jungle clearing not far from here. I expect trouble, and I intend to be prepared for it."

As his subordinates hurried to carry out his orders, Anh turned back to the maps. The message had been unexpected, but not entirely surprising.

As the day wore on and preparations were made, tension built among the troops. By nightfall, a formidable force including two armored vehicles was assembled, ready to accompany their general into what could very well be a trap.

Anh climbed into one of the armored vehicles. As

they set out towards the meeting point, he couldn't shake the feeling that this encounter would change the course of the entire campaign. Whether for better or worse remained to be seen.

Jungle Clearing

The jungle clearing was bathed in the eerie glow of vehicle headlights as General Anh and his forces arrived. In the center stood Spitting Woman, unarmed, her posture relaxed despite the gravity of the situation.

Marines quickly fanned out, surrounding her, while two armored vehicles trained their heavy machine guns on the surrounding jungle. Anh stepped forward, his face a mask of stern authority.

"Surrender now," he demanded, his voice cutting through the night air.

"I'm afraid I can't do that, General. You see, a sniper has his rifle sight centered on your forehead as we speak," said Spitting Woman.

Anh's eyes narrowed, scanning the dark jungle around them. "My snipers will find him before he can pull the trigger."

"I doubt it," Spitting Woman replied calmly. "Granier is very good at his job, and he won't hesitate."

A tense silence fell over the clearing as Anh considered his options. Finally, he spoke, his voice tight. "Alright. What do you want?"

"A trade," Spitting Woman said simply.

"What could you possibly have that I want?"

"The Khmer Rouge lost something valuable recently. I'm willing to give it to you."

Anh's interest visibly grew, though he tried to hide it. "In exchange for what?"

"The lives of the Khmer civilians in Phnom Penh," Spitting Woman stated, her voice taking on a note of urgency.

Anh's face hardened. "It's war. Collateral damage cannot be helped."

"And that is exactly what Pol Pot wants… you and your men to kill a hundred thousand innocent civilians as… collateral damage," Spitting Woman pressed. "Pol Pot has turned the entire city into a fortress. He's using civilians as human shields. Such a massacre would take the spotlight off the genocide committed by Pol Pot and the Khmer Rouge. The world would turn against Vietnam."

"Those are politics. I'm a general. My job is to win wars."

"I doubt Le Duan would agree with you."

"Your relationship with Le Duan is hollow. I have full authority in the field."

"Nobody is going to care about that once the killing starts. They're just going to look for somebody to blame."

"Explain," he demanded.

"Pol Pot has dug massive trenches around the inner city to trap your armor. They're filled with civilians – women, children, the elderly. Any assault will have to go through them first."

She could see the wheels turning in Anh's mind as he processed this information.

"And what is this valuable item you're offering in exchange for... what? Calling off the assault?"

"Not calling it off," Spitting Woman clarified. "Modifying it. Finding a way to minimize civilian casualties. As for what we're offering..." She paused, knowing this was her trump card. "Eight packages, one kilo each. The same shipment the Khmer Rouge were going to trade for American weapons."

Anh's eyes widened almost imperceptibly. The implications of such a trade – both strategically and politically – were enormous.

"How do I know you're telling the truth? About any of this?" Anh asked, his voice low.

Spitting Woman met his gaze steadily. "Because I have no need to lie. We both want to stop Pol Pot. We just disagree on the methods."

A long moment of silence stretched between them. Finally, Anh spoke, "No."

"What do you mean?"

"I mean no deal. You keep your packages. I have a war to win. This will all be over in a few days. I'll deal with you and Granier then."

"If you kill those civilians, the world will hate you."

"Perhaps. But the world never liked me much anyway."

As Anh signaled his forces to withdraw, Spitting Woman remained in the clearing, watching them disappear into the jungle.

In the darkness of the jungle, Granier lowered his rifle, letting out a breath he didn't realize he'd been holding. He rose and walked to Spitting Woman. "How did we do?"

"We didn't. No deal."

"Why not?"

"He doesn't want the opium. He wants a victory."

"He's just going to kill all those people?"

"Yes. Unless we can figure another way to stop him."

They had played their ace-in-the-hole and lost. Granier, Spitting Woman, and Sophal sat quietly around a small campfire, the flames casting flickering shadows on their weary faces.

After a long silence, Granier spoke up, his voice low but determined. "Why does General Anh need to capture Phnom Penh?"

Spitting Woman looked at him, "Because that's where Pol Pot and his government are located. You know that."

"What if they weren't... in Phnom Penh?" Granier suggested.

Sophal leaned forward, intrigued. "Where would they be?"

"Wherever we want them," Granier replied.

Spitting Woman's eyes widened as she realized what he was implying. "You can't be serious... a snatch and grab? That's suicide, Granier."

Sophal shook his head, skepticism clear in his voice. "It's not just suicide, it's impossible. Pol Pot is surrounded by an army. How would we even get close?"

Granier held up his hands, acknowledging their concerns. "I know it sounds crazy but hear me out. If we can somehow lure or drive Pol Pot or key members of his inner circle out of the city..."

"And how exactly do you propose we do that?" Spitting Woman interrupted, her tone sharp. "We're not exactly on their guest list."

"I haven't worked out all the details. It's the beginning of a plan," said Granier. "But anyone can be reached."

"If we can find them. Pol Pot moves every night to a new location. He's the most paranoid man in all of

Southeast Asia."

Sophal nodded in agreement. "Even if we could get to them, what then? We're three people against the entire Khmer Rouge leadership and the troops guarding them."

Granier leaned in, his voice intense. "Your resistance fighters could join us, Sophal. And remember, chaos is our friend. If we can create enough confusion..."

Spitting Woman cut him off again. "Chaos? Granier, we're talking about the most paranoid regime in the world. They're expecting attacks from all sides."

"We can use Pol Pot's paranoia to our advantage. We don't need a full-blown assault. We just need to get him moving and then drive him in the direction we want… out of the city."

"Even if Pol Pot leaves, Ahn will still need to capture the capital to end the war," Sophal added. "He will still attack."

"You're probably right. But with Pol Pot on the run, we might be able to move the civilians out of the trenches and out of harm's way."

"That's a lot of civilians."

"And there's not much time. Ahn will attack as soon as his troops are in position," said Spitting Woman.

"And we still have to find Pol Pot."

Granier sat back, considering their points. "You're both right. It's risky, maybe even impossible. But what other choice do we have? If we do nothing, thousands of civilians die. At least this gives us a chance."

A heavy silence fell over the group as they each wrestled with the implications of Granier's audacious plan.

Phnom Penh, Cambodia

The night air hung thick with diesel fumes and the pungent smell of burning trash. Maly crouched behind a rusted oil drum, his eyes fixed on the entrance of the concrete building that served as Khmer Rouge headquarters. Sweat trickled down his back despite the cool air.

A soft whistle. Maly glanced left. Sokha, the youngest of their team, nodded towards the street. The low rumble of an engine cut through the silence.

A black GAZ jeep rolled to a stop. The rear door opened. A stocky figure emerged, flanked by two armed guards.

Maly's hand tightened on his radio. "Target acquired," he whispered.

Sophal's voice crackled through the static. "Confirmed. Do not lose him."

The man adjusted his thick-rimmed glasses. Even at this distance, there was no mistaking Nuon Chea. Brother Number Two. Pol Pot's right hand.

Chea and his guards disappeared into the building. Maly signaled to Sokha and Chamroeun. They moved swiftly to their waiting Honda Cub, parked in a nearby alley.

Twenty-three minutes passed. Maly's muscles ached from the tension.

The jeep's engine roared to life. Maly started the motorbike, its puttering barely audible over the larger vehicle. As the GAZ pulled away, they followed at a discreet distance.

The jeep wound through the empty streets. Twice, they nearly lost sight of it around corners. Once, they had to kill the engine and coast silently past a Khmer

Rouge checkpoint.

At the city's edge, the road deteriorated. The bike's suspension rattled their teeth as they navigated potholes and debris. Ahead, brake lights flared red.

Maly cut the engine. They pushed the bike into the undergrowth and crept forward on foot.

The jeep had stopped outside a dilapidated storage facility. Chea and his guards entered quickly.

"This isn't right," Chamroeun muttered. "Why come all the way out here?"

Maly silenced him with a look. He keyed his radio. "Sophal, we've tracked him to a facility on the eastern outskirts. Something's off."

"Investigate," came the terse reply. "But do not engage."

They split up, scouting the perimeter. The facility was larger than it first appeared, stretching back into the darkness. Maly counted at least thirty armed guards.

A hand on his shoulder. Sokha pointed to a metal grate set into the ground. A faint breeze issued from it, carrying the scent of damp earth.

"Ventilation," Maly breathed. "This place goes underground."

A twig snapped. They froze. A beam of light cut through the darkness, sweeping dangerously close. Maly held his breath, pressing himself against the rough concrete wall.

The light passed. He exhaled slowly.

"Sophal," he whispered into the radio. "It's a bunker. Connected to tunnels. Heavy guard presence. This has to be where they're hiding."

A long pause. Then: "Understood. Continue your surveillance until we arrive. We'll radio when we are close."

Western Outskirts of Phnom Penh

The pre-dawn air vibrated with anticipation. General Le Duc Anh stood rigid atop his BTR-60, his weathered hands gripping the cold metal. Before him stretched a sea of Vietnamese military might, poised like a coiled spring.

Rows of T-54 tanks, their hulls scarred from previous battles, idled restlessly. Anh could feel the vibration of their engines through the soles of his boots. Behind them, BTR-60s and PT-76s packed tight with infantry, the soldiers inside checking and rechecking their AK-47s with mechanical precision.

The whine of diesel engines filled the air as ZiS-3 field guns and BM-21 Grad rocket launchers maneuvered into position. Anh watched a young lieutenant, barely more than a boy, directing a Grad into place, his movements sharp with nervous energy.

A high-pitched scream tore through the sky. Anh's eyes snapped upward as a formation of MiG-21s roared overhead, their swept-wing silhouettes black against the bruised sky. In their wake came the Su-22s, flying lower, heavy with their payloads of destruction.

Anh's radio crackled. The voice on the other end was tight, controlled. "Thua Tuong, air strike commencing in two minutes."

He acknowledged with a grunt, his eyes never leaving the horizon. The capital lay there, shrouded in early morning mist and the smoke of previous bombardments.

The seconds ticked by, each one stretching like an eternity. Anh's mouth was dry, his tongue like sandpaper. He accepted a canteen from an aide, the water tasting of metal and dust.

A flash on the horizon. Then another. The sound reached them moments later - deep, thunderous booms that Anh felt in his chest. Plumes of smoke and fire erupted from the Khmer Rouge's outer defenses. The air assault had begun.

More explosions followed, walking across the enemy lines. Flashes of light punctuated the smoke - anti-aircraft fire reaching desperately for the Vietnamese planes.

A young officer scrambled up the BTR, his face sheened with sweat despite the morning chill. "Thua Tuong, all units report ready for advance."

Anh nodded, his face an impassive mask. He took the proffered radio handset, feeling the weight of history in his hand.

"All units," he began, his voice gravelly in his own ears. "This is General Anh. The moment has come to crush the Khmer Rouge and liberate Phnom Penh. Our cause is righteous. Our victory is inevitable."

He paused, watching as another wave of Su-22s streaked overhead, rockets blazing from their wings.

"But make no mistake. This battle will test us all. The enemy is entrenched, desperate. They will fight to the last man. And they have shielded themselves with innocents."

Anh's jaw clenched at the thought of the civilians trapped in the city, used as human shields by Pol Pot's fanatics.

"Remember your training. Remember why we fight. For Vietnam. For Cambodia. For humanity itself. Tien len!"

As his words faded, the artillery opened up. The ground shook violently, nearly throwing Anh off balance. Hundreds of guns roared in unison, their muzzle flashes turning night to day. Rockets screamed overhead, leaving smoky trails across the lightening sky.

The tanks lurched forward, treads churning the muddy earth. The air filled with the metallic clank of tank tracks, the roar of engines, the shouts of men.

An aide appeared at Anh's elbow, his young face pale. "Thua Tuong, reconnaissance reports confirm large concentrations of civilians in the enemy's forward positions. Estimates in the tens of thousands."

Anh's stomach churned, but his face remained impassive. "Understood. The plan remains unchanged."

As the aide hurried away, Anh allowed himself a moment of doubt. The use of human shields had been anticipated, but this scale... He pushed the thought aside. There was no turning back now.

A thunderous explosion lit up the sky. A MiG, struck by anti-aircraft fire, spiraled downward trailing black smoke. Anh watched its descent, thinking of the young pilot, until it disappeared behind the smoky horizon.

The noise was overwhelming now - the constant rumble of tanks and APCs, the thunder of artillery, the shriek of rockets, the distant rattle of small arms fire as forward elements engaged the enemy.

Anh climbed down into his command vehicle. As it lurched forward, joining the advance, he felt the weight of countless lives in his hands. The liberation - or destruction - of Phnom Penh had begun, and with it, the final act of a war that had bled Indochina for decades.

The BTR rolled forward, and Anh steeled himself

for the horrors that lay ahead. The fate of two nations hung in the balance, and the next few hours would determine whether history would remember him as a liberator or a butcher.

Trenches Around Phnom Penh, Cambodia

The trenches reeked of fear and filth. Khmer Rouge soldiers crouched behind earthen walls, their hands white-knuckled on their weapons. The lucky ones clutched Chinese-made Type 56 rifles. Others gripped whatever they could find - old French MAT-49 submachine guns, American M16s left over from the civil war, even machetes and farm tools.

Overhead, the scream of jet engines tore through the air. A young soldier, barely sixteen, flinched at the sound. His commander cuffed him hard across the back of the head.

"Eyes forward," the officer snarled. "The Vietnamese will be here soon enough."

In the trench beside them, a group of civilians huddled together. Men, women, children - all pressed into service as human shields. An old woman clutched a crying infant to her chest, trying to muffle its wails.

A whistling sound pierced the air, growing louder by the second. The Khmer Rouge soldiers tensed.

"Incoming!" someone shouted.

The world exploded. Earth and shrapnel erupted skyward as artillery shells found their mark. Screams filled the air - some cut short, others rising to a terrible climax.

When the dust settled, gaps had appeared in the line where soldiers and civilians alike had stood moments before. Blood mixed with the churned earth.

A man stumbled through the haze, his arm a mangled ruin. "Medic!" he cried. "Med—" A bullet caught him in the throat. He fell, gurgling.

"Snipers," a soldier hissed. "Keep your heads down."

In the civilian trench, a young boy, no more than ten, tried to scramble out. His mother pulled him back down, clamping a hand over his mouth to stifle his terrified sobs.

Another whistle. Another explosion. This one closer.

A Khmer Rouge officer strode along the line, his eyes wild. "Stand fast!" he shouted. "Anyone who retreats will be shot. For Angkar! For Democratic Kampuchea!"

His words were drowned out by the roar of low-flying aircraft. Rockets slammed into the ground nearby, showering the trenches with dirt and fragments.

In the distance, the low rumble of tank engines grew steadily louder.

A civilian, an old man with a weathered face, looked to the east. He closed his eyes, murmuring a quiet prayer to whatever gods might still be listening.

The Khmer Rouge soldiers gripped their weapons tighter, eyes straining for the first sight of the Vietnamese advance. In the trench full of civilians, a woman began to weep softly.

The artillery barrage intensified. The tanks grew closer. And still, they waited, soldiers and civilians alike, for the hell that was about to descend upon them.

Underground Bunker - Phnom Penh, Cambodia

Sophal crouched in the undergrowth, his AK-47 held close. Beside him, Granier and Spitting Woman waited in tense silence. The distant rumble of artillery fire punctuated the air.

A twig snapped. Sophal's finger tightened on the trigger. A low whistle, barely audible, sounded from the bush. He relaxed, marginally.

Maly materialized from the shadows, his face streaked with dirt and sweat. He nodded to Sophal, then gestured behind him. Sokha and Chamroeun emerged, moving with the careful precision of men accustomed to staying alive in hostile territory.

Sophal spoke first, his voice a low rasp. "Report."

Maly's eyes darted to the bunker entrance, a nondescript concrete structure a hundred meters away. "No change in the last hour. Guard rotations every thirty minutes. We count at least thirty armed men outside. More inside, we're certain."

Granier leaned in, his voice barely above a whisper. "Any sign of Pol Pot or the other leaders?"

Sokha shook his head. "Nothing. But they're in there. Has to be."

Chamroeun produced a crude map sketched on a scrap of paper. "We've identified three entry points. Main entrance here, heavily guarded. Secondary entrance on the east side, less visible but still watched. And the ventilation shaft we found earlier."

Spitting Woman studied the map, "The shaft. How big?"

"Narrow," Maly replied. "Tight fit."

Sophal's jaw clenched as he processed the information. The sound of artillery grew louder. Time was running out.

"And the tunnel network?" he asked.

Chamroeun shrugged. "Can't be sure, but it's extensive. We've seen supplies being brought in. Enough to last weeks, maybe months."

Granier cursed under his breath. "They're planning to wait out the Vietnamese assault."

Sophal nodded grimly. "While thousands die above ground."

A sudden burst of gunfire in the distance caught their attention.

Maly's voice was tight. "What's the plan, Sophal? The Vietnamese will be here soon. If we're going to move, it has to be now."

Sophal's eyes never left the bunker. When he spoke, his voice was hard with resolve. "We go in. Tonight. And we root Pol Pot out, dead or alive."

The others exchanged glances, a mix of determination and fear on their faces. They all knew the odds. They all knew what failure meant. In the distance, a massive explosion lit up the sky. The final assault on Phnom Penh had begun.

Pol Pot's Underground Bunker

The moon hung low, casting long shadows across the scrubland. Spitting Woman lay on her stomach, eyes fixed on the ventilation shaft. A faint breeze whispered from its depths, carrying the scent of damp earth and fear.

"I'll go," she said, her voice quiet but firm.

Granier's jaw clenched. "It's too dangerous. We don't know what's down there."

She turned to him, her eyes hard in the dim light. "That's exactly why it has to be me. I'm the smallest. The quietest."

Sophal nodded, his face grim. "She's right. It's our best chance."

Spitting Woman began stripping off her excess gear, handing her pistol to Granier. She kept only a knife strapped to her thigh. Her fingers traced the handle of her sniper rifle.

"Lower it down after me," she said. "I'll need it. Also, send a satchel charge down. We'll want to get their attention."

Granier gripped her arm. For a moment, words failed him. She nodded, understanding what he couldn't say. "I'll find another way in and follow in five minutes. Be careful," said Granier.

Spitting Woman approached the shaft. The opening was narrow, barely wide enough for her shoulders. She took a deep breath, then began to lower herself in, headfirst.

The descent was agonizingly slow. The shaft was pitch black, the metal cold against her skin. Every sound - her breathing, the scrape of cloth on metal - seemed deafening in the confined space.

After what felt like an eternity, her hands met open air. She paused, listening intently. Nothing. Slowly, she emerged into a dimly lit concrete room.

Spitting Woman tapped twice on the shaft wall. Moments later, her rifle was lowered down, wrapped in cloth to muffle any sound, then came the satchel charge.

Above ground, Granier turned to Sophal. His voice was low, urgent. "We'll handle Pol Pot. You need to focus on the civilians."

Sophal's brow wrinkled. "What are you talking about?"

"The trenches. Once we create a distraction here, you can hit the Khmer Rouge from behind. It might be the civilians' only chance."

Understanding dawned on Sophal's face, followed quickly by resolve. He nodded sharply. "Agreed. But you're vastly outnumbered. How will you get out?"

Granier's smile was humorless. "We'll figure that out when we get there."

The sound of distant artillery punctuated his words. The Vietnamese assault was drawing closer.

Sophal clasped Granier's shoulder. "Good luck, my friend. See you on the other side."

As Sophal melted into the darkness with his men, Granier turned back to the ventilation shaft. He took a deep breath, steeling himself for what lay ahead.

In the bunker below, Spitting Woman moved silently through the shadows, her rifle at the ready. Somewhere in this concrete labyrinth, Pol Pot was waiting. And one way or another, his reign of terror would end tonight.

Granier moved through the underbrush, his steps measured and silent. The scrubland around the bunker was eerily quiet, the distant sounds of battle muffled by the still night air. His eyes, adjusted to the darkness, scanned the ground methodically.

A glint of metal caught his attention. He froze, muscles tense. Slowly, he crouched down, brushing away loose soil to reveal a metal hinge partially buried in the earth.

Granier's breath caught. A tunnel entrance.

He lay flat, ear to the ground. Faint voices drifted up from below. Two distinct voices, speaking Khmer.

Guards.

Granier unsheathed his knife, the blade dull in the weak moonlight. He took three deep breaths, centering himself. Then, with practiced ease, he grasped the edge of the hatch and lifted it just enough to peer inside.

A narrow ladder descended into darkness. At the bottom, two Khmer Rouge soldiers stood with their backs to him, rifles slung carelessly over their shoulders. They were laughing about something, relaxed. Complacent.

Granier's muscles coiled. He opened the hatch fully and dropped down, landing between the two guards. Before they could react, his knife found the first man's throat, slicing deep. Blood sprayed in a warm arc.

The second guard turned, eyes wide with shock. He opened his mouth to shout, but Granier was faster. The knife plunged into the man's chest, angled up under the ribs. A gurgling gasp, then silence.

Granier lowered the bodies to the ground, his movements economical, devoid of emotion. He wiped his blade clean on one of the guard's uniforms, then retrieved a flashlight from his pack.

The beam illuminated a long concrete tunnel stretching into darkness. The air was stale, heavy with the scent of damp earth and gun oil. Somewhere in the distance, water dripped steadily.

Granier paused at the tunnel's mouth, listening intently. Nothing but the faint echo of the dripping water. He clicked off the flashlight and pocketed it, allowing his eyes to readjust to the gloom.

With one last glance at the dead guards, Granier stepped into the tunnel. The darkness swallowed him whole, the only sound the soft scrape of his boots on concrete and his own measured breathing.

He moved forward, every sense straining for any sign of danger. Somewhere ahead, in this maze of underground passages, lay his target. Pol Pot couldn't hide forever.

The tunnel bent to the left. Granier followed, knife still in hand, ready for whatever might be waiting around the corner.

Spitting Woman moved through the bunker like a ghost, her footsteps silent on the cold concrete floor. The satchel charge weighed heavy against her hip. Her eyes, adjusted to the dim light, scanned every shadow for threats.

She passed several rooms - barracks, storage areas, a primitive infirmary. The air grew thicker as she descended deeper into the complex.

Spitting Woman moved silently through the dimly lit tunnel, her senses heightened. The weight of her sniper rifle across her back was reassuring, but in these close quarters, her knife would be more useful. The satchel charge hung heavy at her hip.

She rounded a corner and froze. Two Khmer Rouge guards stood before a heavy steel hatch, their eyes alert but unsuspecting. Spitting Woman's hand moved to her knife. She advanced silently toward the guards.

In two swift motions, she was upon them. The first guard's throat opened before he could cry out. The second managed a choked gasp as her blade found his kidney. Both crumpled to the floor.

Spitting Woman pressed her ear to the hatch. Muffled voices. One sharp, authoritative. Pol Pot.

She tried the hatch's wheel. It was locked, unmoving. She unclipped the satchel charge. With practiced hands, she set it against the hatch's hinges and armed it. The timer ticked to life.

Spitting Woman sprinted back down the corridor, diving behind a concrete pillar. The explosion rocked the bunker, dust and debris raining down. A ball of flame roared past her hiding spot, the heat searing her skin.

As the inferno subsided, she was moving again. Smoke billowed from the breached hatchway. Knife in hand, she plunged into the choking darkness.

Shapes loomed in the haze. A guard, disoriented, turned towards her. Her blade flashed, plunging into his chest. Two more figures, staff officers in uniforms, met the same fate before they could raise the alarm.

Through the thinning smoke, she saw him. Pol Pot. Their eyes met for a fraction of a second.

Spitting Woman lunged, knife aimed at his heart. A blur of movement. A body interposed itself between them. Her blade sank deep into the chest of Pol Pot's bodyguard. He fell, eyes already glazing over.

She wrenched her knife free, blood slick on her hands. But Pol Pot was gone, escorted by his staff and guards, vanished into the smoke and chaos.

Spitting Woman's eyes narrowed, scanning the room. A hidden door stood ajar in the far wall. The hunt wasn't over yet.

Her grip tightened on the bloodied knife as she moved towards the secret passage. Pol Pot might have escaped for now, but she was far from finished. The echoes of his footsteps beckoned her deeper into the labyrinth.

The muffled thump of an explosion reverberated through the tunnel. Granier's head snapped up, instantly alert. Spitting Woman had made her move.

He quickened his pace, rifle at the ready. The tunnel curved sharply, opening into a wider chamber. Voices echoed from an adjoining passage, growing louder. Guards, responding to the commotion.

Granier pulled a grenade from his vest, thumbing off the pin. He waited, counting heartbeats.

A group of Khmer Rouge soldiers burst into the chamber. Granier lobbed the grenade, then ducked back behind the corner.

The explosion was deafening in the confined space. Screams of pain and confusion filled the air. Granier pivoted around the corner, rifle raised.

Through the haze of dust and smoke, he picked out targets. One, two, three shots in rapid succession. Bodies fell.

More shouts from deeper in the complex. Granier moved forward, retrieving another grenade. He tossed it down the passage the guards had come from, not waiting for the explosion before advancing.

Chaos reigned. Alarms blared. The smell of cordite filled the air. Granier pressed on, deeper into the bunker's heart.

Outside the command center, Pol Pot's face was a mask of barely contained rage. An officer, sweat beading on his brow, delivered his report.

"Comrade, Vietnamese forces have breached our outer defenses. They're assaulting the bunker from multiple directions."

Pol Pot opened his mouth to respond when a bullet smashed into the wall inches from his head, showering him with concrete fragments.

For a moment, all was silent save for the ringing in their ears.

Then Pol Pot's voice, tight with controlled fury: "Abandon the bunker. We retreat to our secondary position."

He turned to Nuon Chea, his eyes cold. "Ensure all political prisoners are eliminated before you join us. Leave no one alive who might talk."

Chea nodded, his face impassive.

Pol Pot surveyed the room one last time, his gaze lingering on the maps and documents strewn across the tables. "Burn everything."

With that, he turned on his heel. A cadre of guards formed up around him as they moved swiftly towards one of the escape tunnels.

As they disappeared into the darkness, another shot rang out. This one found its mark, dropping one of the retreating guards.

In her sniper's nest, Spitting Woman cursed softly. She'd missed her primary target, but the night was far from over.

She slung her rifle over her shoulder and moved out. Somewhere in this maze of tunnels, Granier was fighting his way towards her. And somewhere ahead, Pol Pot was fleeing. The hunt was on.

The Fall

Tuol Sleng - Phnom Penh, Cambodia

The gates of interrogation center S-21, Tuol Sleng creaked open, admitting a black Soviet-made GAZ jeep. Nuon Chea stepped out, his face impassive behind thick-rimmed glasses. His bodyguards fanned out, AK-47s at the ready.

The prison director hurried over, bowing deeply. "Brother Number Two, we weren't expecting-"

Chea cut him off with a sharp gesture. "The bunker has been compromised. Comrade Pol Pot's orders are clear. All prisoners are to be eliminated immediately."

The director's eyes widened. "But... there are hundreds..."

"Was I not clear?" Chea's voice was ice. "Kill them all. Burn the bodies. Leave no evidence."

He turned to his guards. "Assist them. Use whatever means necessary."

The interrogation center erupted into frenzied

activity. Guards rushed to the cells, dragging out emaciated prisoners. Men, women, children - it made no difference.

In the courtyard, the first shots rang out. A woman fell, her child still clutching her hand. The child's wails were cut short by another burst of gunfire.

Inside, prisoners were pulled from their cells and lined up against walls. Some begged. Some prayed. Some stood in silent defiance. The outcome was the same for all.

The rattle of automatic weapons echoed through the complex. Blood ran in rivulets across the concrete floors.

In one cell block, prisoners tried to fight back with bare hands and desperation. Guards responded with grenades, the explosions shaking the building.

Outside, black smoke began to rise as the first bodies were thrown onto hastily constructed pyres. The smell of burning flesh filled the air.

Nuon Chea watched impassively from the jeep, checking his watch occasionally. Efficiency was key. They couldn't linger long.

A guard approached, his uniform spattered with blood. "Brother, the east wing is clear. Moving to the south cells now."

Chea nodded. "Work faster. The Vietnamese will be here soon."

The massacre continued, screams and gunfire blending into a hellish cacophony. Prisoners who had survived years of torture and deprivation now fell in droves.

As the last shots faded, Chea stepped out of the jeep. He surveyed the carnage, smoke stinging his eyes.

"Burn everything," he ordered. "Documents, records, everything. When the Vietnamese arrive, I want them to find nothing but ashes."

With that, he climbed back into the jeep. As they drove away, Tuol Sleng became a pyre, flames licking at the sky, carrying with them the evidence of unspeakable crimes.

Tunnels around Pol Pot's Bunker

Spitting Woman moved through the dimly lit tunnel, her breath controlled, every sense alert. The faint echo of footsteps ahead drove her forward. Pol Pot was close. She could almost taste it.

A heavy metal door appeared on her right, slightly ajar. She paused, listening. Silence. Cautiously, she pushed it open.

The room beyond was a mess of empty weapon racks and scattered ammunition crates. An armory, hastily stripped. Her eyes scanned the chaos, seeking anything useful.

There, in the corner. A single wooden box, its lid askew. She approached warily, knife at the ready. Inside lay a cluster of grenades.

She quickly stuffed her pockets, the weight reassuring against her thighs. One, two, three... eight in total. More than enough.

As she turned to leave, her foot struck something. A discarded gas mask. She kicked it aside, her mind already racing ahead to her quarry.

Back in the tunnel, she paused, orienting herself. The faint sound of voices drifted from the left. Without hesitation, she set off, her footsteps nearly silent on the concrete floor.

The grenades jostled gently with each step, a reminder of the destruction at her fingertips. Pol Pot had escaped her knife, but his luck wouldn't hold forever.

Spitting Woman's eyes narrowed as she moved deeper into the complex. The hunt was far from over. And now, she had the means to flush out her prey.

Pol Pot moved swiftly through the tunnel, his face a mask of contained fury. A cadre of loyal staff and guards surrounded him, their weapons at the ready. The sounds of distant fighting echoed through the passageways.

"We must reach our forces in the city," Pol Pot barked. "They will rally around us."

They passed a side tunnel branching westward. One of his advisors hesitated. "Comrade, perhaps we should—"

"No," Pol Pot cut him off. "Our strength is in Phnom Penh. We press north."

Suddenly, the tunnel ahead erupted in flame and shrapnel. Screams filled the air as the lead soldiers fell.

Granier crouched behind a fallen concrete slab, another grenade already in hand. He lobbed it over his makeshift barricade, ducking as the explosion sent debris raining down.

"Fall back!" someone shouted. The group began to retreat, dragging their wounded.

From the southern tunnel came another explosion. Spitting Woman emerged from the smoke. She'd recognized Granier's handiwork immediately.

She pulled the pin on another grenade, hurling it towards the rear of Pol Pot's group. The blast sent them scrambling forward, caught between two attacks.

Panic set in. Pol Pot's men, hemmed in on both sides, did the only thing they could. They fled down the western tunnel, away from both assailants and away from the city they'd sought to reach.

As the sound of their retreat faded, Granier cautiously stood. Spitting Woman approached from the other direction, her rifle raised. Their eyes met, a moment of recognition and shared purpose passing between them.

"Pol Pot?" Granier asked.

Spitting Woman nodded towards the western tunnel. "With them. Running scared."

Granier checked his ammunition, then gestured down the tunnel.

Without a word, Spitting Woman moved past him, taking point. Granier fell in behind her.

Together, they plunged into the darkness, in pursuit of their prey.

Trench Surrounding City

The pre-dawn sky was tinged with smoke and the flashes of distant artillery. Sophal and his resistance fighters crept through the rubble-strewn outskirts of Phnom Penh, their movements silent and practiced.

As they neared the government area, the sound of weeping and muffled cries reached their ears. Sophal held up a fist, halting the group. He gestured for two of his men to scout ahead.

They returned moments later, they returned. "The trench is just beyond that building," one whispered. "It's filled with civilians. Women, children, old men."

Sophal nodded, his jaw tight. He could see the fear in his men's eyes, mirroring his own. In the distance, the rumble of tanks and the whine of jet engines grew steadily louder. The Vietnamese were coming.

The dawn sky over the trenches outside Phnom Penh was shattered by the roar of jet engines. A squadron of Vietnamese Su-22 attack aircraft screamed in low, their shadows racing across the ground.

In the trenches, Khmer Rouge soldiers scrambled for their weapons. Civilians, pressed into service as human shields, cowered in terror. A young mother clutched her infant to her chest, trying to shield the child with her own body.

The lead Su-22 opened fire, its 23mm cannon spitting death. Rounds tore into the trench, kicking up geysers of dirt and flesh. Khmer Rouge soldiers fell, their bodies shredded by the high-velocity bullets.

But the cannon fire was indiscriminate. Civilians, unable to escape the confines of the trench, were cut down alongside their captors. The young mother's body jerked as rounds found her, her lifeless form falling to cover her now-wailing infant.

The second wave of aircraft unleashed a barrage of rockets. They streaked towards the earth, leaving trails of smoke in their wake. The explosions were deafening, sending shockwaves through the ground and filling the air with deadly shrapnel.

A section of the trench collapsed, burying soldiers and civilians alike in an avalanche of earth and bodies. Screams of the wounded and dying mixed with the continued roar of jet engines.

An elderly man, his face filled with terror and confusion, stumbled out of the trench. He waved his arms desperately at the sky, as if begging for mercy. A burst of cannon fire answered his plea, cutting him down mid-stride.

The attack seemed to last an eternity, though in reality it was over in minutes. As the Su-22s pulled up and away, they left behind a scene of utter devastation. The trench, once a symbol of the Khmer Rouge's desperate defense, was now a charnel house.

Smoke rose from dozens of impact craters. The dead and dying lay strewn about, soldiers and civilians intermingled in death as they had been in life. Those few who survived huddled in shock, unable to comprehend the horror that had just unfolded.

In the distance, the sound of approaching tanks could be heard. The Vietnamese ground assault was beginning, advancing into the carnage left by their air force. The battle for Phnom Penh continued, heedless of the cost in innocent lives.

Through his binoculars, Sophal surveyed the scene. Khmer Rouge soldiers lined the backside of the trench, their backs to the city, all eyes fixed on the approaching forces. The civilians being used as human shields were down in the trench in front of the Khmer Rouge soldiers.

"Listen carefully," Sophal said, his voice low but intense. "We're going to circle around and come up behind them. Chan, take your group left. Rith, go right. I'll lead the center."

His men nodded. Everyone knew what was at stake.

"Remember," Sophal continued, "our priority is the civilians. Protect them at all costs. If you have a clear shot at a Khmer Rouge soldier, take it, but be damned sure of your target. We can't risk hitting the innocent people in those trenches."

He looked each of his fighters in the eye. "This is what we've been fighting for. To save our people from these butchers. Today, we end this nightmare."

With hand signals, Sophal directed his men to their positions. They moved swiftly, using the ruins for cover. As they neared the trench, the cries of the civilians grew louder, punctuated by the harsh shouts of Khmer Rouge officers.

Sophal raised his hand, ready to give the signal to attack. He could see the tension in his men's bodies, the white-knuckled grips on their weapons.

In the trench below, a child began to wail. A Khmer Rouge soldier turned, raising his rifle.

Sophal's hand came down. "Now!" he shouted.

The resistance fighters opened fire, their first volley dropping several Khmer Rouge soldiers before they could even turn around. Chaos erupted as the defenders realized they were being attacked from behind.

"Protect the civilians!" Sophal yelled, charging forward. His men followed.

The battle for Phnom Penh had begun in earnest. And with it, the final reckoning.

Vietnamese Front

General Le Duc Anh stood atop his command vehicle, binoculars pressed to his eyes. Dawn was breaking over the horizon, casting long shadows across the battlefield. The thunder of artillery had faded to a dull, distant rumble.

Through the lenses, Anh watched as chaos erupted along the Khmer Rouge front lines. Muzzle flashes lit up the trenches, but the fire wasn't directed outward. The Cambodians were shooting at each other.

Anh lowered his binoculars, his weathered face

impassive. A young officer approached, saluting crisply.

"Sir, our forward units are in position. They await your order to advance."

Anh raised his hand, silencing the officer. He lifted the binoculars again, studying the unfolding scene. The firefight was intensifying. He could make out civilians scrambling out of the trench searching for cover as Khmer Rouge soldiers fell around them.

"Interesting," Anh murmured.

The officer shifted uncomfortably. "Sir? Should we press the attack?"

Anh was silent for a long moment, his eyes never leaving the battle. Finally, he lowered the binoculars and turned to the officer.

"No," he said, his voice cold and calculated. "Order all units to hold position."

"But sir," the officer protested, "we have the advantage. The enemy is in disarray."

Anh's gaze hardened. "You question my orders, Captain?"

The younger man swallowed hard. "No, sir. Of course not."

"Good." Anh turned back to the battlefield. "Let them kill each other. Why waste Vietnamese blood when the Khmer are so eager to spill their own?"

The officer saluted and hurried off to relay the orders. Anh remained atop his vehicle, watching dispassionately as the Khmer tore themselves apart.

"Fools," he muttered.

In the distance, the gunfire continued unabated. Anh allowed himself a small, grim smile. Sometimes, the best strategy was to simply to do nothing.

Trench

The bitter smell of cordite filled the air as Sophal and his resistance fighters pressed their attack. The horizon was punctuated by muzzle flashes and the screams of the wounded. Sophal moved from cover to cover, his AK-47 chattering in short, controlled bursts.

"Keep pushing!" he shouted over the din. "Drive them away from the civilians!"

To his left, Chan and his group were making steady progress, forcing the Khmer Rouge to abandon their positions in the trench. Rith's team on the right flank was pinned down by a machine gun nest, but they were holding their ground.

Sophal ducked as a grenade exploded nearby, showering him with dirt and debris. He wiped grit from his eyes and signaled to two of his men. They nodded, understanding the unspoken order.

As Sophal provided covering fire, the two fighters sprinted forward, tossing grenades into the Khmer Rouge positions. The explosions were followed by screams and a temporary lull in enemy fire.

"Now! Move!" Sophal ordered.

His men surged forward, leaping into the trench. The fighting devolved into a brutal, close-quarters struggle. Rifles became clubs, knives flashed in the growing light.

A Khmer Rouge soldier lunged at Sophal with a bayonet. He parried the thrust with his rifle, then brought the butt down hard on the man's head. There was a dull crunch, then the soldier crumpled.

"Sophal!" Chan's voice cut through the chaos. "We've breached their line! The civilians—"

Sophal turned to see Chan helping a young woman

out of the trench, a child clutched in her arms. More civilians were emerging, dazed and terrified.

"Get them to safety!" Sophal shouted. He turned to his radioman. "Tell Rith to push hard. We need to open up an escape route."

The radio crackled with Rith's response. His team had finally silenced the machine gun nest and was advancing.

Sophal allowed himself a moment of hope. They were making progress. But he knew the Khmer Rouge wouldn't give up easily.

A bullet whizzed past his ear, snapping him back to the present. Sophal raised his rifle, sighting down on a Khmer Rouge officer rallying his men for a counterattack.

He squeezed the trigger. As short burst of gunfire and the officer fell.

"Keep pushing!" Sophal roared. "For Cambodia!"

His men echoed the cry as they pressed the attack. The trench, once a symbol of the Khmer Rouge's cruelty, was becoming a pathway to liberation. But the cost was high. Bodies of fighters from both sides littered the ground, and the wails of the wounded mixed with the ongoing rattle of gunfire.

Sophal reloaded his rifle. The battle was far from over, but for the first time in years, he could see a glimmer of hope for his people and his country.

The first rays of the sun crept over the horizon, casting a sharp light over the chaos of the battlefield. In the trenches, the sounds of gunfire and explosions began to ebb, replaced by a new noise - the desperate scrambling of terrified civilians.

A young woman clambered out, her fingers clawing at the loose dirt of the trench wall. She pulled herself up, wild-eyed and panting, a small child clinging to her back. For a moment, she froze, exposed and vulnerable, before instinct took over. She ran, stumbling over the uneven ground, heading towards the city.

Her action broke the spell of fear that had paralyzed the others. Suddenly, the trench was alive with movement. Old men helped each other up. Mothers passed children to those already on solid ground before scrambling up themselves. Teenagers pulled younger siblings from the muck.

A frail old woman struggled at the edge of the trench, her strength failing her. Two young men, strangers until this moment, reached down and hauled her up. They supported her between them as they joined the exodus.

The stream of civilians quickly became a flood. They ran in every direction, their only goal to put distance between themselves and the front lines. Some carried makeshift bundles of possessions. Most had nothing but the clothes on their backs.

A man stumbled, falling hard on the debris-strewn ground. A woman he'd never met before stopped, helping him to his feet. They continued on together, strangers united by survival.

The sounds of renewed gunfire spurred them on. No one looked back. Fear and adrenaline propelled them forward, towards the relative safety of Phnom Penh's streets.

As they reached the outskirts of the city, the crowd began to disperse. Some ducked into abandoned buildings. Others continued on, deeper into the urban maze, seeking familiar neighborhoods or rumored safe zones.

A young boy, separated from his family in the chaos, stood alone at a street corner. His eyes were wide with terror and confusion. An elderly couple paused, the woman extending her hand. After a moment's hesitation, the boy took it. Together, the makeshift family disappeared down a side street.

The exodus continued as the sun climbed higher. The civilians of Phnom Penh, long pawns in a brutal war, were taking their fate into their own hands. Behind them, the battle raged on. Ahead lay uncertainty. But for now, they ran, clinging to the hope of survival.

Sophal stood at the edge of the captured trench section, his rifle hanging loosely at his side. He watched as more civilians clambered out, their faces etched with a mixture of terror and desperate hope. A young man helped an elderly woman over the lip of the trench, guiding her trembling steps towards the city.

The sight should have filled Sophal with triumph, but a cold dread settled in his stomach. He turned, surveying the vast trench line stretching in both directions. Their breach was painfully small, a tiny gap in a wall of potential slaughter.

In the distance, he could see the Vietnamese forces arrayed for attack. Tanks and infantry, poised to strike along the entire front. The realization hit him like a physical blow - tens of thousands would die if that assault came.

His eyes fell on a battered bulldozer, abandoned nearby. A plan formed, terrible in its necessity.

"Chan!" he called. His lieutenant jogged over, face streaked with dirt and sweat.

Sophal pointed to the bulldozer. "We need to fill in this section of the trench."

Chan's eyes widened. "But... the civilians. We'd be trapping them."

"I know. But if we don't, the Vietnamese will attack the whole line. This way, we might funnel them through our breach."

He watched understanding dawn on Chan's face, followed quickly by the same grim resolve he felt himself.

"I'll find someone who can operate it," Chan said quietly.

As Chan hurried off, Sophal turned back to the trench. More civilians were emerging, helping each other up the muddy slope. A mother passed her infant to waiting hands before scrambling out herself.

Sophal closed his eyes briefly, the weight of his decision settling heavily on his shoulders. When he opened them, his voice rang out, clear and commanding.

"Everyone who can move, get out now! We're sealing this section. Spread the word down the line!"

His words sparked a new frenzy of activity. Those still in the trench redoubled their efforts to escape. Resistance fighters rushed to help, pulling people up and over.

The bulldozer roared to life behind him. Sophal watched as it lurched forward, its rusted blade lowering. The first scoop of earth cascaded into the trench.

A woman's scream cut through the air. "My son! He's still down there!"

Sophal's heart clenched. But he couldn't stop now. "Keep going," he ordered the bulldozer operator. To his men, he shouted, "Find that child!"

The bulldozer continued its work, slowly filling in

the trench. Sophal's fighters searched desperately in the shrinking space. Just as the blade was about to make another pass, a fighter emerged, a small boy in his arms.

Sophal allowed himself a moment of relief before turning back to the larger battle. In the distance, the Vietnamese lines were shifting. He prayed his gamble would pay off.

The trench that had been a lifeline minutes ago was now disappearing under mounds of earth. With each pass of the bulldozer, Sophal felt the weight of lives saved and lives potentially lost.

The bulldozer's engine roared as it pushed another mound of earth into the trench. Dust filled the air, choking and blinding. Among the civilians trapped in the trench, panic spread like wildfire.

A young woman, Mai, tried to scramble up the steep sides, her fingers clawing at the loose dirt. Beside her, an old man stumbled, falling back as the wave of earth cascaded down.

"Help!" Mai screamed, but her voice was lost in the chaos.

The dirt came faster now, an avalanche of soil and debris. Mai felt it hit her legs, then her waist. She fought desperately, trying to keep her head above the rising tide.

To her left, a child disappeared beneath the earth, one small hand reaching out before being swallowed by the deluge. The old man was already gone, buried without a sound.

Mai's world narrowed to a pinpoint of sky above her. She took one last, desperate breath before the dirt covered her face.

Minutes passed. Then, a hand burst from the earth. Mai clawed her way out, gasping and sobbing. She looked around wildly, hoping to see other survivors.

But she was alone. The only one to emerge from the impromptu grave.

Mai collapsed on the newly formed ground, her body shaking with shock and grief. Around her, the battle for Phnom Penh raged on, indifferent to the small tragedy that had just unfolded.

The bulldozer's engine roared as it pushed the last mound of earth into place, completing the pathway over the trench. The operator, his face streaked with sweat and grime, looked to Sophal for further instructions.

Sophal nodded, a grim satisfaction in his eyes. "Good work. Now, pull back."

As the bulldozer reversed, leaving deep treads in the newly formed earth, Sophal surveyed the scene. The pathway stood as a stark interruption in the long line of trenches, a potential lifeline for the advancing Vietnamese forces.

But his work wasn't done. Sophal's gaze shifted to the stretches of trench still filled with terrified civilians, struggling to climb the steep earthen walls.

"Take it further down the line," Sophal ordered, pointing towards a section of trench about a hundred meters away. "We need to give these people a way out."

The bulldozer operator nodded, understanding immediately. He maneuvered the massive machine, its engine growling as it moved parallel to the trench line.

Upon reaching the designated spot, the operator lowered the blade. With practiced skill, he began to cut into the trench wall, creating a gradual slope. Earth cascaded down, forming a ramp that led from the bottom of the trench up to ground level.

Sophal watched as comprehension dawned on the

faces of the trapped civilians. A murmur of hope rippled through the crowd. As soon as the ramp was passable, people began to scramble up, helping each other, passing children hand to hand.

"Keep going," Sophal called to the bulldozer operator. "Cut more exits. Space them out."

The bulldozer moved on, repeating the process. With each new exit, more civilians poured out of the trenches, a stream of humanity flowing towards the relative safety of the city.

Sophal turned to his lieutenants. "Spread the word. Tell everyone to head for the city center. And keep an eye out for any Khmer Rouge trying to blend in with the civilians."

As his men moved to comply, Sophal allowed himself a moment to absorb the scene. The bulldozer continued its work, the sound of its engine now mingling with the cries of relief from escaping civilians. It wasn't a perfect solution - the trenches still held thousands - but it was something.

Sophal crouched behind a crumbling wall, his AK-47 at the ready. He signaled to his men, scattered in small groups along the edge of the trench line. The Khmer Rouge forces were in disarray, struggling to maintain their defensive positions while keeping control of the civilian hostages.

"Now!" Sophal shouted.

His resistance fighters opened fire, a coordinated barrage that caught the Khmer Rouge soldiers off guard. The air filled with the crack of rifle fire and the dull thud of grenades.

In the chaos, more civilians saw their chance. A middle-aged man grabbed his young daughter's hand and made a break for it, scrambling up the side of the trench. Others followed, a stream of desperate humanity clawing their way to freedom.

Sophal's men provided covering fire, their shots precise and disciplined. They were careful to avoid hitting the fleeing civilians, instead focusing on the Khmer Rouge soldiers who tried to stop the escape.

"This way!" one of Sophal's lieutenants shouted, waving the civilians towards their lines. "Quickly!"

The Khmer Rouge, caught between the resistance fighters attacking their flank and the advancing Vietnamese forces to their front, began to fall back. Their retreat was hasty and disorganized, leaving more gaps for civilians to slip through.

Sophal moved along his line, encouraging his fighters. "Keep pushing! Don't let up!"

The resistance fighters advanced, leap-frogging from cover to cover. They were a far cry from the ragtag group that had started this fight - now they moved with the coordination and purpose of a seasoned military unit.

As the Khmer Rouge retreated further, more sections of the trench were freed. Civilians poured out, seeking escape from their captors. They ran past Sophal's men, tear-streaked faces showing a mix of terror and relief.

"Get them to the rear!" Sophal ordered. "Set up a safe zone!"

The battle was far from over, but for these freed civilians, a nightmare was ending. As they passed the resistance fighters, some reached out to touch them, murmuring thanks. Others were too shell-shocked to do more than stumble forward.

Sophal allowed himself a moment of satisfaction. They were making a difference. Every civilian freed was a life potentially saved from the coming firestorm.

But there was no time to dwell on it. He turned back to the fight, knowing that many more still needed their help. The resistance would keep biting at the Khmer Rouge flank, freeing as many as they could before the full might of the Vietnamese assault came crashing down.

In the distance, Sophal could see dust clouds rising. The Vietnamese were on the move. Time was running out. Sophal gripped his rifle and started towards the nearest exit ramp. The bulldozer's roar faded into the background as Sophal moved forward.

Vietnamese Front Lines

General Le Duc Anh stood motionless atop his command vehicle, binoculars fixed on the distant front line. The early morning light revealed an unexpected sight: a battered bulldozer methodically filling in a section of the Khmer Rouge trenches.

"Curious," Anh muttered, his weathered face betraying no emotion.

A staff officer approached, saluting crisply. "General, we've confirmed the activity. They appear to be creating a pathway through their own defenses."

Anh lowered his binoculars, his eyes narrowing. "Indeed."

Another officer spoke up, his voice tinged with concern. "Sir, this could be a trap. They might be funneling us into a kill zone."

Anh considered this, his mind working through the tactical implications. The breach could significantly accelerate their advance, potentially saving thousands of Vietnamese lives. But the risk...

"Your assessment?" Anh asked his chief of staff.

The man frowned. "It's... unprecedented. The strategic advantage is clear, but so is the danger."

Anh nodded, turning back to survey the battlefield. The bulldozer continued its work, the gap in the enemy line growing wider.

After a long moment, he spoke. "Prepare a team of combat engineers and our best recon unit. I want that breach thoroughly examined for booby traps and signs of ambush."

"Yes, sir," his chief of staff replied, already moving to relay the orders.

Anh raised his binoculars again, studying the area around the breach. He could see movement - civilians fleeing towards Phnom Penh. This complicated matters further.

"Have the forward artillery units hold their fire on that sector," Anh ordered. "And get me a detailed report on enemy movements in the area. I want to know if they're repositioning to take advantage of this... invitation."

"Sir," an aide approached, radio in hand. "The engineering team is assembled and awaiting your final order."

Anh took one last look at the growing breach. It was a risk, but war was built on such moments.

"Send them in," he commanded. "But tell them to proceed with extreme caution."

As the recon team moved out, Anh settled in to wait. The next few hours would determine whether they had been handed a victory or were walking into a slaughter. He had made his decision. Now, he could only watch as events unfolded.

General Anh watched intently as the Vietnamese

recon team cautiously approached the breach. Through his binoculars, he could see them moving in a careful formation, engineers sweeping for mines while combat troops provided cover.

"Report," he barked to his radioman.

The soldier listened intently to his headset before responding. "Sir, the team reports no signs of mines or other explosives in the immediate approach. They're proceeding into the filled-in trench area now."

Anh nodded, his eyes never leaving the scene. The tension was palpable among his staff.

Minutes ticked by. The recon team had disappeared into the breach, their progress hidden from view. Anh's grip tightened on his binoculars.

Suddenly, the radio crackled to life. The radioman's eyes widened. "General, they've cleared the breach! No booby traps detected. They report..." he paused, listening intently, "They report evidence of a firefight, but between Khmer factions. Bodies wearing different insignia."

A murmur ran through the assembled officers. Anh raised a hand, silencing them.

"Any sign of an ambush force?" he asked.

The radioman shook his head. "Negative, sir. The area behind the breach appears to be clear of enemy combatants. They've spotted civilians fleeing towards the city, but no organized military presence."

Anh lowered his binoculars, his mind racing. This was an opportunity, but one that required swift action.

"Order the 1st Armored Division to advance through the breach," he commanded. "Infantry to follow closely. Tell them to secure a perimeter on the other side and prepare for potential counterattack."

As his staff rushed to relay the orders, Anh turned

to his chief of operations. "Redirect our artillery to provide covering fire on the flanks of the breach. I want to discourage any attempt by the Khmer Rouge to seal it."

The officer nodded, hurrying off to coordinate the fire plan.

Anh climbed down from his command vehicle, striding towards a nearby tank. He could see the dust cloud rising as the armored division began to move.

"Sir," his aide called, jogging to catch up. "Should we inform Hanoi of this development?"

Anh paused, considering. "Not yet. Let's see how this plays out. If we can exploit this breach, we might be able to report the fall of Phnom Penh instead."

As he watched the first tanks rumble towards the gap in the enemy lines, Anh allowed himself a moment of cautious optimism. The path to victory had suddenly become clearer.

As the Vietnamese armored units approached the breach, General Anh climbed into a BTR-60 armored personnel carrier. He was determined to witness the advance firsthand.

The vehicle lurched forward, joining the flow of tanks and infantry fighting vehicles moving towards the gap. Inside the carrier, Anh studied a map spread across his lap, occasionally glancing out the viewport.

"Sir," his communications officer called out, "1st Armored reports they've passed through the breach. No resistance encountered."

Anh nodded, his face impassive. "Tell them to fan out and secure a bridgehead. I want room for the follow-up forces to deploy."

The BTR-60 rattled as it crossed the filled-in trench. Anh felt a momentary tension, half-expecting an ambush. But they passed through without incident.

On the other side, chaos reigned. Civilians streamed towards the city, while scattered groups of Khmer Rouge soldiers fled in disarray. Some surrendered on the spot, throwing down their weapons at the sight of the Vietnamese armor.

Anh's vehicle came to a stop. He climbed out, surveying the scene. To his right, a T-54 tank crushed an abandoned Khmer Rouge machine gun nest. To his left, Vietnamese infantry were already setting up defensive positions.

His radioman approached, face taut with excitement. "General, our forces report minimal resistance along the entire front. The Khmer Rouge lines are collapsing!"

For the first time that day, Anh allowed himself a thin smile. "Push forward. I want our lead elements in the heart of Phnom Penh by nightfall."

As the orders were relayed, Anh turned his attention to the stream of civilians. Many looked malnourished, their eyes wide with a mixture of fear and hope.

"Set up aid stations," he commanded. "And find interpreters. I want to know what these people have endured."

A young officer approached, saluting sharply. "Sir, we've captured several high-ranking Khmer Rouge officials. They're requesting to speak with you."

Anh's eyes hardened. "Secure them for interrogation. Their fates can wait. Our priority now is taking the city."

He climbed back into the BTR-60, gesturing for the driver to move forward. As they advanced towards Phnom Penh, Anh considered the broader implications of the day's events. The war might be ending sooner than anyone had anticipated.

But as the vehicle rumbled on, passing scenes of destruction and human suffering, Anh knew that the real challenge lay ahead. Winning the war was one thing. Building a lasting peace would be another battle entirely.

Bunker Complex and Tunnels

The tunnel was a claustrophobic nightmare, barely wide enough for two men to walk abreast. Spitting Woman led, her movements silent and predatory, with Granier close behind. The stale air reeked of fear and gunpowder.

Ahead, voices echoed off the concrete walls. Pol Pot and his entourage had stopped. Spitting Woman raised a fist, halting their advance. She and Granier pressed themselves against the tunnel wall, straining to listen.

"We must contact the front," Pol Pot's voice, taut with barely controlled panic. "They need to hold the line."

The crackle of a radio. "Comrade, the signal is weak. We need to get closer to the surface."

Granier met Spitting Woman's eyes in the dim light. They couldn't let that happen. She nodded, understanding without words.

Spitting Woman reached for a grenade, pulling the pin. With practiced precision, she lobbed it down the tunnel. Granier was already moving, rifle raised.

The explosion was deafening in the confined space. Screams and chaos erupted from Pol Pot's group. Before the dust could settle, Granier opened fire, short controlled bursts cutting through the smoky air.

"Go, go!" Spitting Woman shouted, surging forward.

They advanced, using the confusion to their advantage. Another grenade from Spitting Woman sent Pol Pot's men scrambling further down the tunnel.

"The radio!" Pol Pot's voice, shrill with desperation. "We must reach the commanders!"

Granier's rifle cracked twice. The distinctive sound of electronics shattering echoed back to them, followed by curses.

"Keep moving!" one of Pol Pot's officers shouted. "We'll find another way to communicate."

Spitting Woman and Granier pressed on, relentless in their pursuit. The tunnel continued to wind westward, taking Pol Pot further from his disintegrating forces in Phnom Penh.

"We're driving them out of the city," Granier said between breaths.

Spitting Woman's reply was cold. "Good. Let's make sure they never come back."

They paused at a junction, listening for movement. The sound of running footsteps echoed from the right-hand passage.

Without hesitation, they followed. The hunt continued, deeper into the earth, further from the Khmer Rouge's crumbling regime. Pol Pot might escape today, but his power was slipping away with every step.

Front Lines Around City

The sky over Phnom Penh roared with the sound of jet engines as Vietnamese MiG-21s swooped low over the city. Below, Khmer Rouge forces scrambled to establish a new defensive line, their previous positions now overrun.

A squadron of Su-22 attack aircraft appeared on the horizon, their wings heavy with bombs and rockets. As they approached, the lead pilot's voice crackled over the radio.

"Target acquired. Commencing attack run."

The first bombs fell, their whistling descent ending in thunderous explosions that shook the earth. Plumes of smoke and debris erupted where Khmer Rouge troops had been hastily digging in.

On the ground, a Khmer Rouge commander shouted frantically into a radio. "We need anti-aircraft support! They're tearing us apart!"

His words were drowned out by another wave of explosions as the Su-22s made a second pass, rockets streaking from their wings to devastate vehicle columns and ammunition dumps.

In the distance, the deep boom of artillery added to the cacophony. Soviet-made 130mm guns, their barrels raised to the sky, unleashed a relentless barrage. Shells arced high over the city before raining down on Khmer Rouge positions with terrifying accuracy.

A group of Khmer Rouge soldiers attempted to move an anti-aircraft gun into position. They never got the chance to fire. A precisely placed artillery shell landed in their midst, leaving nothing but a smoking crater.

The MiGs circled back, strafing the ground with their 23mm cannons. Lines of dust and debris kicked up as bullets tore through makeshift barricades and sent Khmer Rouge troops diving for cover.

In the chaos, a Khmer Rouge officer tried to rally his men. "Stand your ground! We must hold the—"

His words were cut short as a bomb landed nearby, the concussion throwing him to the ground. When he looked up, half his unit had disappeared.

The Vietnamese attack was relentless. Every time the Khmer Rouge tried to regroup or establish a strong point, it was met with overwhelming firepower from the air and long-range artillery.

As the smoke began to clear, revealing the devastation, the sound of tank engines grew louder. The Vietnamese ground forces were advancing, ready to exploit the chaos sown by their air and artillery support.

The Khmer Rouge line, such as it was, began to crumble. Soldiers threw down their weapons and fled. Others raised their hands in surrender, shell-shocked and defeated.

The battle for Phnom Penh was entering its final stages, and the sky continued to rain fire on those who would resist.

Tunnel Exit

Pol Pot emerged from the tunnel, blinking in the harsh daylight. His once-pristine uniform was now caked with dirt and sweat. His staff and remaining guards stumbled out behind him, faces filled with exhaustion and fear.

One of his officers immediately produced a radio, frantically adjusting the dials. "Comrade, we've reestablished contact with the front."

Pol Pot snatched the radio, his knuckles white around the handset. "Report!" he barked.

The voice that crackled back was filled with panic and the sounds of distant explosions. "Brother

Number One, the Vietnamese... they've broken through. Our lines have collapsed. They're in the city streets now."

Pol Pot's face remained impassive, but his eyes betrayed a mix of rage and despair. "How far have they advanced?"

"They're approaching the city center. Our forces are in disarray. We can't hold them back."

A heavy silence fell over the group. Pol Pot's mind raced, calculating options that were rapidly dwindling.

Finally, he spoke, his voice cold and decisive. "Pull our remaining forces out. Abandon the capital."

His staff exchanged shocked glances. One of them dared to speak up. "But Comrade, if we lose Phnom Penh—"

"Phnom Penh is already lost," Pol Pot cut him off sharply. Into the radio, he continued, "Order all commanders to disengage and regroup in Battambang. We'll consolidate our forces near the Thai border."

He paused, then added, "This is not the end. We will become the shadows in the jungle, the whispers in the night. The Vietnamese may take our cities, but they will never hold our country."

As his orders were relayed, Pol Pot turned to his inner circle. "Our war enters a new phase. We will melt into the countryside, become one with the people. Every village will be our fortress, every farmer our soldier."

His eyes gleamed with a fanatical light. "The Vietnamese think they've won, but they've merely stepped into a quagmire. We will bleed them with a thousand cuts until they abandon our sacred soil."

The group nodded, their resolve hardening. They knew the road ahead would be long and brutal, but their faith in Pol Pot's vision remained unshaken.

As the sounds of battle echoed from the distant capital, Pol Pot and his cadre began their journey west. The jungle would be their new home, the mountains their citadels. The war for Cambodia was far from over; it was merely changing form.

Behind them, Phnom Penh burned, its fall marking the end of one era and the beginning of another equally bloody chapter in Cambodia's tragic history.

City Center – Phnom Penh, Cambodia

The once-bustling streets of Phnom Penh's city center were now eerily quiet, save for the sound of hurried footsteps and hushed, urgent voices. Khmer Rouge soldiers moved swiftly through the abandoned boulevards.

"Move, move!" a commander shouted, urging his men forward. "We head west! Abandon your positions!"

Trucks laden with whatever supplies and weaponry they could salvage rumbled past. Some soldiers cast longing glances back at the city they were leaving, the capital they had held with an iron grip for so long.

As the last stragglers disappeared down the western roads, a heavy silence fell over the city center. The Khmer Rouge flag, once fluttering proudly over government buildings, now hung limp and forgotten.

Royal Palace – Phnom Penh, Cambodia

Miles away, on the outskirts of the city, a column of Vietnamese T-54 tanks ground to a halt before the ornate front gates of the Cambodian Royal Palace. The lead tank commander emerged from his hatch, surveying the scene with wary eyes.

"No sign of resistance," he reported into his radio. "The gates appear unguarded."

After a tense moment of silence, the order came through. "Proceed with caution. Breach the gate."

The lead tank's engine roared to life. It lurched forward, picking up speed. With a thunderous crash, it smashed through the golden gates, splinters of wood and metal flying in all directions.

The tanks rolled into the palace complex, their treads leaving deep imprints in the once-immaculate gardens. Infantry soldiers fanned out, weapons at the ready, expecting an ambush at any moment.

But the courtyards were empty. No shots rang out. No defenders appeared.

A young Vietnamese soldier cautiously pushed open the grand doors of the main palace building. He peered inside, then turned back to his comrades, his face a mask of disbelief.

"It's abandoned," he called out. "They're gone."

The news rippled through the Vietnamese forces. The Khmer Rouge, the fearsome regime that had held Cambodia in its grip for years, had fled without a fight.

As the Vietnamese flag was raised over the Royal Palace, replacing the Khmer Rouge standard, a sense of anti-climax settled over the conquering forces. The expected final, desperate battle for Phnom Penh had not materialized.

The city had fallen, not with a bang, but with the whisper of retreating footsteps and the echo of an empty palace.

Tunnel Exit - Phnom Penh, Cambodia

Spitting Woman emerged from the tunnel first, her eyes squinting against the sudden brightness. The forest around them was deceptively quiet, the distant sounds of battle barely audible.

Granier followed close behind, his rifle at the ready. "Anything?" he whispered.

Before she could answer, the world erupted in gunfire. Muzzle flashes lit up the underbrush as Pol Pot's guards, hidden in carefully prepared positions, opened fire.

"Ambush!" Spitting Woman shouted, diving behind a fallen tree. Bullets splintered the wood around her.

Granier threw himself to the ground, crawling rapidly to a small depression. Dirt kicked up inches from his face as rounds impacted all around him.

"I count at least five positions," Spitting Woman called out, her voice barely audible over the gunfire. She popped up briefly, squeezing off two shots before ducking back down.

Granier nodded, his eyes scanning the treeline. He spotted movement and fired a quick burst, rewarded by a cry of pain.

They were pinned down, the guards' superior positions giving them a clear advantage. Any attempt to move would be met with a hail of bullets.

Spitting Woman checked her ammunition. "We're going to run out of ammo before they do."

Granier's mind raced, assessing options. The guards were well-trained, patient. They could wait all day if necessary.

A grenade landed near Granier's position, rolling towards him. Without thinking, he snatched it up and hurled it back. The explosion sent shrapnel tearing through the leaves.

"Nice throw," Spitting Woman said.

Granier didn't respond, his attention focused on a slight movement to their left. He raised his hand slowly, signaling to Spitting Woman.

She nodded, understanding. In one fluid motion, she rose to a crouch, laying down suppressing fire towards the main guard positions.

Granier used the distraction to sprint to a new position, diving behind a large rock just as bullets chipped away at its surface.

Now they had a crossfire. It wasn't much, but it was something.

"Any bright ideas?" Spitting Woman called out, reloading her rifle.

Granier's response was drowned out by another fusillade of gunfire. They were running out of time and options. Pol Pot was slipping away with every second they remained pinned down.

The forest echoed with gunfire as the two sides remained locked in a deadly stalemate, neither able to gain the upper hand. For now, survival was the only objective, the hunt for Pol Pot temporarily forgotten in the desperate struggle to stay alive.

The sound of engines roaring to life cut through the gunfire. Pol Pot's guards had managed to commandeer a small convoy of vehicles - a mix of battered trucks and civilian cars.

Pol Pot climbed into the back of a covered truck. His remaining staff hurried to join him, their movements urgent and fearful.

"Quickly!" one of the senior guards shouted. "We must reach Battambang before the Vietnamese can regroup!"

The guards maintaining the ambush began to fall back in stages, providing covering fire for their retreating comrades. The intensity of their assault on Granier and Spitting Woman's position increased, pinning the two down even more effectively.

From his hidden vantage point, Granier caught a glimpse of the convoy through the trees. He raised his rifle, trying to line up a shot on Pol Pot, but a hail of bullets forced him back into cover.

"They're getting away!" he shouted to Spitting Woman.

Spitting Woman knew as well as Granier did that they were powerless to stop the escape. Their ammunition was running low, and the guards had them too well pinned.

The convoy began to move out, engines revving as they picked up speed. The guards nearest the vehicles jumped aboard, hanging onto the sides of the trucks as they pulled away.

Pol Pot's voice, faint but audible, drifted back to them. "To Battambang! We will regroup and continue the struggle!"

As the last of the vehicles disappeared down a dirt road, the remaining guards intensified their fire one last time. It was a final, vicious barrage meant to keep Granier and Spitting Woman's heads down long enough for a clean getaway.

Then, suddenly, silence fell. The guards had melted away into the forest, leaving only spent cartridges and the smell of gunpowder behind.

Granier cautiously raised his head, scanning the area. "I think they're gone," he said, his voice hoarse.

Spitting Woman stood slowly, her eyes narrow as she surveyed the now-empty battlefield. "Pol Pot?"

Granier shook his head, frustration evident in every line of his body. "Gone. Heading for Battambang."

They shared a look of understanding. Their quarry had slipped away, leaving them behind with nothing but bruises, empty magazines, and the bitter taste of a mission unaccomplished.

In the distance, they could hear the fading sound of engines as Pol Pot and his entourage sped towards Battambang, towards an uncertain future of guerrilla warfare and continued bloodshed. For now, at least, the hunt was over.

Granier slumped against a tree, his breathing heavy. He exchanged a look with Spitting Woman, both of them coming to the same realization.

"We can't keep this up," Granier said, wiping sweat from his brow.

Spitting Woman nodded, her face filled with frustration and exhaustion. "We're outgunned and outmaneuvered. Pol Pot's heading for Battambang with an army. We're just two people."

Granier reached for the radio they'd been carrying. It had survived the firefight, miraculously unscathed. "Time to bring in the big guns," he muttered.

He fiddled with the dials, searching for the right frequency. After a moment of static, a voice came through, speaking rapid Vietnamese.

Spitting Woman took the radio, responding in kind. After a brief exchange, she handed it back to Granier. "General Anh is on the line."

Granier took a deep breath, composing himself. "General Anh, this is Granier. We have critical information on Pol Pot's movements."

There was a pause, then Anh's voice came through, cold and precise. "Speak quickly."

"Pol Pot and his staff have abandoned Phnom Penh. They're heading for Battambang, near the Thai border. They plan to regroup their forces there and wage a guerrilla war."

"When did you acquire this information?" Anh demanded.

"Minutes ago," Granier replied. "We were in pursuit until just now. They've commandeered vehicles and have a head start."

"I see," Anh said, his tone neutral. "We'll verify and act on this intelligence as we see fit."

Spitting Woman leaned in, adding, "General, be advised that Pol Pot intends to blend his forces with the civilian population. He's switching to guerrilla tactics."

"Noted," Anh responded curtly. "What's your current status?"

Granier and Spitting Woman shared a weary look. "We're withdrawing from pursuit. We'll be returning to Phnom Penh."

"Very well," Anh said, his voice devoid of emotion. "Report to headquarters upon your return. Anh out."

As the radio fell silent, Granier and Spitting Woman sat in momentary quiet, the weight of their complicated position settling over them.

"Not exactly a warm reception," Spitting Woman said softly.

Granier nodded, slowly getting to his feet. "We're still outsiders to them. Come on, we've got a long walk back to the city."

As they began their journey back to Phnom Penh, the sound of distant aircraft could be heard. The Vietnamese war machine was moving into action, the hunt for Pol Pot now in their hands.

TWILIGHT OF WAR

Granier and Spitting Woman trudged through the underbrush, the sounds of distant combat fading behind them. They walked in silence for a while, each lost in their own thoughts. Finally, Granier spoke, his voice low and weary.

"You know what's waiting for us at Anh's headquarters, don't you?"

Spitting Woman nodded, "The brig, most likely. Followed by a show trial for treason."

Granier snorted. "Some gratitude for the intel we just gave them, not to mention decapitating the Khmer Rouge command."

They paused at the crest of a small hill, surveying the war-torn landscape before them. The sky was tinged orange with the setting sun and the glow of distant fires.

Spitting Woman turned to Granier, her eyes filled with a mixture of exhaustion and resolve. "We don't have to go back."

Granier raised an eyebrow. "What are you suggesting?"

"Home," she said simply. "Back to the north. Our war is over, Granier. We've done what we came to do."

He considered her words, weighing their options. The thought of facing Anh's cold judgment and likely punishment held no appeal. And she was right - they had accomplished their mission, even if the outcome wasn't exactly what they'd planned.

"You're right," he said finally. "There's nothing left for us here. And I've had enough of other people's wars."

Spitting Woman allowed herself a small smile. "So, north then?"

Granier nodded, a weight seeming to lift from his

shoulders. "North. It's a long walk, but I think we've earned the break."

They adjusted their course, now heading away from Phnom Penh and towards the Vietnamese-Laotian border. The sounds of battle continued to fade behind them, replaced by the natural rhythms of the forest.

As they walked, Granier glanced at Spitting Woman. "What will you do, when we get back?"

She was quiet for a moment before answering. "Find some peace, if I can. You?"

"The same," he replied. "Maybe we can find it together."

Spitting Woman's hand found his, squeezing gently. No more words were needed.

They continued their journey north, leaving behind the chaos and violence of Cambodia. Their war was indeed over, and while the road ahead was long and uncertain, it was theirs to choose.

The jungle swallowed them up, two weary soldiers finally heading home.

General Anh's Headquarters

General Anh stood at the window of his command post, hands clasped behind his back. The evening sky bled red over the distant jungle. Anh knew that Granier and Spitting Woman had no intention of returning to his headquarters. He would need another way to deal with them. He didn't turn as Colonel Bui, the Ranger battalion commander, entered.

"You summoned me, General?"

Anh's voice was cold as he slid two personnel folders across the table. "Two operatives have deserted. They've stolen sensitive intelligence."

The colonel stiffened as he opened the folders and saw photos of Granier and Spitting Woman. "The scouts who helped secure Phnom Penh?"

"The same. They know troop movements, supply lines. In enemy hands, this information could cripple our entire Cambodian operation."

"What are your orders?"

"Take your battalion of Rangers. Set up a series of ambushes along the Laotian border. They must not escape."

"Sir, how can we be certain they'll attempt to cross into Laos? Wouldn't entering Vietnam directly be simpler?"

Anh's eyes narrowed. "They're too smart for that. They know we'd expect it. Laos offers a chance to disappear, to perhaps sell their information to other interested parties."

"Understood. And if we capture them alive?"

"Preferably, you won't. But if you do, there will be a field trial. Swift. Followed by immediate execution."

The colonel nodded. "We'll deploy immediately."

"One more thing." Anh's voice dropped. "These two are not to be underestimated. They're skilled, resourceful. Treat them as you would the most dangerous of enemies."

"Yes, sir."

"Dismissed."

As the colonel left, Anh turned back to the window. The sky had darkened, the jungle now a sea of black. Somewhere out there, two people who knew far too much about his dealings were trying to disappear. He wouldn't let them.

Laotian-Cambodian Border

The jungle thinned as Granier and Spitting Woman approached the Laotian border. Sweat plastered their clothes to their bodies, a week of hard travel etched in the lines of exhaustion on their faces. They moved with the practiced stealth of seasoned operatives, but fatigue had begun to dull their usual razor-sharp awareness.

"I've been thinking…" said Spitting Woman.

"About what?" said Granier.

"Our hut back in the village… we should move it closer to the river."

"Why? It's fine where it's at. We've got a nice shade tree overhead and it's close to the community lodge."

"Not enough privacy. Besides, I like swimming at night."

"It's not like we can just lift the thing up and carry it."

"Of course not. We'll build a new one. Two rooms this time. You have to admit, it would be nice to have a bedroom."

"Well, yeah, but I've never built a hut before."

"I have. I'll show you how. I'll be construction manager and you can be the labor."

"That hardly seems fair."

"Welcome to life."

Granier held up a hand, signaling a halt. He cocked his head, listening intently. The forest had gone unnaturally quiet.

"What is it?" Spitting Woman whispered, her hand instinctively moving to her weapon.

After a tense moment, Granier shook his head. "Nothing. Thought I heard… never mind."

They pressed on, unaware of the danger surrounding them.

Fifty meters to their left, a Vietnamese Ranger lay motionless, his body seeming to melt into the forest floor. Only his eyes moved, following the targets. He keyed his radio twice, a silent signal to the men waiting ahead.

Granier consulted a worn map. "Should hit the border in about two klicks. There's a stream just on the other side. Good place to rest."

Spitting Woman nodded, allowing herself a small smile. "A wash and some sleep sound like heaven right now."

As they neared a small clearing, a twig snapped underfoot. Both froze, eyes darting, searching for threats. After a moment, they relaxed slightly, attributing the noise to their own passage.

Two hundred meters north, another Ranger team shadowed their flank. One soldier raised his rifle, tracking Granier through his scope. The team leader placed a restraining hand on his shoulder, shaking his head. Not yet.

Granier paused again, scanning the path ahead. This time, the hairs on the back of his neck stood up. Something felt off.

"What's wrong?" Spitting Woman asked, tension evident in her voice.

"I don't know," Granier muttered. "It's too quiet. No birds, no insects."

They stood in silence, every sense straining. The jungle seemed to hold its breath.

Finally, Spitting Woman spoke. "We can't stay here. We're too exposed."

Granier nodded reluctantly. "You're right. Let's move. Carefully."

They advanced, hyperaware now, but still unable to

spot the Rangers hidden mere meters away. Fingers near triggers. Muscles coiled, ready to spring.

"Almost there," Granier murmured. "Just over that rise, and we're in Laos."

Spitting Woman allowed herself a small sigh of relief. "First thing I'm doing is soaking my feet in that stream."

As they crested the rise, the hidden Rangers tensed. The moment had come.

The jungle's suffocating heat pressed down as the Vietnamese Ranger sniper tracked his targets through his scope. Sweat trickled down his face, but he remained motionless, his breathing slow and controlled. Years of training had prepared him for this moment.

He focused on the woman first. She moved with a fluid grace that spoke of years in the field. The sniper adjusted his aim, compensating for wind and distance.

His finger tightened on the trigger. Just a little more pressure and...

She stopped suddenly, hand flying to her hip. The sniper paused, curious. Was she hit? Injured?

No. She was retrieving something. A map? The sniper's pulse quickened. This could be the evidence they needed.

But before he could take the shot, his view was obscured. The man - Granier - had moved in front of her. The sniper cursed silently, waiting for a clear line of sight.

Granier gestured at something in the distance, then turned back to his companion. The sniper shifted his aim, centering his crosshairs on Granier's head. His orders were clear: eliminate the targets, retrieve any intelligence they carried.

He drew a deep breath and let half of it out, steadying himself for the kill.

Granier took a step forward, his foot landing on loose stones. He stumbled slightly.

The sniper's finger squeezed the trigger.

Suddenly, Spitting Woman jerked to a stop, caught on something. Granier turned back to help her.

The sniper's shot, perfectly aimed a split second before, now whistled harmlessly past Granier's head, thudding into a tree trunk.

The jungle erupted in chaos as the Rangers opened fire.

The air exploded with gunfire. Granier and Spitting Woman dove in opposite directions, instinct overriding coordination. Granier rolled behind a massive fallen tree, its rotting trunk offering meager protection. Spitting Woman disappeared into a shallow depression, her body pressed flat against the damp earth.

Ten feet of open ground separated them, but it might as well have been miles. A hail of bullets tore through the space between, shredding leaves and splintering bark. The staccato of automatic weapons fire was deafening, punctuated by the sharp crack of sniper rifles.

Granier dared a quick glance over his cover. A bullet whizzed past his ear, forcing him back down. He caught a glimpse of movement - Rangers advancing in teams, using the trees for cover as they tightened the noose.

He shouted over the din. "You, okay?"

A burst of return fire from her position answered his question. Three quick shots, then silence. She was conserving ammunition.

From her position, Spitting Woman tried to get a bead on their attackers. The Rangers were good, damned good. They moved like beasts between the trees, offering only fleeting targets. She fired again, rewarded by a grunt of pain. One down, but how many more? She saw movement on her right side.

"We need to move!" she called to Granier. "They're flanking us!"

Granier nodded. They were being herded, driven away from the border and deeper into the jungle. But any attempt to break out of the encirclement would mean crossing that exposed stretch of ground between them.

A grenade arced through the air, landing just beyond Spitting Woman's position. She scrambled backwards as it exploded, showering her with dirt and shrapnel. A cry of pain escaped her lips.

"Are you hit?" Granier shouted, his voice raw with fear and rage.

Spitting Woman felt her torso where the pain was. There was a wet spot – blood. She pulled up her shirt revealing the wound – a small puncture, bleeding.

"It's small. I'm alright," she called back.

Granier glanced at her position, saw her grimace as she tried to stem the blood flowing from her side.

"You don't look alright."

"It's small. I'll live."

The Rangers pressed their advantage, their fire intensifying. Granier and Spitting Woman were pinned down, options dwindling with each passing second. The trap had sprung, and they were caught.

Granier pressed his back against the fallen tree, his mind racing. The Rangers were closing in, their coordinated fire keeping him and Spitting Woman pinned, separated.

They were out of options. Out of time.

A terrible clarity settled over Granier. There was only one way this could end with at least one of them surviving.

Granier shouted over the gunfire. "When I move, you run! Head for the river!"

Spitting Woman's head snapped up, her eyes widening as she realized his intent. "No! We go together or not at all!"

Granier shook his head, a sad smile crossing his face. "Not this time."

Before she could protest further, Granier took a deep breath. He checked his weapon - half a magazine left. It would have to be enough.

Granier burst from cover, firing wildly as he sprinted away from Spitting Woman's position. The gambit worked - the bulk of the enemy fire shifted to him, bullets kicking up dirt at his heels.

Spitting Woman watched in horror as Granier drew the Rangers' attention. Every instinct screamed at her to go after him, but she knew that would negate his sacrifice. Tears stinging her eyes, she took advantage of the distraction and slipped away in the opposite direction.

Granier ran, dodging between trees, his lungs burning. He could hear the Rangers crashing through the underbrush behind him. Good. The further he led them from Spitting Woman, the better her chances.

A bullet grazed his side, the sharp pain nearly causing him to stumble. He pushed on, emptying his magazine in a final act of defiance.

As Granier burst into a small clearing, he knew he'd reached the end of his run. Rangers materialized from the trees, weapons trained on him. He raised his hands slowly, hoping against hope that Spitting Woman had made it to safety.

The last thing Granier saw was the Ranger commander raising his hand, signaling to his men. Then rifle but slammed into the back of his head and darkness claimed him.

Spitting Woman crashed through the dense undergrowth, her breath coming in ragged gasps. The sounds of pursuit faded behind her, but the echo of gunfire still rang in her ears. She ran until her legs burned and her lungs screamed for air.

Finally, she stumbled to a halt, collapsing against a massive banyan tree. As the adrenaline ebbed, the reality of what had just happened hit her. Granier. Gone. Sacrificed himself so she could escape.

She closed her eyes, fighting back tears. Then, with a deep breath, she steeled herself. No. She wouldn't leave him behind.

Spitting Woman turned, orienting herself. The forest was quiet now, an eerie calm after the chaos of the ambush. She moved silently, every sense on high alert.

Her bare feet made no sound on the soft forest floor. Years of hunting had taught her to step lightly, to blend with the natural rhythms of the jungle. She became a shadow, slipping between trees, freezing at the slightest sound.

After twenty minutes of careful backtracking, she heard voices. Vietnamese clipped and professional. The Rangers.

Spitting Woman climbed a nearby tree, her movements fluid and practiced. From her perch, she saw them. A group of six Rangers, Granier's limp form slung between two of them.

Her jaw clenched at the sight of Granier's bloodied face, but she forced herself to remain still. Patience. Wait for the right moment.

As the Rangers moved out, Spitting Woman followed from above. She leapt from tree to tree, her steps sure despite the wound in her side. When the canopy thinned, she dropped to the ground, using the underbrush for cover.

The Rangers were good, constantly scanning their surroundings. But they didn't look up enough. Spitting Woman used this to her advantage, climbing back into the trees whenever the terrain allowed.

Hours passed. The sun dipped low, casting long shadows across the forest floor. Still, Spitting Woman followed. Her body ached, her wounded side throbbed, but she pushed the pain aside. Nothing mattered except staying on their trail.

As night fell, the Rangers made camp in a small clearing. Spitting Woman watched from the darkness as they secured Granier to a tree, his head lolling forward. She noted the placement of sentries, the location of their weapons.

Her mind raced, formulating a plan. The odds were impossible, but she'd faced worse. Somehow, some way, she would get Granier out of there.

Spitting Woman settled into a comfortable position, her eyes never leaving the camp. She would wait, conserve her strength. And when the moment came, she would be ready.

The jungle night closed in around her, alive with subtle sounds and movements. But Spitting Woman remained motionless, a predator poised to strike, determined to save the man who had sacrificed everything for her.

The next morning, Granier had regained consciousness. He had a splitting headache, but he was alive. After being forced to hike nine miles through heavy jungle, Granier entered a more permanent Ranger camp and was immediately tied up with his legs bound.

The makeshift Ranger camp was a study in efficient military organization, hastily established yet meticulously arranged in the heart of the dense Cambodian jungle. A small clearing, no more than one hundred meters across, served as the camp's center, ringed by the towering trees of the surrounding forest.

At the clearing's edge, a perimeter of sharpened stakes had been driven into the ground, angled outward to deter any frontal assault. Camouflage netting was strung between trees, breaking up the camp's outline from aerial observation.

Olive-drab tents were arranged in a rough semicircle, each large enough to house four to six men. The command tent, slightly larger and adorned with antenna for field radios, stood at the far end of the clearing. Outside it, a folding table held maps and communication equipment, guarded by two alert sentries.

Near the center of the camp, a makeshift interrogation area had been set up. A sturdy tree served as an anchor point, with ropes dangling ominously from a low-hanging branch. Nearby, a small generator hummed, powering work lights and equipment.

The Rangers moved about with purpose. Some cleaned weapons, others pored over maps or maintained equipment. The atmosphere was charged with the gravity of their mission.

At the opposite end from the command tent, a crude holding area had been fashioned. Here, Granier was kept under constant guard, his hands bound behind him and secured to a metal stake driven deep into the ground. The area was open to the elements, offering no shelter from the oppressive heat or the occasional downpour.

Cooking fires smoldered at the camp's edge, the smell of military rations mixing with the heavy scent of the jungle. Stacks of ammunition crates and supply boxes were neatly arranged, evidence of the Rangers' preparedness for a prolonged operation.

Despite its temporary nature, the camp exuded an air of efficiency. Every element served a purpose, from the strategically placed sentry positions to the carefully maintained paths that allowed for quick movement throughout the area. It was a spartan outpost, designed for a single, uncompromising mission – one that centered on the battered man bound at its edge.

The first light of dawn filtered through the jungle canopy as the Ranger commander approached Granier. They had moved him to a makeshift interrogation area, away from the main camp. Granier's wrists were bound tightly to a tree trunk, his face bruised and covered with dried blood.

"Where is the stolen intelligence?" the commander demanded, his voice cold.

Granier spat blood, meeting the commander's gaze defiantly. "There is no stolen intelligence. It's all a lie."

A sharp backhand snapped Granier's head to the side. "Do not play games. We know you took sensitive documents. Where are they hidden?"

Granier's laugh was bitter. "You've been fed a story, Commander. Ask yourself why General Anh wants us dead so badly."

The commander's eyes narrowed. "Explain."

"Weapons for opium," Granier said, his voice raw. "Anh's been trading arms to the Khmer Rouge in exchange for drugs that he can sell. We stumbled onto his operation. That's why he wants us silenced."

A moment of doubt flickered across the commander's face, quickly replaced by hardened resolve. "A convenient tale. But it changes nothing. You will tell us what we want to know."

He nodded to one of his men, who stepped forward with a car battery and jumper cables.

Fifty meters away, concealed in the dense foliage of a tall tree, Spitting Woman watched the scene unfold. Her knuckles were white as she gripped a branch, every muscle in her body tense with the need to act.

She saw the cables touch Granier's skin, saw his body convulse as electricity coursed through him. His scream of pain was muffled, but it tore at her heart.

Spitting Woman closed her eyes briefly, forcing herself to remain still. She knew Granier could endure tremendous pain. She had witnessed his strength firsthand during their years together. But knowing his resilience didn't make watching his suffering any easier.

The interrogation continued, a brutal dance of questions and pain. Granier's responses became more slurred, but he gave them nothing. Spitting Woman's admiration for his strength warred with her desperate need to end his torment.

As the sun climbed higher, she noted the Rangers' movements, their patrol patterns. She counted weapons, assessed vulnerabilities. Her mind worked furiously, crafting and discarding plans.

An opportunity would come. It had to. And when it did, she would be ready. For now, she forced herself to be patient, to wait. Every fiber of her being screamed to rush in, to save the man she loved. But she knew that would only end in both their deaths.

So she watched, and waited, her heart breaking with each grunt of pain from Granier. The jungle grew hotter, insects buzzing incessantly. Still, Spitting Woman remained motionless, a statue of focused determination. She would save him, or die trying.

She hated the idea of attacking the Rangers. Under normal circumstances they would be her ally, but these were far from normal circumstances. If forced to choose between the Rangers and Granier, she would save Granier and kill them all if needed.

As the interrogation of Granier continued, Spitting Woman silently retreated deeper into the jungle. She moved with purpose, her eyes scanning the forest floor and canopy for what she needed.

She found a suitable branch first - young, flexible wood with just the right amount of spring. Using her knife, she carefully stripped the bark and began shaping the bow. Her movements were swift and practiced, honed by years of crafting similar weapons in her youth.

Next, she harvested sturdy vines for the bowstring. As she worked, plaiting the fibers into a strong cord, her ears remained attuned to any sound from the Ranger camp.

For arrows, she selected straight branches, meticulously smoothing and straightening them over a small, smokeless fire. The heat helped remove any slight bends, ensuring true flight.

The most challenging part was the fletching. Spitting Woman moved through the jungle, searching for the telltale flash of color that would indicate a parrot's presence. Fortune smiled on her – She crept through the underbrush, eyes scanning the canopy. A flash of crimson caught her attention - a scarlet macaw perched on a low branch, unaware of the danger below.

She drew her knife, its weight familiar in her hand. With a swift, fluid motion, she sent the blade spinning through the air. The knife struck true, embedding itself in the bird's chest. The macaw let out a strangled squawk before falling to the forest floor with a soft thud.

Retrieving her knife and the bird, Spitting Woman quickly plucked the vibrant feathers she needed. She murmured a quiet thanks to the creature for its unwilling sacrifice.

Back at her impromptu workspace, Spitting Woman split the feathers with exquisite care. She attached them to the arrow shafts using sap as an adhesive, her fingers working nimbly despite the urgency of the situation. She needed the arrows to fly true to save Granier.

As she crafted each arrow, her mind replayed the layout of the Ranger camp, planning her approach. The bow took shape under her skilled hands, a deadly weapon born from the jungle itself.

Once her arrows were complete and the bow strung, Spitting Woman knew she needed to test her handiwork. She selected a tree about thirty meters away, its trunk scarred by weather and time.

Nocking an arrow, she drew the bow to full extension. The wood creaked slightly but held firm. She took a deep breath, sighting along the shaft.

The arrow flew true, burying itself deep into the trunk with a satisfying thunk. The bow would serve its purpose.

She retrieved the arrow, not wanting to leave any sign of her presence. As she made her way back towards the Ranger camp, her steps were silent but purposeful. The weight of the bow in her hand was reassuring.

Spitting Woman waited until an hour after sunset before moving into her assault position. It wasn't pitch dark, but close. She would need a small amount of light to site her targets. She used the time before the assault to clear her thoughts of fear and anxiety. She needed to focus. The odds were heavily against her and Granier. She was outnumbered and outgunned. The Rangers were a force multiplier. One Ranger was worth two to three normal soldiers. The only advantages she had were her experience and stealth. She hoped for Granier's sake that those would be enough.

It was time. Spitting Woman moved through the underbrush, her feet finding purchase on the soft earth without a sound. She came to the camp once again. Her eyes, accustomed to the gloom, scanned the makeshift compound. The soft glow of shielded lanterns cast long shadows, creating a patchwork of light and dark. She searched for Granier and saw nothing. The holding area where she'd last seen him was empty, the metal stake driven into the ground a mocking reminder of his captivity. She worried that she was too late. Even without knowing his location, she decided to continue with her plan and hope to find him once she entered the camp. Steadying her breathing, Spitting Woman nocked an arrow. The familiar weight of the bow grounded her, clearing her mind of fear and doubt. She'd faced impossible odds before. She would do so again.

Thirty meters away, a Ranger sentry stood at the camp's perimeter, his eyes scanning the treeline. Spitting Woman drew the bow, the wood creaking softly. She held her breath, aiming carefully. The arrow flew true, catching the sentry in the throat. He fell without a sound, disappearing into the tall grass.

Without giving soldier's life a second thought, she moved to her next position. Another sentry fell to her arrows, then a third. Each shot brought a heightened tension. How long before they noticed the missing guards?

Inside the command tent, Granier was shoved roughly before a makeshift tribunal. His face was a map of bruises, dried blood caking his split lip. The Ranger commander stood before him, face impassive.

"Rene Granier," the commander's voice was cold, "you stand accused of treason and espionage against the Socialist Republic of Vietnam. How do you plead?"

Granier's laugh was harsh, ending in a cough. "This isn't a trial. It's a farce, and you know it."

The commander's eyes narrowed. "Your plea is noted. Given the evidence against you, this tribunal finds you guilty of all charges."

As the commander spoke, Spitting Woman crept closer to the camp. Another sentry fell to her arrows. She moved swiftly between shots, using the lengthening shadows to her advantage.

"The sentence," the commander continued, "is death by firing squad, to be carried out immediately."

Granier's face remained defiant as two Rangers

grabbed his arms, dragging him away from the tribunal.

As Granier emerged from the command tent, Spitting Woman saw him and felt her chest tighten. He was alive... at least for now. She quickened her pace, knowing time was running short.

Granier was marched to a large tree at the edge of the clearing. His hands were cuffed behind him, the metal biting into his wrists. A squad of six Rangers formed a line twenty paces away, rifles at the ready.

Spitting Woman's breath caught as she saw the execution unfold. She abandoned stealth for speed, sprinting towards a small rise that would give her a clear shot. She dropped her bow as she unslung her sniper rifle.

The commander began to read out the sentence formally. "Rene Granier, for your crimes against the people of Vietnam..."

Spitting Woman dropped to her stomach on the rise, the cool metal of her rifle pressed against her cheek. Through the scope, she could see the sweat on Granier's brow, the tense set of his jaw. He wasn't giving an inch. That's who he was in life and that is who he would be in death.

"Ready!" the commander shouted. The firing squad raised their rifles.

Spitting Woman's finger curled around the trigger. She drew a slow breath, steadying her aim.

"Aim!"

The crack of Spitting Woman's rifle shattered the tense silence. The commander's head snapped back, a spray of crimson in the fading light. Before the others could react, she fired again and again. Three more Rangers fell in quick succession, their bodies crumpling to the ground. The remaining three Rangers dove for cover, turning their weapons away from Granier and to the tree line.

Chaos erupted in the camp. Shouts of confusion and alarm filled the air. Granier, seizing the moment, bent over and raised his cuffed hands behind his back high. Spitting Woman's next shot severed the chain with surgical precision, the bullet whistling mere centimeters from Granier's skin.

Freed, Granier dove for a fallen Ranger's weapon. He came up firing, the AK-47 bucking in his hands. The clearing erupted in chaos as Granier grabbed a bandolier of ammunition from a dead Ranger and sprinted towards Spitting Woman. His muscles screamed in protest, days of captivity and torture taking their toll. But adrenaline coursed through his veins, pushing him forward. The stolen AK-47 bounced against his chest, its weight a reassuring promise of retribution.

Spitting Woman's rifle cracked repeatedly, the muzzle flash briefly illuminating her position to the Rangers. Each shot found its mark with deadly precision. A Ranger dropped as he raised his weapon, another fell mid-stride as he charged towards Granier.

Bullets kicked up dirt around Granier's feet, uncomfortably close. He zigzagged, presenting a harder target, his eyes fixed on Spitting Woman's position. The distance between them seemed to stretch endlessly.

"Down!" Spitting Woman's voice cut through the din.

Granier dropped instantly, feeling the wind of a bullet passing overhead. He rolled, coming up in a crouch and unleashing a burst from his AK-47. The Ranger who'd nearly shot him fell, clutching his chest.

Spitting Woman's cover fire intensified, keeping the bulk of the Rangers pinned down. Each report followed by a cry of pain or the thud of a body hitting the ground.

Granier was close now, only meters away from Spitting Woman's position. A grenade arced through the air, landing near Spitting Woman. Without hesitation, Granier changed direction. He scooped up the grenade and hurled it back in one fluid motion. The explosion sent two Rangers flying, buying them precious seconds.

With a final burst of speed, Granier reached Spitting Woman. He slid into cover beside her, his back pressed against the fallen log that had been her sniper's nest.

"Took you long enough," Granier shouted over the gunfire.

"You're welcome. Next time, listen to me and try not to get captured," she replied.

They shared a brief look, volumes spoken in that silent exchange. Then, as one, they turned to face the advancing Rangers. The night was still young, and their fight for survival had only just begun.

They fought side-by-side, their movements synchronized from years of working together. Spitting Woman's rifle cracked repeatedly, each shot finding its mark with deadly accuracy. Granier's stolen AK-47 chattered, keeping the Rangers' heads down and preventing them from organizing an effective counterattack.

"We need to get out of here before reinforcements arrive!" Spitting Woman called, gesturing towards a gap in the perimeter she'd created earlier.

"Good plan," said Granier. "Which way?"

Spitting Woman motioned the direction with a nod.

They ran, bullets kicking up dirt at their heels. Granier winced as a shot grazed his arm, but he didn't slow down.

Just as they were about to disappear into the treeline, a burly Ranger burst from the underbrush, swinging his rifle like a club. Granier ducked the blow, countering with a swift uppercut that sent the man staggering. Spitting Woman finished him off with a precise shot.

They plunged into the jungle, its familiar darkness enveloping them. They ran until their lungs burned, putting as much distance between themselves and the camp as possible.

Finally, when the sounds of pursuit had faded, they paused to catch their breath. Leaning against a massive tree trunk, Granier turned to Spitting Woman, his eyes filled with gratitude and something deeper.

"I knew you'd come," he said between ragged breaths.

Spitting Woman's response was simple, but laden with meaning. "Always."

As their breathing steadied, they shared a look of understanding. There would be time for words later. For now, they needed to keep moving. The jungle night closed in around them as they pressed on, two soldiers melting into the shadows, leaving chaos and unanswered questions in their wake.

Dawn's first light filtered through the jungle canopy as Granier and Spitting Woman approached the border. They moved in tandem, every step calculated, communicating with hand signals honed over years of partnership.

Granier held up a fist, signaling a halt. He pointed

to a barely visible tripwire stretched across their path. Spitting Woman nodded, her eyes scanning the surrounding foliage. The Rangers had laid their ambush well.

They backtracked, finding a massive fallen tree. Using it as cover, they observed the area. Granier spotted a camouflaged sniper nest in a tree thirty meters to their left. Spitting Woman noticed the telltale signs of a machine gun emplacement to their right.

Spitting Woman returned the smile, nocking an arrow. "I'll take the sniper. You handle the MG nest."

Granier nodded, checking the ammunition in his stolen AK-47. "On three."

Spitting Woman's bullet caught the sniper in the throat before he could react. Simultaneously, Granier opened fire on the machine gun position. The Rangers there returned fire, bullets splintering bark around them.

A grenade arced through the air, landing near their position. Granier snatched it up and hurled it back. The explosion sent the two Rangers in the machine gun nest flying.

Spitting Woman picked off Rangers as they emerged from cover. Her shots were precise, each one finding its mark.

Granier provided covering fire as they leapfrogged from tree to tree, slowly advancing.

They reached a small stream, its rushing water masking their movements. Submerging themselves, they pulled themselves underwater along the rock bed. They use the stream as cover to flank the Ranger position.

Emerging on the other side, they caught the Rangers off guard. Granier's AK-47 chattered, cutting down three men before they could turn. Spitting Woman's rifle cracked twice more, eliminating the last visible threats.

As they approached the border, they stopped to survey the area for possible ambushes. There were none. They crossed the invisible line that marked the border, slipping into Laos. As the adrenaline faded, fatigue set in.

As they disappeared into the Laotian jungle, the sounds of distant engines could be heard. Vietnamese reinforcements, arriving too late.

Road to Battambang

The convoy of battered vehicles sped along the dusty road towards Battambang, engines straining under the urgent pace. Pol Pot sat in the back of a covered truck, exhausted. The mood among his entourage was tense, a mixture of fear and desperate hope.

Suddenly, the roar of jet engines filled the air. A guard's shout cut through the noise: "Aircraft! Vietnamese MiGs!"

Pol Pot's eyes widened. "Scatter! Into the jungle!"

But it was too late. The lead MiG swooped low, its cannons blazing. The first truck in the convoy erupted in flames, flipping over and skidding off the road. Screams of the dying mixed with the shriek of twisting metal.

The convoy broke formation, vehicles swerving wildly as drivers sought escape. A second MiG streaked overhead, dropping bombs that cratered the road and sent shrapnel tearing through the fleeing cars.

Pol Pot's truck lurched violently as the driver veered off the road, crashing through the underbrush. Branches whipped at the canvas covering, threatening to tear it away.

Behind them, another explosion lit up the sky. One of the staff cars had taken a direct hit, its occupants vaporized in an instant.

"Keep moving!" Pol Pot shouted, his usual composure cracking. "We must reach the forest!"

The air was filled with smoke and the smell of burning fuel. More MiGs appeared, strafing the scattered convoy with merciless precision. A truck carrying Khmer Rouge officers was hit, its gas tank exploding and sending a fireball into the air.

Pol Pot's driver pushed the truck harder, the engine screaming in protest as they plunged deeper into the jungle. Branches and vines tore at the vehicle, slowing their progress.

In the sky above, the MiGs circled like vultures, searching for targets. The sounds of explosions continued, each one marking the end of more lives, more of Pol Pot's dwindling inner circle.

As the truck finally reached the deeper cover of the forest, Pol Pot looked back at the road they'd left behind. Pillars of smoke rose into the sky, marking a trail of destruction. His convoy, once a symbol of his power, now lay in ruins.

His face hardened, rage and fear etched into every line. The Vietnamese had found them far quicker than he'd anticipated. Survival was now the only objective.

The truck pushed on into the gathering darkness, carrying Pol Pot towards an uncertain future, the sounds of destruction slowly fading behind them.

TWILIGHT OF WAR

General Anh's Headquarters

General Le Duc Anh stood in the mobile command center, his eyes fixed on the large map of Battambang and its surroundings. The room was a flurry of activity, with officers relaying updates and coordinating movements.

Anh addressed his assembled commanders. "Gentlemen, intelligence reports confirm that the remnants of the Khmer Rouge forces have concentrated in Battambang. This is our opportunity to end this conflict decisively."

He turned to his artillery commander. "Colonel Nguyen, I want a continuous barrage on the city's outskirts. Soften their defenses and keep them pinned down."

Nguyen nodded sharply. "Yes, General. Our guns are in position and ready to fire."

Anh then addressed his armor commander. "Major Tran, your tanks will lead the assault. Drive straight for the city center. Show no mercy to any armed resistance."

"Understood, sir," Tran replied.

To his infantry commander, Anh said, "General Pham, your men will follow the armor. Secure each sector as you advance. I want every street, every building cleared."

Pham saluted. "It will be done, General."

Finally, Anh turned to his air force liaison. "I want helicopter gunships providing close air support. Any large concentrations of enemy troops are to be engaged immediately."

The liaison nodded, already reaching for his radio

to relay the orders.

Anh surveyed the room, his voice rising with authority. "Our objective is clear: surround Battambang and destroy what remains of the Khmer Rouge forces. Leave them nowhere to hide, nowhere to run. This ends today."

He paused, his eyes hard. "But remember, there may be civilians still trapped in the city. We are not the Khmer Rouge. Avoid unnecessary casualties where possible. But no matter what… do not let the enemy escape."

The commanders nodded in understanding.

"Any questions?" Anh asked. The room remained silent. "Good. Commence the operation."

As his officers hurried to their posts, Anh turned back to the map. In the distance, the first rumbles of artillery fire could be heard. The final battle for Battambang had begun.

Anh allowed himself a small smile. After years of conflict, the end was finally in sight. Or so he thought.

Battambang

The streets of Battambang buzzed with frantic activity as Khmer Rouge soldiers fortified positions and distributed ammunition. Pol Pot stood in a hastily established command center, surrounded by his remaining commanders. The room was tense, filled with the nervous energy of men who knew they were cornered.

A young officer entered, saluting sharply. "Comrade, we've completed the count. We have approximately 40,000 troops remaining. Most of our armor and artillery were destroyed in Phnom Penh or on the road to Battambang."

Pol Pot's face remained impassive, but his eyes betrayed a flicker of dismay. He turned to a large map of the region spread across a table.

"And the Vietnamese?" he asked.

Another officer stepped forward. "Our scouts report at least 100,000 troops advancing on Battambang, supported by armor and air power."

A heavy silence fell over the room. The odds were overwhelming.

Pol Pot traced a line on the map with his finger, from Battambang to the Thai border. His mind raced, calculating options.

Finally, he spoke. "If we stay and fight, we will be annihilated. The Khmer Rouge cannot die here."

His lieutenants exchanged glances, relief and uncertainty on their faces.

"What do you propose, Brother Number One?" one of them asked.

Pol Pot's finger moved across the map to Thailand. "We cross the border. The Thai government, for all their public statements, will not turn us away. They fear Vietnamese expansion more than they hate us."

Murmurs of agreement filled the room. Pol Pot continued, his voice gaining strength. "In Thailand, we can regroup, rearm. The jungle will hide us, and from there, we can wage a guerrilla war that will bleed the Vietnamese dry."

He looked up, his eyes blazing with fervor. "Cambodia may be lost to us for now, but our struggle continues. We will return, stronger than ever."

Orders were quickly disseminated. The Khmer Rouge army began to move, abandoning their hastily prepared defenses.

The night sky over Battambang erupted in chaos as Pol Pot's remaining forces launched their desperate breakout attempt. The air was thick with smoke and the metallic tang of blood. Khmer Rouge soldiers surged forward in waves, their faces contorted with fanatical determination.

"Push through! For Angkar!" commanders shouted, their voices hoarse from hours of battle. They urged their men onward even as Vietnamese machine guns cut swathes through their ranks. Bodies fell in heaps, the dead and wounded alike trampled underfoot by the relentless advance.

At the weakest point of the siege ring, a team of Khmer Rouge sappers crawled forward under heavy fire. Their clothes were torn and bloodied, but they were filled with purpose. With shaking hands, they set their explosives, the devices barely visible in the flickering light of nearby fires.

The detonation was thunderous. Earth and debris erupted skyward, momentarily creating a gap in the Vietnamese lines. The shock wave rippled through the battlefield, leaving ears ringing and vision blurred.

The surviving Khmer Rouge soldiers charged through the breach firing their weapons and yelling like banshees. The Vietnamese soldiers were stunned by the blast and disorganized. They dove for cover.

Behind the front lines, Pol Pot and his inner circle waited in a convoy of the remaining armored vehicles, engines idling. The moment the explosion cleared, drivers gunned their engines. Tires spun in the loose earth before finding purchase, and the lead vehicles plowed through the chaos, crushing anything in their path including their own soldiers.

Hundreds of Khmer Rouge soldiers were left

behind to keep the breach open, sacrificed to secure their leaders' escape. They fought on, knowing they were abandoned but driven by years of indoctrination and the simple will to survive.

The roar of helicopter rotors cut through the cacophony of battle. Vietnamese Mi-24 gunships appeared like vengeful specters, their searchlights cutting harsh white beams through the darkness. Rockets streaked from their pods, leaving trails of smoke before exploding among the fleeing Khmer Rouge columns.

"Westward! Don't stop for anything!" Pol Pot's voice crackled over the radio, tension evident even through the static. His convoy sped on, bouncing violently over the uneven terrain.

The gunships continued their relentless assault. Their cannons spit streams of tracer fire that stitched deadly patterns across the retreating forces. Vehicles exploded in balls of flame, illuminating the night and casting twisted shadows. Bodies were torn apart, the screams of the wounded rising above the din of engines and gunfire.

Yet still the remnants of the Khmer Rouge army pushed on, driven by desperation and their leader's iron will. Soldiers clung to the sides of trucks, jumped onto passing vehicles, anything to escape the closing jaws of the Vietnamese forces.

Miles away, in the Vietnamese command center, General Le Duc Anh stood rigid, his eyes fixed on the tactical displays. As reports of the breakout filtered in, his face darkened with each passing second.

Suddenly, he slammed his fist on the table, sending maps and reports flying. "How did they break through?" he roared at his subordinates, spittle flying from his lips. "I want air support redirected immediately! Cut them off before they reach the border!"

Officers scrambled to relay orders, their faces pale under Anh's furious glare. But the chaos of the battlefield made coordinated action difficult. Communications were garbled, units were out of position, and the Khmer Rouge's desperate gambit had caught them off guard.

Anh's eyes blazed with fury as he watched Pol Pot's forces slipping away like sand through an hourglass. "Months of fighting," he seethed, his voice dangerously low, "and we let them escape at the final hour."

Thai Border

The western horizon glowed faintly with the promise of dawn as Pol Pot's battered army raced towards the Thai border. The air was thick with dust kicked up by dozens of vehicles and thousands of feet, all moving with desperate urgency.

Pol Pot himself sat in the back of a Soviet-made UAZ jeep, his once-immaculate uniform now stained with sweat and soot. His eyes darted nervously to the sky, searching for signs of pursuit.

"How much further?" he barked at the driver.

"Less than two miles, Comrade," came the terse reply.

Suddenly, the distinctive roar of jet engines cut through the rumble of vehicles. Pol Pot's head snapped up, his eyes widening in fear.

"Vietnamese MiGs!" someone shouted.

The lead jet screamed overhead, so low that Pol Pot

could see the pilot's helmet. It banked hard and came around for an attack run.

"Scatter! Take cover!" officers shouted, their voices nearly drowned out by the approaching jets.

"No! Continue to head for the border. We will only be safe when we are in Thailand. The Vietnamese wouldn't dare follow us," shouted Pol Pot.

The MiG opened fire, its cannons spitting death. A truck in front of Pol Pot's jeep exploded, sending flaming debris in all directions. The driver swerved hard, nearly tipping the vehicle.

Soldiers on foot dove for whatever cover they could find, many simply throwing themselves flat on the ground. But on the open road, there was little protection to be had.

Another jet swooped in, releasing a cluster of bombs. They fell with a whistling sound that ended in a series of thunderous explosions. Earth and bodies were thrown skyward.

"Keep moving!" Pol Pot screamed, his usual composure shattered. "We must reach the border!"

The convoy pushed on, leaving their dead and wounded behind. Those on foot who could still walk broke into a run, driven by pure survival instinct.

The jets came around again. This time, they fired rockets that streaked across the sky before finding their marks. Vehicles erupted in balls of flame. Men screamed as shrapnel tore through flesh and bone.

A young Khmer Rouge soldier, barely more than a boy, stumbled and fell next to Pol Pot's jeep. For a moment, their eyes met. The boy's face was filled with terror and confusion. Pol Pot looked away as the jeep sped on, leaving the soldier in the dust.

The border was now visible, a thin line of trees

marking the frontier. But so was another wave of Vietnamese jets, approaching fast.

"Faster!" Pol Pot urged, his knuckles white as he gripped the jeep's frame.

The jets opened fire once more, their cannons raking the earth. Men fell by the dozens, their bodies joining the trail of destruction that marked the Khmer Rouge's retreat.

But still, the army pushed on. Those who could run, ran. Those who could crawl, crawled. The border drew nearer with each passing second.

As they crossed into Thai territory, the Vietnamese jets pulled up, unable to pursue further without risking an international incident.

Pol Pot slumped in his seat, exhaustion and relief washing over him in equal measure. Behind him lay the ruins of his army and his dreams of power. Ahead, an uncertain future as a fugitive.

The sun finally crested the horizon, casting long shadows across a landscape littered with the dead and dying. The Khmer Rouge had escaped, but at a terrible cost. And the war, despite this moment of respite, was far from over.

Anh's Headquarters

As reports continued to flood in, detailing the Khmer Rouge crossing into Thailand, Anh's anger gave way to cold determination. He turned to his staff, his voice now calm but filled with menace.

"This isn't over," he declared. "Pol Pot may have escaped today, but he's just ensured that our fight will follow him beyond Cambodia's borders." He swept his hand across the map, encompassing not just Cambodia but Thailand and beyond. "Prepare for extended operations. We'll hunt them to the ends of the earth if necessary."

The command center buzzed with renewed activity as Anh's orders were disseminated. Outside, the sound of jet engines roared as more aircraft were scrambled in a last-ditch effort to stop the escaping Khmer Rouge.

But Anh knew, with a sinking feeling that he refused to acknowledge, that they were already too late. The war was entering a new phase, one that would drag on for years to come. As he stared at the map, his mind was already racing, planning the next moves in a conflict that had just become infinitely more complex.

Anh paced in his command tent, barely containing fury. The radio operator sat nervously at his equipment, waiting for the connection to be established with Hanoi. The air was thick with tension and cigarette smoke.

Finally, the radio crackled to life. "Hanoi here. Go ahead, General Anh."

Anh snatched up the microphone. "This is Anh. I need to speak with Comrade Le Duan immediately. It's urgent."

There was a pause, then the gravelly voice of Le Duan, the General Secretary of the Communist Party, came through. "Anh, what's the situation?"

Anh's words tumbled out in a rush. "Comrade Secretary, Pol Pot and a significant portion of his forces have crossed into Thailand. We have them on the run, but they're regrouping just across the border. I'm requesting immediate permission to pursue them into Thai territory."

He paused, then added with barely restrained

intensity, "If we strike now, we can end this once and for all."

The silence that followed seemed to stretch for an eternity. When Le Duan finally spoke, his voice was measured and calm. "No, Anh. Do not cross into Thailand."

Anh's face contorted in disbelief. "But Comrade Secretary, we can't let them escape! They'll only come back stronger, and—"

Le Duan cut him off. "I said no, General. We cannot risk expanding this conflict. An incursion into Thailand could draw in other powers, perhaps even the Americans. The international repercussions would be severe."

"With all due respect, Comrade Secretary, we're throwing away years of sacrifice. The Khmer Rouge will use Thailand as a base to continue their resistance. This war could drag on for years!"

"Perhaps," Le Duan replied, his tone hardening. "But that's a problem for another day. Our immediate goal has been achieved. Cambodia is under our control. We must consolidate our gains, not risk everything on a reckless pursuit."

Anh opened his mouth to argue further, but Le Duan continued, "This is not a request, General. It is an order. Secure the border, but do not cross it. Is that understood?"

The tent fell silent. The staff officers present held their breath, watching their commander carefully. Anh's jaw worked silently, the muscles in his neck standing out with tension.

Finally, he spoke, his voice tight with suppressed emotion. "Understood, Comrade Secretary."

"Good," Le Duan said. "I expect a full report on the

situation within the hour. Hanoi out."

The radio went silent. Anh stood motionless for a long moment, the microphone still clutched in his hand. Then, with a roar of frustration, he hurled it across the tent. It smashed against a map of the region, leaving a dent in the board right over the Thai border.

He turned to his stunned staff, his eyes blazing. "You heard the orders. Secure the border. Not one of our troops sets foot in Thailand." His voice dripped with bitterness.

As his officers hurried to comply, Anh turned to stare at the map, his gaze fixed on the spot where Pol Pot's forces had slipped away. The war might be over for Hanoi, but Anh knew in his bones that this was far from the end.

Outside the tent, the sounds of victory celebrations could be heard as the order to standdown spread. But inside, the atmosphere was one of foreboding for the challenges that lay ahead.

White House – Washington DC, USA

President Jimmy Carter sat at the head of the long table in the White House Situation Room, his brow furrowed in concern. The room was filled with the murmur of worried voices as his advisers and cabinet members debated the unfolding situation in Cambodia.

National Security Advisor Zbigniew Brzezinski stood, addressing the room. "Mr. President, our latest intelligence confirms that the Vietnamese forces have effectively taken control of Phnom Penh and Battambang. It's clear their intention is not just to remove the Khmer Rouge, but to occupy Cambodia entirely."

Secretary of State Cyrus Vance interjected, his voice grave. "If Vietnam succeeds, we're looking at a significant expansion of communist influence in Southeast Asia. There's a real risk they could annex Cambodia outright."

Carter leaned back in his chair. "And what of the Khmer Rouge? Pol Pot?"

CIA Director Stansfield Turner cleared his throat. "Our sources indicate that Pol Pot and a significant portion of his forces have fled to Thailand. They're regrouping, presumably to wage a guerrilla war against the Vietnamese occupation."

The room fell silent as the implications sank in. Carter looked around at his advisers, seeing the conflict written on their faces.

Secretary of Defense Harold Brown spoke up. "Mr. President, as abhorrent as it may seem, supporting Pol Pot's resistance might be our best option to check Vietnamese expansion."

Carter's jaw tightened. "Pol Pot is a war criminal. His regime has committed unspeakable atrocities."

"You're right, sir," Brzezinski acknowledged. "But we have to consider the larger geopolitical picture. A Vietnamese-controlled Cambodia poses a significant threat to regional stability and U.S. interests in Southeast Asia."

The president stood, pacing the room. The weight of the decision was evident in every line of his face. After a long moment, he turned to face his advisers.

"I never thought I'd hear myself say this," Carter began, his voice heavy. "But we cannot allow Vietnam to expand its communist revolution unchecked. The stability of the entire region is at stake."

He paused, taking a deep breath. "We will provide

support to Pol Pot's resistance efforts against the Vietnamese occupation. But let me be clear - this is a strategic necessity, not a moral endorsement. We will do what we must to stop communist expansion, but we will not forget the crimes of the Khmer Rouge."

The room was silent, the gravity of the decision palpable.

"God help us," Carter muttered, almost to himself. Then, louder, "Prepare a detailed plan for covert support. And may history judge us kindly for what we're about to do."

As his advisers hurried to comply, Carter turned to look out the window, the weight of his decision heavy on his shoulders. The lines between right and wrong, once so clear to him, had become blurred in the harsh reality of global politics.

Royal Palace - General Ahn's Headquarters

General Anh trudged up the ornate staircase of the Royal Palace, his boots echoing off the marble floors. The day's events weighed heavily on him - the escaped prisoners, the failed ambush, the mounting pressure from Hanoi. He rubbed his temples, longing for the solitude of his quarters.

As he pushed open the heavy wooden door, Anh froze. A figure sat in his chair, feet propped casually on the antique desk. The room's only illumination came from a small lamp, casting long shadows across the intruder's face.

"Bonsoir, General," the man said, his Corsican accent thick. "I hope you don't mind that I let myself in."

Anh's hand moved instinctively towards his

sidearm. "Liccioni. This is unexpected."

Vincent Liccioni, the Corsican mob's representative, smiled coldly. "As unexpected as your man failing to show up for our scheduled exchange?"

Anh closed the door behind him, mind racing. "There were... complications. Resistance fighters intercepted the shipment."

Liccioni's eyebrow arched. "Is that so? How very inconvenient."

"A temporary setback," Anh assured him, moving further into the room. "I've already arranged for a replacement shipment from our Burmese suppliers. It will arrive within the week, and we can conclude our deal then."

Liccioni stood slowly, his movements deliberate. "I'm afraid that won't be possible, General. My associates have lost faith in your ability to deliver. We've decided to cut out the middleman and deal directly with the Burmese."

Anh's face darkened. "Now, wait just a minute. We had an agreement. You can't simply—"

"Can't we?" Liccioni interrupted, his tone dangerously soft. "I'm afraid you misunderstand the nature of our relationship, General. We tolerated your involvement because it was convenient. That convenience has vanished."

Anh's anger flared. "You ungrateful bastard. After everything I've risked—"

The sound of a gun being cocked cut through the air. Liccioni now held a pistol, its barrel fitted with a long silencer. "Your risks are no longer our concern," he said calmly.

Anh's eyes widened. He opened his mouth to speak, to bargain, to threaten - but Liccioni pulled the trigger twice in rapid succession. The silenced shots were no louder than a cough.

General Anh crumpled to the floor, blood spreading across the priceless carpet. Liccioni regarded the body dispassionately, then carefully wiped down any surfaces he might have touched.

As he slipped out of the room and into the night, Liccioni pulled out a radio. "It's done," he said simply.

The palace remained quiet, its other occupants unaware that power had just violently changed hands in the ornate room upstairs.

Liccioni exited the palace through a side entrance, then through a guarded gateway. He handed the guard an envelope filled with cash as promised, then slipped into shadows and disappeared. As always, the Corsicans had made a statement that failure was not tolerated, and that business would go on as usual. Opium was king in Southeast Asia.

Village in Northern Vietnam

The sun was setting over the lush green hills of northern Vietnam as Granier and Spitting Woman crested the final ridge. Below them, nestled in a valley carved by a winding river, lay their village. Smoke rose lazily from thatched roofs, and the distant sound of children's laughter drifted up to them on the evening breeze.

Spitting Woman paused, her weathered face softening as she took in the familiar sight. "It's been so long," she murmured, almost to herself.

Granier stood beside her, his own eyes misty with emotion. "Seems like a lifetime ago."

They began their descent, their weary bodies

protesting after the long journey. As they approached the outskirts of the village, an old woman tending to her garden looked up. Her eyes widened in recognition.

"Linh?" she called out, using Spitting Woman's given name. "Is that really you?"

Word spread quickly. By the time they reached the village center, a small crowd had gathered. There were gasps of surprise, cries of joy, and not a few tears.

An elderly man pushed his way through the crowd. Spitting Woman's father, his face lined with age but his eyes bright with joy. "My daughter," he said, his voice cracking. "You've come home."

As night fell, the village erupted in an impromptu celebration. There was food, rice wine, and music. Granier and Spitting Woman found themselves at the center of it all, fielding questions about their adventures, their time away.

But they shared little, deflecting inquiries with vague responses and changing the subject. The horrors they'd seen, the things they'd done - those were burdens they would carry alone.

Later, as the celebration wound down, Granier and Spitting Woman stood at the edge of the village, looking out over the moonlit valley.

"Do you think we can do this?" Granier asked softly. "Just... live?"

Spitting Woman was quiet for a long moment. "We have to try," she finally said. "I'm tired of death, Granier. Tired of war."

He nodded, understanding completely. "Peace and quiet," he mused. "Sounds like heaven."

She took his hand, squeezing it gently. "It won't be easy. The memories..."

"I know," he said. "But we're home now. That's a

start."

They stood there in comfortable silence, watching as the last lights in the village winked out. The war, the violence, the chaos - it all seemed very far away now.

Tomorrow would bring its own challenges. Learning to live as civilians again, dealing with the trauma of their experiences, finding their place in a village that had moved on without them. But for now, in this moment, they allowed themselves to hope.

Hope for peace. Hope for quiet. Hope for a life beyond war.

As a cool breeze rustled through the trees, Granier and Spitting Woman turned and walked hand in hand back to the village. Their long journey was finally over. They were home.

Politburo - Beijing, China

In a grand hall within Zhongnanhai, Beijing's leadership compound, Deng Xiaoping sat at the head of a long table, surrounded by his top advisors. The room was thick with the smell of cigarette smoke.

Wang Dongxing, the chief of Chinese intelligence, cleared his throat. "Comrade Deng, our latest reports confirm that Vietnamese forces have occupied Phnom Penh and Battambang. It appears they intend to control all of Cambodia."

Deng's face remained impassive, but his eyes narrowed slightly. "And the Soviets?"

Li Xiannian, the senior vice premier, leaned forward. "We have reason to believe Moscow is supporting Hanoi's actions. They see this as an opportunity to expand their influence in Southeast Asia."

Geng Biao, the minister of defense, added, "If we allow this to continue, we risk Soviet-backed Vietnamese dominance in the region. It could threaten our southern border."

Deng sat silently for a moment, tapping his fingers on the table. The room waited, the only sound the soft ticking of a large clock on the wall.

Finally, Deng spoke, his voice quiet but firm. "We cannot allow Vietnam to become the Cuba of Asia. The consequences for regional stability would be severe."

He turned to Geng Biao. "What is the readiness of our southern forces?"

"They can be mobilized within days, Comrade Deng," Geng replied.

Deng nodded, then addressed the room. "We have given Vietnam many chances to correct its behavior. We have tried to be patient, to guide them as an elder brother should."

His voice hardened. "But now, the child is getting naughty. It is time he got spanked."

The advisors exchanged glances, understanding the weight of Deng's words.

"Prepare plans for a limited punitive action against Vietnam," Deng ordered. "We will teach them the cost of their ambitions. But remember, this must be swift and decisive. We cannot risk a prolonged conflict that might draw in the Soviets directly."

As his advisors hurried to comply, Deng turned to look out the window at the Beijing skyline. The decision to go to war was never easy, but he was convinced of its necessity.

"Let Hanoi learn," he murmured, "that there are consequences for defying the will of China."

The wheels of war once again began to turn, setting in motion events that would reshape the geopolitics of Southeast Asia for years to come.

Letter to Reader

Dear Reader:

I hope you enjoyed *The Forgotten War*. I was shocked when I researched the conflict between the Cambodians and Vietnamese. The disregard for life was disturbing. Anyway, I hope you liked it. The next novel in the Airmen Series is **Retribution** – Book 24. Here's a quick snapshot:

Granier and Spitting Woman return home looking for peace and a long rest. They find the opposite when Chinese long-range reconnaissance team is found operating on the Vietnamese side of the border. With most of the Vietnamese military focused on Cambodia, Granier and Spitting Woman must defend their village until the military can be redeployed to stop the Chinese from invading. I can't tell you anything more or I will spoil it. Oh, and there're lots of historical battles and suspense. I hope you like it.

Sharing my work with your friends and reviews are always welcome. Thank you for supporting The Airmen Series.

Regards,

David Lee Corley, Author

TWILIGHT OF WAR

Author's Biography

Born in 1958, David grew up on a horse ranch in Northern California, breeding and training appaloosas. He has had all his toes broken at least once and survived numerous falls and kicks from ornery colts and fillies. David started writing professionally as a copywriter in his early 20's. At thirty-two, he packed up his family and moved to Malibu, California, to live his dream of writing and directing motion pictures. He has four motion picture screenwriting credits and two directing credits. His movies have been viewed by over fifty million movie-goers worldwide and won a multitude of awards, including the Malibu, Palm Springs, and San Jose Film Festivals. In addition to his twenty-four screenplays, he has written fourteen novels. He developed his simplistic writing style after rereading his two favorite books, Ernest Hemingway's *The Old Man and the Sea* and Cormac McCarthy's *No Country For Old Men* An avid student of world culture, David lived as an expat in both Thailand and Mexico. At fifty-six, he sold all his possessions and became a nomad for four years. He circumnavigated the globe three times and visited fifty-six countries. Known for his detailed descriptions, his stories often include actual experiences and characters from his journeys.

Milton Keynes UK
Ingram Content Group UK Ltd.
UKHW031953281024
450365UK00008B/349